Elmore Leonard

Unknown M   #89

Also by Elmore Leonard

FICTION

Raylan

Djibouti

Comfort to the Enemy and
    Other Carl Webster Stories

Road Dogs

Up in Honey's Room

The Hot Kid

The Complete Western Stories
    of Elmore Leonard

Mr. Paradise

Fire in the Hole (previously
    titled When the Women
    Come Out to Dance)

Tishomingo Blues

Pagan Babies

Be Cool

The Tonto Woman and Other
    Western Stories

Cuba Libre

Out of Sight

Riding the Rap

Pronto

Rum Punch

Maximum Bob

Get Shorty

Killshot

Freaky Deaky

Touch

Bandits

Glitz

LaBrava

Stick

Cat Chaser

Split Images

Gold Coast

City Primeval

Gunsights

The Switch

The Hunted

Swag

52 Pickup

Mr. Majestyk

Forty Lashes Less One

Valdez Is Coming

The Moonshine War

The Big Bounce

Hombre

Last Stand at Saber River

Escape from Five Shadows

The Law at Randado

The Bounty Hunters

NONFICTION

Elmore Leonard's 10 Rules of Writing

ELMORE LEONARD

UNKNOWN MAN #89

wm

WILLIAM MORROW
An Imprint of HarperCollins*Publishers*

UNKNOWN MAN #89. Copyright © 1977 by Elmore Leonard, Inc. All rights reserved. Printed in the United States of America. No part of this book may be used or reproduced in any manner whatsoever without written permission except in the case of brief quotations embodied in critical articles and reviews. For information address HarperCollins Publishers, 10 East 53rd Street, New York, NY 10022.

HarperCollins books may be purchased for educational, business, or sales promotional use. For information please write: Special Markets Department, HarperCollins Publishers, 10 East 53rd Street, New York, NY 10022.

FIRST AVON BOOKS PAPERBACK PUBLISHED 1984.
FIRST HARPERTORCH PAPERBACK PUBLISHED 2002.
FIRST WILLIAM MORROW PAPERBACK PUBLISHED 2013.

Library of Congress Cataloging-in-Publication Data has been applied for.

ISBN 978-0-06-218928-8

22 23 24 25 26 LBC 8 7 6 5 4

For Peter

———————

A Prompt Man Is a Lonely Man

—*Andrew Donahue*

1

A FRIEND OF RYAN'S SAID TO HIM ONE TIME, "YEAH, but at least you don't take any shit from anybody."

Ryan said to his friend, "I don't know, the way things've been going, maybe it's about time I started taking some."

This had been a few years ago. Ryan remembered it as finally waking up, deciding to get off his ass and make some kind of run.

His sister drove him down to the Detroit police car auction, where he bought a 1970 maroon and white Cougar for $250. His sister didn't like the Cougar because it had four bullet holes in the door on the driver's side. Ryan said he didn't mind the holes. Didn't *mind*; he loved them.

The friend of Ryan's who told him about the car auctions was a police officer with long hair and jeans and a big Mag under his leather jacket who worked out of the Criminal Investigation Division at 1300 Beaubien. His name was Dick Speed. He showed Ryan around the Frank Murphy Hall of

Justice and what went on behind the courtrooms and told him about serving papers and how a guy could do pretty well if he didn't mind driving around in his car all day. The way Dick Speed explained it, it didn't look too hard.

Ryan met a few process servers. He studied them to see if there was a process server "look." There didn't seem to be one. They could have been working on the line or delivering dry cleaning. Only one of them stood out, a short and sort of fat Jewish guy who wore leisure suits and seemed to know everybody in the Frank Murphy Hall of Justice. His name was Jay Walt. Ryan couldn't figure out what made the guy so sure of himself.

Ryan was thirty-six by then and starting to worry that maybe he was a misfit, a little out of touch with reality, that all the people strapped to their boring nine-to-fives were right and he was wrong.

He had sold insurance one time, for three weeks. He had sold new cars for several different Detroit dealerships; but, each place, the sales manager or the owner turned out to be a pain in the ass. He'd worked construction and driven a truck. He'd been with Local 299 of the Teamsters as a business agent for a while and got into a couple of fistfights that were interesting. He'd worked on the line at Chevrolet truck assembly in Flint, quit before he went out of his mind, and got a job at Abercrombie's store in Troy, but only lasted two weeks. One day during the Christmas rush he told a lady if she didn't like the service why didn't she go someplace else. He'd said to her, "Why should a nice person like you stand around taking a lot of shit?" Ryan was always polite. He had also been into a little breaking and entering when he was much younger and working for a carpet-cleaning company; but it was more for fun than profit: see if he could get away with it. He had been arrested only once, for felonious assault—belting a migrant crew chief the summer he picked cucumbers up in the Thumb—but the charge was dismissed. He had never served time.

What he got into serving was legal papers and it surprised him he liked it and was good at it. It surprised him that he was patient and had a knack for finding people. He wasn't afraid to walk up and hand someone a writ or a summons. As long as he didn't know anything about them personally it was all right. What they did, whatever trouble they were in, was their business, not his. He was polite, soft-spoken. He never hassled anybody. He would identify the individual and hand over the paper and say thank you, best of luck, and that was it. He couldn't remember many of the faces and he liked it that way.

He decided he liked process serving because he was his own boss. He could work two hours a day or twenty-four; and because he liked it, he usually put in at least twelve. He didn't mind being in the car most of the day. He liked to drive around and listen to music or, about a hundred days a year, a Detroit Tigers baseball game. It didn't matter what place they were in. Ryan's ambition, up until the time he was twenty, was to be a major league third baseman. He'd looked good enough to get a tryout with the Red Sox; but he couldn't hit a breaking ball if the guy hung it up there in front of him. They told him he'd never make it. He had connected with that Chicano crew chief, though: hit him with a baseball bat on the hardpacked clearing in the cucumber fields when the guy came at him with a knife. Ryan had learned early that in street fighting, if there was no way to get out of it, you hit first and made it count and usually it was over. It was a good thing to know and keep with you.

The only problem he anticipated in his work was taking shit from people who didn't want to be served: people who'd give him a hard time, like he was the one taking them to court. But he handled it in a way that surprised him. He just didn't let these people bother him. He realized they were frightened or reacting without thinking. They were so pissed off at the first party, the plaintiff, they had to take it out on somebody and he was standing there, responsible. He realized they didn't mean it personally, so why get mad or upset?

He was told process serving was a dangerous occupation and that most process servers carried a gun. But Ryan never packed. A friend of his—not the cop, Dick Speed, another one—said, "But look, this guy sees you come in, he knows if he gets served he's going to lose his ass maybe. What if he's got a gun? The guy's scared shitless, he sees you come in, *bam*, you're dead."

Ryan had been threatened with getting his head taken off. He had had guns pointed at him and waved in his face. He had served a guy, in a child-custody case, who had beaten up a couple of policemen. He had walked into the headquarters of a blacks-against-the-world group and had gotten all the looks and the bullshit and had walked out with an adding machine, a repossession.

"You're not even that big," his friend said, "that you'd scare anybody."

"In this work," Ryan told his friend, "you can be a boy scout, a humanitarian, you can be an ass chaser, there's plenty of that. I mean broads, ones that're lonely or grateful. You can lean on people, stick it to them if you get a kick out of that. Christ, like a guy I know, he's in the collection business now, Jay Walt. He likes to torture people, get them to squirm and whimper. You can do that. Or you can wish them luck and not horse them around any. We're all making the same trip, right? Trying to get along. Why should we fuck each other over and make life miserable?"

But never get personally involved, he might have added. That was rule number one. Don't get too close and start feeling sorry for people. You want to do that, go work for the Salvation Army.

The second week on the job, when he was still a little nervous, Ryan did buy a .38 Smith and Wesson Chiefs Special; but he never got around to carrying it. He could if he wanted to, it was legal, and it was in his top dresser drawer if he ever needed it. In his wallet he had a shield that was in the shape of a star and identified him as a constable, Oakland County, and business cards that advertised his private practice, SEARCH AND SERVE ASSOCIATES, JACK C. RYAN. He worked mainly in Wayne, Oakland, and Macomb counties, which took in the Greater Detroit and Pontiac areas and as far east as Grosse Pointe and Mount Clemens on Lake Saint Clair.

By the end of his first year, Ryan had a list of attorneys who were sending him their service work. He'd stop by the Troy Municipal Court and pick up a batch there from the clerk two or three times a week and then stop by the Oakland County Circuit Court in Pontiac. He was getting enough business that he didn't have to go all the way downtown to the Detroit courts too often. What surprised him the most, he was organized. He planned his calls carefully, sometimes knocking on a door as early as four in the morning and handing the guy the paper before he had his eyes open. He served on the average of fifteen to twenty legal papers in a twelve-hour day, put upwards of two thousand miles a month on his car, and grossed between twenty and twenty-five thousand a year. Not bad, considering he was getting five or six bucks a service from the courts—zip if he failed to serve the paper—and twelve or fifteen, plus mileage, from the attorneys. Ryan was good and he knew it, and so did the court clerks and the attorneys who called him to handle the tough ones. They could take Ryan's word for it: if a defendant couldn't be found, then he wasn't around anymore, or he was dead. They knew his word was good and that he never signed the affidavit on a service he didn't complete—like the Belle Isle Bridge servers, guys who were known to drop a summons in the Detroit River (or a trash can) if locating the defendant appeared too difficult, or if it took them into a rough, inner-city neighborhood.

Ryan lived alone. He had a small one-bedroom unit in a fairly new apartment building in Royal Oak. He had been married once. He married a nice quiet girl who came into her own during the five years of their marriage and turned into a tough little hard-headed woman who liked to pick and find fault and was always right. He'd ask her, "What's it like being always right?" And she'd say, "You should hear yourself. No more Mr. Nice Guy, huh? Boy, have you changed." And things like that. He hadn't changed. He had gone by the book and pur-

posely picked a sweet little June Allyson and discovered too late that when you take the girl next
door into a different life she isn't the girl next door
anymore. So he said fuck it—going through the
motions of playing house, being someone he didn't
want to be—and got a divorce.

His sister and brother-in-law, stuck in their little
ranch house with four kids and a lamp in the picture
window, told him he'd probably never grow up: he
was like a little brat who always wanted his own
way. He had dinner there and listened to them about
three times a year. Every once in a while he would
ask them what was so great about growing up.

Lately, he was seeing a girl by the name of Rita
who was a legal secretary. Ryan told her, with her
blond hair, she didn't look like a Rita at all. Rita
thought he was nuts. She was a little nuts herself,
unpredictable; though Ryan noticed she worked at
it. Rita had thought that going out with a process
server—actually making calls with him—would be
a kicky thing to do. Until she realized Ryan was
probably doing the same thing: getting an extra
kick out of scoring with a legal secretary, a girl who
handed him papers to serve. She wasn't sure, with
his straight face, when he was kidding or being serious. So she'd tell him he was a nut and that would
somehow cover it either way.

Sometimes on Saturdays Rita would ride with
him, keep him company, and once in a while she'd

help him serve a paper. He'd call her and Rita would say, "What have you got, another doctor?" Doctors, scared to death of malpractice suits, were hard to get to. One time Ryan tried to make an appointment with a doctor and found out the guy was a gynecologist. So he went in with Rita for her rabbit test, the concerned hubby. But when he tried to serve the paper, the doctor actually ran. They followed him out of the clinic, saw him get in his Buick Electra and take off. A mile and a half later they finally caught him at a stop light. The doctor was locking his doors, closing the power-operated windows as Ryan got out and walked around to the Buick. The doctor stared straight ahead and wouldn't look at Ryan when he knocked on the side window. So Ryan lifted the windshield wiper in front of the doctor's face and let it snap back to hold the court papers against the windshield. He said to the doctor, "This is a domestic litigation. You're being sued for divorce, not malpractice." Like turning it around and telling the doctor his tumor was benign. The doctor, behind the windshield, seemed to sag with relief. Ryan heard him say, "Oh, shit, is that all? Thank you."

Ryan got his picture in the paper when he served a rock group with a summons during their performance at the Masonic Temple Auditorium. He didn't do it as a stunt. It was the only way he saw to get close to them. The lead-in to the picture caption said

"*Show Stopper*!" Rita had the newspaper photo
blown up in a photostat and mounted and hung it in
Ryan's living room. He showed a nice amount of
poise there on the stage in front of the rock group,
the freaks gaping at him, the paper extended, and
the calm, deadpan expression on his face. Ryan
liked the blowup. He would never have thought of
hanging something like that in his living room.

The only things he didn't like about the paper-
serving business were evictions and repossessions.
Kicking people out of their home was awful. Getting ten bucks a room for the job and usually having to bring boxes for all their pitiful junk. Going in
and taking a color TV or a chrome and Formica
dinette set was bad enough. He couldn't get used to
it, sticking it to some poor cluck who'd been laid
off and was behind on his payments.

"He shouldn't have bought the item in the first
place," Jay Walt said. "Who's supposed to eat it,
the bank? The store? No, they'd be out of business
carrying deadbeats. They got no choice in the final
analysis but go to court."

Jay Walt ran a collection agency now with a high
turnover of personnel; he still served some paper,
but more as a sideline. Ryan had got to know him,
picking up some of his paper work for a split of the
fee when Jay Walt was overloaded and Ryan didn't
have much to do. In a way, Jay Walt fascinated him;
it was like the guy was playing a part, the little hot-

shot in his tinted glasses and leisure suit. Everything was a big deal, but the guy never paid an in-
voice sooner than ninety days. Ryan figured he was
so tight with a buck he must still have his bar mitz-
vah money. Ryan didn't know he was being a smartass when he thought this; he believed he was being
funny. He didn't own a leisure suit and hadn't gotten a dime when he made his first communion.

One time Jay Walt took Ryan along to show him
how to handle a repossession. With them were two
outside men who waited by the U-haul van and
would do the lifting once Jay Walt cleared the way.
Unbelievable. He walked right in, brushed past the
woman in hair curlers who opened the door, and
started looking around, hands on his hips, locating
the stereo outfit and the color TV, where the little kid
was sitting on the floor with a bowl of Spaghetti-Os
watching *General Hospital*. The woman was asking Jay Walt who he was, what he wanted. Jay Walt
said, "Honey, all the times we've talked on the
phone, we're old friends. Allied Credit Service, Mr.
Walt. Yeah, *now* you remember."

The husband came out from the kitchen wiping
his hands on his T-shirt. Jay Walt didn't give him a
chance.

"What's this, you're on your vacation? Taking a
holiday? Your wife said you were working."

"What? I'm working," the husband said. "Over
at Ranco, second shift." He was anxious, on the

defensive in his own home, not even knowing what was going on.

"So how come you haven't made any payments?"

"For what?"

"For *what*? The home entertainment center. Hi-fi, speakers, nineteen-inch color TV. You're four payments behind. I told your wife, I didn't get it last week, on my desk, attention Mr. Walt, that's it, you don't own it anymore."

"See, I've only been working the past two weeks."

"You get paid?"

"We had some bills piling up. Specially doctor bills."

"You got some bills—what am I, at the end of the line? Screw Mr. Walt, huh?"

"We had to pay the doctor. Stevie's got this allergy they found out about—"

"Hey," Jay Walt said. "I'm allergic too. I break out when somebody gives me the runaround, when they lie to my face, tell me they refuse to meet a contractual obligation."

"Nobody lied to you. See, I was laid off, I was out five months, drawing just unemployment. What am I supposed to do?"

"You turn the music off and the TV?" Jay Walt asked. "No, you stop paying, but you keep entertaining yourselves." He looked over at Ryan by the door. "Tell them okay."

Ryan didn't know what he meant at first. The two guys outside. He felt funny motioning to them, like he was part of this.

As they came through the door, Jay Walt said, "The TV, the home entertainment setup, the étagère, everything."

"The what?" one of the outside men said.

"The fake shelves."

"Now wait a minute," the husband said, getting a little something into it; but he didn't move from where he was standing.

"Wait your ass," Jay Walt said. "Waiting time's over. Come on, get this crap out of here."

One of the outside men unplugged the TV. *General Hospital* disappeared and the little kid on the floor started to whine, making a sound like he was going to cry.

"They drop that TV on the kid, it's not our fault," Jay Walt said. "Get him out of the way." The mother yelled at the little boy, grabbed him, and marched the bewildered kid out of the room. She had to take it out on somebody.

Jay Walt said to the husband, "I was going to give you another month, you know that? But you blew it, give me that shit about the doctor."

"I can show you. Stevie's got this allergy." The husband didn't know what to do. He was getting frantic.

"Forget it," Jay Walt said.

When they were in Jay Walt's light-blue Mark IV, Ryan said, "He could've called the cops, you know that? Had you arrested."

"Sure I know it," Jay Walt said, "but asshole doesn't. Listen, you can tell them, Christ, *anything*, you wouldn't believe it."

"I'd believe it," Ryan said. "What do you do with his stuff?"

"Wait twenty-one days, that's the law, put three notices in the paper nobody can find, and supposedly sell it at auction," Jay Walt said. "How'd you like a home entertainment center, Jackie? Pretty good speakers, the étagère, everything, seventy-five bucks."

Rita told him he should have taken it, get rid of the Mickey Mouse record player he had. What the heck, seventy-five bucks, if he didn't grab it somebody else would. Ryan said listen, the cluck still had to make his payments; you realize that? Okay, Rita said, so it's a shitty deal. Life's full of shitty deals.

Well, maybe, but he wasn't going to get involved in that kind of stuff. He wouldn't mind having a light-blue Mark IV and an expensive hi-fi setup and a few other things. He wouldn't mind having a box at the ball park, right behind the Tigers' dugout, so he could get a good look at the guys as they came off the field and hear some of the things they said. It was possible. But he wasn't going to get a hernia trying, or give anybody else one.

He was doing all right.

At the end of three years he'd put 83,000 miles on the Cougar and traded it in on a Pontiac Catalina two-door, light-blue, with air and heavy-duty shocks, forty-six fifty-eight delivered. He was glad to finally get rid of the Cougar, though he'd still think about it every once in a while. There weren't many cars around with four bullet holes in the door.

2

JAY WALT WAS GETTING A COFFEE, cream and sugar, to go.

Ryan slid onto a stool between a couple of black girls with coats on, visitors, and hunched over the menu. He didn't feel like talking to Jay Walt in the coffee shop of the Frank Murphy Hall of Justice, ninth floor: Jay Walt talked out loud wherever he was, even on an elevator. When Ryan was with him he'd feel people looking at them.

"Jesus Christ, hey, where you been? Move down one, honey, okay? You mind? Thank you, sweetheart."

Ryan looked up at the beige leisure suit and trench coat over one arm—belt and rings and epaulets—and the alligator attaché case and the coffee to go with the plastic lid, all of it being wedged in against the counter, close to him.

"What're you, so busy you don't call your answering service anymore? I been trying to get you, two days I been calling. I figure you're shacked up with some broad filed for divorce. Needs a little sympathy, huh? I know, don't tell me, buddy, I been there."

Jay Walt's back filled and stretched the double-knit suit. The black girl next to him looked over. It was close in here, humid, the stools filled shoulder to shoulder.

"I figure you had some paper," Ryan said, "no hurry. I was going to call you today or tomorrow. But I don't think I can handle it right now."

"Jesus, you eat in here?" Jay Walt pulled his tinted glasses off to look at the vapor forming.

"Not too often. Usually I'm downtown, I go around to the Hellas—"

"Eat that Greek shit?"

"—or the Athens." Sounding like he was apologizing.

"I grab a cup," Jay Walt said, "drink it in the car, make a few phone calls."

"You got a phone in the Mark now?"

"Naw, new Cadillac Seville. It's small, you know, but it's okay. With the phone, shit, I could drive to Miami handle all my business I don't have to do personally." Jay Walt was peeling the lid off his coffee to go.

Ryan was hot in his raincoat. He ought to take it off. He looked past Jay Walt to get the waitress. Get something and get out. Jay Walt glistened. His styled hair, like a grayish ace cap, glistened with spray. His nose glistened, and his tinted wire-frame glasses glistened and reflected the overhead light. The waitress wouldn't look this way. She'd made up her mind, nothing was going to make her look. He could get up and leave. He wasn't sure why he'd come in here anyway, or why he'd come downtown. He hadn't been downtown in a month. He hadn't seen Jay Walt in about two months. He didn't like fast-food counter places with slow service. Tell Jay Walt he'd changed his mind.

Christ, walk out if you want. You don't have to explain anything.

Ryan said, "Well, I think I'm going to give up on getting served."

"You want the waitress?"

"No, never mind." The guy would probably yell at her to get her ass down here, then call her honey and sweetheart and give her a lot of bullshit with everybody listening. Ryan started to turn the stool to ease out of there. "I'll call you later on, okay?"

"Wait a minute, sit still." Jay Walt laid his hand on Ryan's arm and left it there. "I got you, let me tell you what I want."

"I'll come by. I'd have to pick up the papers, anyway." He'd do it, just to get out of here.

"It's not papers. I want you to find a guy for me."

Ryan could see it coming. A guy ran out on his car payments and took the car, disappeared. Something like that. He said, "What do you need me for? Call the police."

"It's not that kind of a thing," Jay Walt said. "No paper, no summons, anything like that. I just want you to locate a guy for me. A Robert Leary, Jr. He's probably around sixty. Say fifty-five to sixty-five. Find out where I can reach him and let me know. That's all. You don't have to hand the guy anything or even talk to him."

"So he's not in the phone book or the city directory." Ryan turned back to the counter, but Jay Walt's hand remained on his arm.

"A lot of people aren't. But this guy, he doesn't even have a credit record. Can you imagine that today, no credit record? Not even a rotten one. I put some of my guys on it, that's as far as those shitheads could go, phone book and a credit check. It's going to take a pro, I can see that. So who do I think of first, immediately?"

"What'd the guy do?"

"He didn't do anything. There's nothing illegal, it's a business thing. Client of mine, guy I do business with, wants to find him. Why would you have to know anything about it? You understand?"

"How much?"

Jay Walt finally let go of Ryan's arm. He took a sip of coffee and touched a napkin to his mouth. "Guarantee you a hundred and a half for three days. No, shit, say two days. You're fast, the way you work. You don't locate him in two days, you get paid anyway and we talk about it some more, see if there's any point in continuing."

"This client of yours—he pays the bills?"

"Sure he does, he's looking for the guy, I'm not. I'm helping him out strictly as a favor."

Ryan got out his notebook. "How do you spell his name? The guy I'm looking for."

"Robert Leary. L-e-a-r-y. Junior. J-u-n-i-o-r." Jay Walt glanced over to see if the girl next to him was listening, appreciating him. She was biting into a club sandwich, then wiped some mayonnaise from the corner of her mouth. "Last known address 146 Arden Park."

Ryan looked at him with a question.

"I know," Jay Walt said, "it's all colored down there now, but it's still a pretty good street—big houses, mansions. I think a lot of colored doctors must live there, or else it's all whorehouses, I don't know."

Ryan was sure the girl was still listening. Dumb guy. That's what it was, not his confidence, he was just dumb, he didn't have any feelings. Ryan said, "When did Robert Leary, Jr., live there? How long ago?"

"Nineteen forty-one. It was still solid white then, a very classy address."

"That was thirty-five years ago—you don't have anything else? Something current?"

"Jackie, if I had something current I'd have called the guy up by now. This is why I'm talking to the pro, guaranteeing a hundred and a half."

The "Jackie" stopped Ryan. Jay Walt was the only person he knew who ever called him that. Ryan didn't consider himself a Jackie. It hooked him, Jay saying it in his loud voice.

"You want me to do it," Ryan said, "it'll be twenty bucks an hour. A hundred and a half gets you one day. But I'll probably have to make some inquiries and they'll have to be followed up the next day or maybe even the day after, so it looks to me like we're talking about three hundred guaranteed. If that's too steep for you, then put your shitheads back on it."

Jay Walt was staring at him through his tinted glasses. "What'd I say?"

"You didn't say anything."

"All of a sudden, on the muscle."

"I'm telling you the terms, my rate on something like this." Ryan kept his voice low, calm but with a little edge to it. "Since you're not paying, what do you care what I charge, right? Or do you have to get an okay?"

"I got a little flexibility in negotiating," Jay Walt said. "Naturally. It's pretty much up to me."

"So maybe I'm low," Ryan said, "and we should start over."

"No, I think you did pretty good. You're coming along, Jackie."

"Also, a hundred and a half in advance," Ryan said. "I don't mean in ninety days, I mean before I do anything."

"I'll call the guy," Jay Walt said, "have him mail you a check." He hesitated. "No, wait a minute—"

"How about if I pick it up? Save him the trouble."

"Well, actually, see, he doesn't want to deal with too many people. This guy, he's from out of town, doesn't have a lot of time." Jay Walt was thinking and talking at the same time.

Ryan saw it. "If he sends me a check, I'm going to know who he is, anyway. What's his name?"

"Let's keep it simple." Jay Walt had his billfold out and his thoughts in order. "I give you the advance, you won't have to worry about it anymore. We keep the deal simple, strictly between you and me."

"Why don't you want me to know who it is?"

Jay Walt was holding the billfold open, looking inside.

Ryan watched him. The girl was eating her sandwich, not paying any attention. "Hey, Jay? What's the big secret? What's it about?"

"You wouldn't know the guy, anyway. He's from out of town."

"Then what's the difference?"

"You want the hundred and a half or not?"

Ryan didn't ask any more questions.

He got right on it, beginning with the Detroit City Directory for 1941. Then looked up the next few years.

Robert Leary, Jr., was not listed as a resident of 146 Arden Park in any of the volumes. Allen Anderson was the only name that appeared.

Next he visited the records section, Detroit Department of Health. Robert Leary, Jr., finally showed up. Born at Harper Hospital. Parents, Robert J. and Clara Anne. Date of birth . . .

Ryan paused, looking at the date. Right there—July 20, 1941—his job ceased to be routine. Or else somebody had made a mistake. Robert Leary, Jr., at least the one on record, was not sixty years old. He was thirty-five.

Board of Education records confirmed it. Robert Leary, Jr., had attended Cass Technical High School during the years 1957–58. There was no record of his having graduated.

At the Wayne County Clerk's office Ryan found out that Robert Leary, Jr., and a Denise Leann Watson had been issued a marriage license August 11, 1973.

There was no Denise Leary or Watson listed in the telephone directory.

Ryan was in a phone booth in the lobby of the Detroit City-County Building. He called his friend Dick Speed and arranged to meet him at the Athens Bar on Monroe, around the corner from police headquarters.

In an hour, Dick Speed said.

That was fine with Ryan. It would give him a chance to look up probate court records and see if he could learn something about the Allen Anderson family, who were living at 146 Arden Park the year Robert Leary, Jr., was born. There was a connection, or else Leary wouldn't have been listed with that address.

Ryan had another idea. Before he left the phone booth he called both the *Detroit News* and the *Free Press* and dictated an insertion for their personal columns in the classified section. Both for tomorrow's editions.

He almost called Jay Walt, to tell him what he had learned so far, then decided no, don't appear eager. Make it look easy.

Ryan and Dick Speed had gone to high school at the same time, Catholic Central. Both had played varsity football and baseball and American Legion ball. Both their dads had worked at Ford Highland Park. Ryan remembered Speed's brush cut in '62, the year he graduated from Western Michigan with a Phys. Ed. major. He had tried out as a free-agent defensive back with the Browns, Bengals, Redskins, and Lions and finally put in his application at the Detroit Police Academy. Ryan had thought he'd make the pros on his name alone, Christ, Dick Speed, six-one, two-ten; but Speed found out he couldn't back-pedal worth a shit and those skinny black wide receivers would show him a hip and be on their way.

Dick Speed had hair now, layers of it, and choker beads and tight faded Levi's and a .357 Mag that was almost as big as Clint Eastwood's.

Sipping his Stroh's in the Athens Bar, he told Ryan he was with Squad Six now—a special unit of the Criminal Investigation Division that handled drug-related homicides: a lot of execution-type killings where the guy was tied up and gagged and shot in the head.

"Like in the movies," Ryan said.

"The movies, shit," Dick Speed said. "I mean you can't imagine the mess, a guy gets hit in the head. All over the wall, the floor. Jesus, it's something."

"You ever get sick?"

"No, I never did. These other guys, the old pros, they'd wait to see how you're going to take it. But I never have been sick. Knock wood. Shit, knock Formica in this place."

"I wanted to ask you if you could do me a favor."

"The movies, listen, you want to see the real

thing," Dick Speed said, "I can arrange it, ride in the meat wagon sometime. Shit, you'd die."

"Then what would I want to do it for?"

"Sunday morning early's the best time. Come back to Receiving with the meat wagon, then stop by the morgue, see all the Saturday night hotshots, the good time they had."

Ryan was polite and listened and made a few comments, but he wasn't buying him beer to learn about dope-related executions or Sunday mornings at the morgue.

"Listen," Ryan said, "I got to get over to Probate before it closes"—where he had just come from—"and I was wondering if you could do me a favor. Look and see if you got a sheet on a Robert Leary, Jr."

"What's he supposed to've done?"

"Nothing I know of," Ryan said. "But if a guy's hard to find, I was wondering maybe it's because he's got something to hide. Am I wrong?"

"There could be all kinds of reasons," Dick Speed said. "Maybe he owes money, hasn't paid his alimony. You sure this guy's still around?"

"No, I'm not, but I started thinking—what if he's in jail? I'm looking up all the records and he's sitting there waiting."

"You know something you're not telling me?"

"No, it's just a thought," Ryan said. "Something I might've overlooked."

3

THE TWO-INCH NOTICE that appeared in the Personal columns of the *News* and the *Free Press* said:

Robert Leary, Jr.
Urgent!
Call 355-1919

Ryan planned to stay in the apartment all day if he had to. By midmorning he was restless, not used to sitting around. Pacing and looking out the window didn't help much until a Detroit Edison crew came along and started tearing up the street with jackhammers. Watching them dig into the pavement, making gradual progress, was better than only listening to the noise. They'd stop for a while and stand around in their yellow slickers and he'd watch TV, popping from one channel to another to find something interesting. *Search for Tomorrow* wasn't too bad. He was going to have a sandwich when he got hungry, then decided to cook one of his specials. He sautéed onions and green pepper, threw in a can of tomatoes, peas, and cut-up ham, and dished it over Minute rice. He could do a lot with a can of tomatoes: tomatoes and lima beans, tomatoes and corn. Brown some chicken or chuck roast first, put it back in the tomatoes and onions to simmer awhile and dish it out over rice or noodles. Ryan loved it. Rita said everything he cooked tasted the same.

When the phone rang the first time, he took his time walking over to the footlocker that served as a coffee table and cleared his throat before he picked up the phone and said hello.

It was his sister, Marion. She hadn't called in at least six months, but she picked today. She was wondering how things were going, *living alone*. He had been living alone for four and a half years, but Marion was still wondering and asked him when did he want to come over for a home-cooked meal. Ryan said anytime, you name it. Marion was not that much of a cook. In fact, she was pretty bad. But he always said that, anytime. She never picked a date beforehand but always waited until she got him on the phone and then would have to go and get her calendar and study it and try to remember what nights Earl bowled or had Cub Scouts or an Ushers Club meeting. Ryan told her he was expecting an important phone call, but it still took another ten minutes.

He knew it was a remote chance the guy would see the notice in the personals, or that a friend might see it and tell him—if the guy had a friend and if he hadn't moved away and a few more ifs. Still, he had to give it a chance. And if the guy did call and the line was busy—he didn't know anything about the guy, if he was impatient or if he'd wait and try again. He wanted at least to cover all the bases, so he could hand in a full report and show them what he did for the three hundred. It surprised him a little that he felt this way, that he was conscientious.

By the time the phone rang again, at a quarter past four, Ryan had decided sitting by a telephone was a pretty dumb way to make a buck, and if the guy didn't call by five, he'd go for a ride and lay some paper on somebody.

Ryan said hello and the voice on the other end said, "What do you want?" There were faint sounds in the background, voices and music. Country music.

"Who is this?"

"That's what I want to know. Who're you?"

"My name's Ryan. I represent someone who's looking for—"

"What is it?"

"Ryan. R-y-a-n."

"You want Robert Leary, it said call this number. What do you want?"

"I'm trying to tell you," Ryan said. "Are you Robert Leary, Jr.?"

"What is it you want?"

"Tell me something. What year were you born?"

"What year . . ." There was a pause. "You said call this number. What do you want?"

"I want to know if I'm talking to Robert Leary, Jr."

"This is him."

"You in a bar? . . . You drinking?"

There was a pause again and the background sound was blocked out, as though a hand had been placed over the phone.

"Hey," Ryan said. "You still there?"

"What do you want?"

The voice was low and husky. Ryan pictured it coming from an old man.

"You want to see me?"

"I want to see Robert Leary, Jr. Tell me what year you were born."

"Listen, you want to see me or not?"

"All right," Ryan said. "Where do you live?"

"Meet me—you know where the bus station is?"

"Downtown?"

"Yeah. Nine o'clock tonight. Park on the roof of the bus station—wait a minute." Another pause, silence. "What kind of car you drive?" Ryan told him. "Okay, park up on the roof, take the elevator down. Go over and stand—wait a minute." Again a pause, longer this time. "Hello?"

"Yeah."

"Go over and wait by the door to the men's room."

"How'll I know you?" Ryan said.

"Nine o'clock. You want to see me, be there."

"Let me ask you something."

Robert Leary, Jr., or whoever it was, hung up.

Ryan called Dick Speed. He was out on assignment. So Ryan sat around again, wondering if he should bother going all the way down to the bus station. He was reasonably sure the guy on the phone wasn't Robert Leary, Jr. In fact, he knew it wasn't. The guy could have been calling for Leary, though, getting instructions from Leary during the pauses. That was a possibility. So he'd have to go down to the bus station, go through the motions, and put in the report.

The second Robert Leary, Jr., called at five to seven, while Ryan was changing his clothes. This time he forgot to clear his throat before picking up the phone.

"Your number 355-1919?"

"That's right."

"Who am I talking to?" A slow, quiet voice; maybe a southern accent.

"My name's Ryan. What's yours?"

"You put that in the paper today?"

"I'm the one," Ryan said. "Are you Robert Leary, Jr.?"

"I don't know you," the voice said.

"No, I don't know you either," Ryan said. "Are you Robert Leary?"

"Yeah. What do you want?"

"You mind I ask you when you were born?"

There was a silence as the man waited, still on the line.

"I want to be sure I'm talking to the right party," Ryan said. "If you are, all I need to know is where I can get in touch with you, or where you live."

The second Robert Leary, Jr., hung up.

Shit.

Ryan waited around until eight-fifteen. There were no more calls.

Dick Speed returned his call at eleven-thirty that evening.

"I've been trying to get you for a couple of hours."

"I had to go down to the bus station."

"The *bus* station?"

"It's a long, boring story."

"Well, this Robert Leary, Jr., I hope to shit you don't have to serve him papers."

"Why?"

"The guy's a fucking beauty."

Ryan listened then for several uninterrupted minutes while Dick Speed read the sheets on Leary. Ryan listened and said, reverently, when he finished, "Jesus Christ."

Ryan didn't get hold of Jay Walt until the next morning. He said over the phone, "I don't think twenty bucks an hour is going to make it. The three hundred for openers, okay, you've spent that. But now, what I've found out so far, I think it's possible I could get killed if I keep at it. But not for any twenty bucks an hour. We make another deal and you tell me what's going on before I tell you anything."

Jay Walt got back to Ryan within fifteen minutes. He said he had to do a little talking, but finally arranged a meeting. Ryan was to go to the Pontchartrain Hotel and ask for a Mr. Perez.

"Aren't you going to be there?"

"Well, not right away. He said he wanted to see you alone."

Jay Walt didn't sound too happy about it.

4

"THERE'S NOTHING MYSTERIOUS ABOUT IT," Mr. Perez said with his soft accent. "My business is finding lost stockholders. People who own stock in a company but don't know it."

"Why don't they know it?" Ryan asked him.

"We'll get to that if you're interested." Mr. Perez uncrossed his legs and pulled himself out of the deep chair. "I'm sorry, I didn't ask you what you drink." He picked up a glass from the coffee table and moved away.

"Nothing, thanks," Ryan said.

"Too early, huh? I have my dinner at noon. So I start anytime a half hour before." The way he said "my dinner" with the soft drawl sounded good, something he enjoyed, though he didn't look like a big eater. He was bony, in fact, with a long, bony nose that was discolored with broken blood vessels. He looked more like a drinker than an eater.

"Where's your home?" Ryan asked him.

"Baton Rouge, when I'm not somewhere else. I

also have a home at Pass Christian, on the Gulf. But
I haven't seen much of it lately, been spending most
of my time up this way."

Ryan sat in a straight chair with arms, his damp
raincoat across his lap. He was having a hard time
typing Mr. Perez. Light-skinned Cuban or old
Louisiana Spanish maybe, with a halo of hair that
had receded to the top of his head and an air of relaxed self-confidence. The man knew who he was.
It didn't bother him that his white shirt was rum-
pled or his necktie had slipped and was off-center.
Ryan watched him go over to a low bookcase that
was set up with several bottles of liquor and glasses
and a silver ice bucket. Next to the bar, an alcove
window of tinted glass reached to the floor, framing
a view of the Detroit River and the Ambassador
Bridge to Canada. It was still raining, coming down
out of a washed-out gray sky that had been hanging over the city for days.

Ryan wondered how much the hotel suite cost.
There was a desk piled with folders and papers and
a thick briefcase on the chair next to it. Beyond the
desk, through an open doorway, he saw twin beds
with gold spreads and gold headboards. He bet it
was costing the guy a hundred a day, at least. He
wondered if the guy was a lawyer. He looked like
one: not the corporate lawyer, but the downtown
city-hall lawyer.

"What do you call what you do?"

Mr. Perez was coming back with his whiskey over ice, taking his time.

"My title? Well, my card says I'm an investment consultant. How's that sound?" Mr. Perez smiled easily.

"I suppose you're a lawyer, too."

"Why do you suppose that?" He lowered himself carefully, holding the lowball glass in front of him, and sank down in the chair.

"I guess I just assumed you were."

"You hire lawyers," Mr. Perez said. "You don't have to be one. Thank God."

"Can I ask you, how do you happen to know Jay Walt?"

"I don't know him. Least I didn't," Mr. Perez said. "I used him once before, he was all right. You see, locating people, a very good way to find out about them is through their credit rating. So I generally use somebody in the business. I believe he was the first or second one in the Yellow Pages, Allied Credit something or other. Let me ask you, are you a friend of his?"

"No," Ryan said.

"You don't care too much for him either."

Ryan didn't say anything.

"I have kind of a negative feeling myself," Mr. Perez said. "Man talks out loud in elevators. I was thinking, there's not much reason to keep him around. That's if you've got something to tell me."

"A few things," Ryan said. "But I don't know what I'm into yet. I don't know what's going on."

"You're trying to locate a lost stockholder who, I hope, doesn't know he's lost," Mr. Perez said. "See, the way I go about it, I pick out a company that was around during the depression, when the value of their stock was quite low or maybe worthless. I go to the company and I say, 'If you give me the names of any stockholders you've lost track of, I'll see if I can locate them for you, at my own expense. Get the dead wood out of your stockholder list and bring it up to date.' See, what happens from time to time, the company will get back a dividend check they sent out. Or their annual report comes back. Maybe the person died and the company wasn't notified. Or moved and didn't leave a forwarding address. The company usually doesn't make much of an effort to find the person. They go through the motions, then after a while, if they still haven't located the party, they put the name on their list of lost stockholders."

"What I was wondering before," Ryan said, "the stockholder, I mean if he's alive, he knows he owns the stock, doesn't he?"

"You'd be surprised," Mr. Perez said. "He might've put it away thirty years ago and forgot about it. Or he thought the company went broke during the depression. Or, what happens, he inherits the stock but never looks at it to see what it is.

Now it's buried under some old papers in the bottom of a desk. So, I get the list from the company and go to work."

"They just give it to you?"

"Why wouldn't they?" Mr. Perez stared, interested in Ryan's answer.

"Well, I'd think it would be privileged information. I can't see the company taking the chance, exposing their stockholders to, well, they don't know what, do they?"

Mr. Perez smiled. "You were going to say exposing them to some kind of con. Believe me, Mr. Ryan, there's nothing questionable or suspicious about what I do. You're right, though. Some companies are hesitant. They feel they have to consider my proposition very carefully, discuss it, get approval from the board, all that. Well, in those cases, what I do, I get on friendly terms with one of the third- or fourth-level executives of the company and ask him to let me have the list—he knows I'm not going to do anything illegal—and avoid a lot of red tape and confusion."

"What's that cost you?"

"Not a thing. Oh, I may send him a case of scotch, something like that." Mr. Perez paused, but Ryan didn't say anything. "It's done all the time."

"So then you try to find the lost stockholder."

"That's right. I locate the individual and I tell

him I have knowledge of a certain property in his name that's of some value."

"You don't tell him it's stock."

"No, that might be telling too much. I ask him to sign an agreement first, giving me a percent of the value as a finder's fee. He does that, then I tell him what it is."

"Can I ask you, what percent do you get?"

"Well, it depends. Sometimes, if there's a lot of work involved, as much as half." Mr. Perez took a sip of his whiskey and lit a cigarette. He was comfortable in the deep chair, at ease talking about himself. "So now the guy scratches his head and tries to think of what it is he owns or if something could have been left to him or what. Or he might want to talk to a lawyer first. That's fine. Sometimes they'll dig around and find the stock or remember it from years and years ago and I'm out of luck. I say thank you, I'll be on my way. But if he doesn't know what it is, then he signs the agreement and gives me power of attorney to handle the transaction. We sell the stock back to the company or on the open market, I take my percent, and everybody's satisfied."

"What if he doesn't want to sell it?"

"That's all right, he can pay me the equivalent of my percent."

Ryan was trying to picture it. He said, "I can't

imagine the stockholder being too happy, splitting something he owns with a guy walks in off the street."

"You get different reactions," Mr. Perez said. "Most people are very grateful. I've found something that's been lost and they look on it as paying a reward for its return."

"I suppose, if you look at it that way," Ryan said. Like Mr. Perez was doing them a favor. Maybe he was. But there was something about it, something about warm, friendly Mr. Perez that bothered Ryan. He wondered about other sides of the man; what he was like when he was pissed off, or when a deal fell through, or when he didn't like somebody. Mr. Perez had already, no trouble at all, crossed off Jay Walt.

"Now tell me what you've got," Mr. Perez said, "that's worth more than two hundred dollars a day."

"I told Jay Walt a hundred and fifty," Ryan said. "Not two hundred."

"Well, I guess he added on a commission, then." It didn't seem to bother Mr. Perez. "What you got?"

Ryan told him that Robert Leary, Jr., first of all, was thirty-five, not sixty; had gone to school in Detroit, briefly, and had married a Denise Leann Watson a few years ago.

"You see," Mr. Perez said, "I assumed he was an adult back in 1941 when the stock was listed in his name. But he would've just been born then, wouldn't he?"

"We're getting to that," Ryan said. He told Mr. Perez that Robert Leary, Jr., was never listed as a resident of 146 Arden Park. But Probate records showed the owner and resident, a man by the name of Allen Anderson, died in 1941 and left his entire estate to his wife and children, with the exception of fifteen hundred shares of common stock, with a value at the time of a dollar a share, that was left to a Robert Leary, a household employee of the Andersons for some twenty years.

"Did the record say what the stock is?"

"I don't think so. It said other considerations, including stock certificates."

Mr. Perez nodded. "So it was his father. The stock's left to him, his son's born about the time and he reassigns the stock in his son's name. Pay for his college education, so he won't have to be a servant like his father. That must be what happened."

"Well, I don't know about college," Ryan said, "but the man you want has spent some time in institutions." He took folded sheets of paper out of his inside coat pocket and looked at Mr. Perez as he opened them. "I have a friend, he's with the Detroit police."

"That's a good place to have one," Mr. Perez said.

"I stopped off this morning, made these notes. You ready?"

"I can't wait," Mr. Perez said.

"Robert Leary, Jr., also known as Bobby Lear," Ryan began. . . .

Born in Detroit. Both parents deceased by the time he was ten. Raised in foster homes. . . .

"I can get the names if I need them."

. . . attended Cass Technical High School, dropped out, was drafted and sent to Vietnam, where, according to U.S. Army psychiatrists, he suffered a severe nervous breakdown during a mortar barrage near Chu Lai. Leary was hospitalized and returned to duty on a "maintenance dosage" of Thorazine. Evacuated again for treatment and hospitalized for psychiatric disorders in Japan, in Hawaii, and finally at Valley Forge General, Phoenixville, Pennsylvania, from which he was discharged as one hundred percent psychiatrically disabled. Leary was given an honorable discharge, and a guaranteed income for life, and returned to Detroit to begin killing people.

"My," Mr. Perez said. He was holding his glass, about to take a drink. "That's what it says?"

"That's the way I put it down," Ryan said.

He beat a woman to death with his fists. Her name was Thelma Simpson and she was said to be his girl friend.

Ryan looked up. "Leary was married at the time, but none of the police reports mention his wife."

Two days later he shot and killed Eugene Bailey,

a known dope dealer who Leary believed was fooling around with Thelma Simpson. Leary's attorney, at the trial, called in V.A. hospital psychiatrists to testify. Leary was declared insane and sent to the state hospital at Northville. Within six months he was judged to be normal and released.

Leary was arrested for armed robbery—charged, along with two others, with the holdup of a savings and loan company—then acquitted when the witnesses, in court, changed their previous testimony and could not make a positive identification of Leary.

Leary was arrested for the attempted murder of Ronnie J. Hughes in a dope pad on Orchestra Place and released on bond. A week later Ronnie J. Hughes was killed in front of a bar on Twelfth Street by an unknown assailant. Three days later the two men who had witnessed the dope-pad shooting were found at the foot of Twenty-third Street near the river; both had been bound and shot through the head at close range.

Leary walked into the Veterans Administration Hospital in Allen Park claiming to be the President of the United States. A week later he checked into the Battle Creek V.A. hospital and remained under observation five days.

Leary shot and severely wounded a man in a bar on Cass Avenue over a ten-dollar gambling debt. The charge was reduced to felonious assault, and

Leary was sent to Jackson to serve a three and a half to four. His lawyer appealed, basing his case on Leary's history of mental illness, and he was transferred to the Ionia State Hospital. Three months later he was released.

Leary shot and killed a man by the name of Teddy "Too Much" Smith in his white Eldorado while Teddy Smith's three-year-old son, sitting in the front seat, watched.

A police informant who knew Leary said, "Bobby told me one time he never had to worry about going to jail for very long on account he had a act he put on." The man pointed to his head.

Leary told a state psychiatrist he had probably killed twenty people. Following the shooting of Teddy Smith, he gave the police the names of ten victims after he was promised immunity from prosecution. The police believed he was telling the truth about eight of the victims and closed those cases. Most of the victims lived in Leary's neighborhood and were involved commercially in narcotics. Few, if anybody, would miss them; especially the police. Leary was brought to trial for the murder of Teddy Smith, was again judged insane, and was committed to the state's Center for Forensic Psychiatry at Ypsilanti.

In five years of arrests, convictions, plea bargaining, and insanity judgments, shuttling between Jackson and several different state hospitals, Leary spent only a few months at a time in prison. Psychiatrists from Valley Forge General, Jackson, Ionia, Northville, Battle Creek, and the forensic center came to Leary's trials and hearings during the five-year period and testified repeatedly, unequivocally, that Robert Leary was suffering from paranoid schizophrenia, an essentially incurable mental illness. Finally, making his most recent appeal from the forensic center, Leary insisted he had lied to the psychiatrists in an attempt to make them believe he was insane. He then made a statement that he was, as of now, sane and, in a probate hearing, demanded his release. The jury believed Robert Leary and he was allowed to return to the street. That had been two months ago.

"Mmmm, that's not so good, is it?" Mr. Perez said. "Sounds like a mean bugger, doesn't he? Hard to talk to."

"I'll tell you something else that's not so good," Ryan said. "Somebody's looking for him besides me. I put an ad in the personals. Robert Leary, Jr., urgent, and a number, phone number. Two different guys called, both saying they're Robert Leary, Jr., and what do I want to see him about. One of them says he'll meet me at the Greyhound station nine o'clock. Nobody showed up. At least that I know of. Maybe he did, whoever it is, and got a look at me, my car, and now I'm being watched. I don't know. One, let's say, is the real Robert Leary. The other one, I've got a feeling he's looking for Robert Leary, too, and he thinks maybe I can help him."

"How about his parole officer? You talk to him?"

"Leary, Bobby Lear, isn't out on parole, he was released, clean."

"So the assignment, you might say, has taken on a different complexion. Might be a little more difficult than it looked at first, uh?"

"It isn't that it's more difficult so much as I'm getting mixed up with people who shoot each other," Ryan said, "and it's a little different than what I'm used to."

"Well, maybe if you had more of an incentive," Mr. Perez said, in his quiet tone. "I don't want you to feel I'm pushing you or talking you into continuing, you understand. It's entirely up to you. I can understand why you might be apprehensive, the fact he's killed people." Mr. Perez paused, and for a moment his mouth showed the trace of a smile. "He does sound like a mean son of a bitch, doesn't he? Bobby Lear." He took a drink before looking at Ryan again. "But I don't see why it would be necessary for you to confront him or have any conversation with him. All I'd like you to do is locate him for me. Get on his trail and follow it, anywhere he might have gone."

Ryan waited for him to finish. "You mentioned something about more of an incentive."

"Yeah . . . I was thinking maybe a percentage

rather than an hourly rate or a per diem," Mr. Perez said. "That is, if you locate him and I'm able to make a deal. Say, oh . . . ten percent?"

"Ten percent of what, the stock?"

"Yeah, the whole thing."

"The stock's only worth a buck a share, isn't it?"

"In 1941 it was," Mr. Perez said. "Its cash value now, I'd say, would be around a hundred and fifty thousand. We'd have to look into the accumulated dividends, so it could be several thousand more."

Ryan saw the figure in his mind, fifteen grand, a clean round figure. But he wanted to be sure. "I get ten percent of a hundred and fifty thousand?"

"If you find him and *if* I make a deal, get him to agree."

"Ten percent of the hundred and fifty," Ryan said, still wanting to be sure. "Not ten percent of what you get."

"Say fifteen thousand minimum," Mr. Perez said. "I'll draw up an agreement, give it to you in writing."

"What do you think the chances are? I mean of you getting him to go along with it?"

"Four to one. I sign eighty percent of the people I locate," Mr. Perez said. "Ah, but locating them, that's the bugger. It comes down to a question of how much time to allow in relation to the potential gain. I can afford to put a little more time in on this one. I can afford to hire you and sit here and discuss a proposition. Otherwise, Mr. Ryan, I doubt we'd have sufficient reason to be talking to each other about anything."

Mr. Perez spoke and revealed little glimpses of himself, what the real Mr. Perez thought and felt. That was fine with Ryan. It was a business deal. They weren't going to the ball game together.

"So now I'll ask you," Mr. Perez said, "what you think your chances are of locating him."

Ryan thought a moment. He almost told the truth and said he didn't know, that maybe he wouldn't even come close. But he didn't.

He said, "I usually hit about ninety percent. As you say, time's a factor. If I wasn't concerned with that, I'd probably do better." Ryan picked up his raincoat from his lap and draped it over one arm. He seemed about to get up, then sank back into the chair again.

"I almost forgot. You said something about a written agreement, didn't you?"

Mr. Perez picked up the phone to call room service for his noon dinner, then changed his mind and placed a person-to-person call to Mr. Raymond Gidre in New Iberia, Louisiana. He took the phone over to the deep chair and sank down comfortably.

After a moment he said, "Raymond, how you doing, boy? I bet you got a big plate of crawfish in front of you and a glass of cold beer. . . . What?"

Mr. Perez laughed. "That's just as good. You can't get nothing like that up here. . . . Uh-huh. Listen, Raymond? How'd you like to come to Detroit for a few days? . . . No, this one's a little different. Man turns out, he likes to shoot people. . . . I'm telling you the truth." Mr. Perez listened, then began to grin. "Now you're talking. We got one here, Raymond, I believe we can go all the way. . . . You bet. You get ready and I'll call you back, tell you when exactly I need you. . . . Fine, Raymond. Be good now, I'll see you."

Mr. Perez picked up the phone again and asked for room service.

"How you doing?" Mr. Perez said. "You got any crawfish? . . . No, I don't want crayfish, I want *craw*fish. . . . I didn't think so. How about boiled shrimp? . . . With the shells on. You peel 'em, dip 'em in hot sauce. . . . What? All right, I'll call you back."

Mr. Perez went over to the desk and shuffled through the papers and file folders. He opened the drawer then. There it was. Mr. Perez took the room-service menu back to his chair, looking at it.

Bunch of shit.

About all he could do was get this deal done and hope it didn't take too long.

5

"THE THING THAT BOTHERS ME ABOUT HIM," RYAN SAID, "here's this businessman, investment consultant—he's staying in this suite at the Pontch has got to cost him a hundred bucks a day—I tell him about Robert Leary, about the people he's killed, and he grins and says, 'Sounds like a mean bugger, doesn't he?'"

"Maybe he was being cool," Dick Speed said. "Trying to impress you."

Dick Speed was driving an unmarked Ford sedan, turning off Saint Antoine now and heading out Gratiot Avenue, creeping along about twenty-five.

"I don't think so," Ryan said. "It was real, the way he sounded. See, it bothered me that it didn't bother him, the idea of doing business with a homicidal maniac. Christ, a guy like that out on the street."

"Maybe he is, we don't know."

"You don't care, is what you mean," Ryan said. "You only care about him if he kills somebody else."

"Like you maybe, messing around with him."

"Shit, I don't even want to see the guy."

"Well, I promise you this, buddy," Dick Speed said. "Make you feel better. If he kills you, I promise I'll get the son of a bitch if it's the last thing I do."

"Thanks," Ryan said. "What I'd really like is if you could find out something about Mr. Francis X. Perez. How would you do that? Teletype Baton Rouge? New Orleans maybe?"

"I'd pick up the phone. You know, they think I'm working, all this shit I'm doing for you."

"I appreciate it. Don't think I don't."

"When do I get this big dinner?"

"You name it. Whenever you're free."

"I can see it," Dick Speed said. "You call up say come on over, I got this tomato surprise shit." He crept along the inside lane, his gaze on the storefronts and the people on the sidewalk. Most of them were black. "Tomato and fucking cornflakes or something."

"I never tried that. Where's the place?"

"Few blocks. He could be walking. I've never seen him drive."

"How do you know he'll be there?"

"I called. They said he'd probably be in. He's due for his fix."

Ryan said, "Listen, I don't want to be taking up all your time."

"Then what're you doing it for?"

"I said I'd talk to the guy. You don't have to come."

"You talk to him, but he won't talk to you," Dick Speed said. "Not alone. Be looking over his shoulder all the time. Ask him what it's like, being a police snitch. You'll see him trying to act cool, but he's scared shitless. There it is, next to the drugstore."

Dick Speed coasted past the storefronts, the drugstore and the one with the show windows painted white and the posters Ryan couldn't read from the car, and pulled into a parking place on the street, a few stores down in the block of fifty-year-old two-story buildings that were scarred and worn out before their time, some of them with collapsible iron grating over the display windows.

"I expected a sign," Ryan said. "Methadone center."

Dick Speed was watching the sidewalk, turning to look through the rear window at the painted storefront.

"They know where it is. The ones that need it."

"This guy was a junkie?"

"He was everything, if you believe him. You got to weed out the bullshit."

"What's the guy's name?"

"Tunafish."

"That's all, just Tunafish?"

"You got a name like that, what else you need?"

Ryan kept looking at his watch. When they'd

been there thirty minutes he said, "Doesn't look like he's going to show, does it? Maybe we ought to come back." He was antsy; he could never stand sitting around very long.

"You want to talk to the guy or not?" Dick Speed said. "I could be at the Athens instead of out in the fucking rain so I can get invited to the big dinner."

Ryan told him not to think he didn't appreciate it, and looked at his watch again.

An hour and ten minutes passed.

"There he is," Dick Speed said. "See, you're patient, God rewards you. The skinny jig with the afro."

Ryan ducked his head to look through the rear window. There were two black guys in front of the place, moving away from each other but still talking.

"They both got afros."

"No, the finger waves, that's a superfly," Dick Speed said. "Don't you know your hairstyles? That's our boy in the leather coat. Turning his collar up. Ahhh, coming this way now, finished their chitchat. The other one's name is Lonnie. He talks to the narcs, tells them interesting stories, and they let him deal a little grass. How do you like the fucking shoes? He's about five-foot nothing in his socks."

"He's coming," Ryan said. "Tunafish."

"Don't worry. I got him."

Tunafish was almost even with the unmarked car, his head turned against the misty rain. Dick Speed opened the door and stood up outside. He said over the top of the car, "Get in the back."

The skinny black guy didn't say anything. He looked back over his shoulder as he got in. Dick Speed pulled out, turned the corner at the first side street, and parked in front of a vacant lot. There were old frame houses farther down. Dick Speed switched off the ignition. The sound of the engine and the windshield wipers stopped. It was quiet in the car. Tunafish sat on the right side of the back seat, his hands folded in his lap. His hair glistened with drops of moisture.

"My associate here," Dick Speed said, "wants to get hold of Robert Leary . . . Bobby Lear. Where does he go to find him?"

"Bobby Lear," Tunafish said, as if trying to picture him.

"Let's cut the shit, okay?" Dick Speed said. "Bobby Lear."

Ryan had the twenty in his raincoat pocket. His hand came out with the bill, folded twice, and reached over the backrest with it.

Tunafish took it and looked at it, then looked at Ryan as he put the twenty in his shirt pocket, under the leather coat. His expression didn't say if he was happy with it or not; his expression didn't say anything. His eyes moved from Ryan and he seemed to be staring straight ahead, at the rain filming the windshield.

"Nobody know where he is," Tunafish said. "Nobody seen him."

"He's out," Dick Speed said. "Why should he hide?"

"I don't know. Maybe he heard something."

"People talking about him?"

"They say some friends of his. They get together and decide somebody should put a gun next to Bobby Lear's head."

"Kill him?" Ryan said.

"For the sake of humanity and everybody's ass," Tunafish said. "Nobody feel safe with him anymore."

"Who're the friends?" Dick Speed asked him.

"Man, that's a hard one."

Dick Speed looked at Ryan.

Ryan reached into his pocket and came out with another twenty. Tunafish took it.

"You're doing all right," Dick Speed said, "for a relatively shitty afternoon. Who'd you say these friends are?"

"See, most of them talking big, bullshitting each other, saying how they gonna burn that motherfucker, put him out of his misery. But only one might do it, get out of bed in the morning pure, not on any high, and do it. You know who I mean?"

"Tell us," Dick Speed said.

"Bobby Lear, only armed robbery bust he ever had. You remember it? About four years ago."

"Wyandotte Savings and Loan," Dick Speed said.

Tunafish nodded. "That's the one. Bobby Lear and two others. Bobby Lear got off, no positive I.D. Wendell Haines is dead. That leaves one more. Look on your job sheet."

"Virgil Royal," Dick Speed said. "He went to Jackson."

"He went and he come back."

"So what's the talk?"

"That Virgil have a private reason to see him. Besides helping humanity, help Virgil Royal, too. You dig?"

Ryan had a question. He waited, listening to them talking about Virgil Royal. He didn't understand most of it. When Tunafish paused, Ryan said, "How about his wife? You know where I can find her?"

Tunafish was thoughtful again, shaking his head.

Dick Speed said, "Come on, you been paid."

"No, man," Tunafish said, "I didn't know that, the man had a wife. There was a lady I used to see him with—I can't think of her name."

"Thelma Simpson," Dick Speed said.

"No, Thelma—he got her in the closet, she couldn't move, and beat on her till she was dead. No, I mean another lady, before he went to the hospital. Had real long hair, blond color, you know?

I'd see them once in a while, the lady have on these beads, fake African shit, was always drinking wine."

"What's her name?" Ryan asked him.

"Let's see—I believe it was Lee." Tunafish thought about it. "Yeah, he call her Lee."

"Where'd you see them?"

"Different places." Tunafish paused and his face almost came alive for the first time. "Hey, I seen her a week, two weeks ago. Was in the afternoon, she was alone. She had the blond hair and the beads, drinking wine. I said to myself, Who is that? Then I remember, yeah. But she look different."

"Where was it?" Ryan said. "A bar?"

"Yeah, on Cass," Tunafish said. "Shit, I don't know the name. Down near Masonic Temple."

"You think she lives around there?"

"I don't know, she might." Tunafish nodded then, still picturing her. "Yeah. I don't see any reason she be in the place unless she live around there. Trashy, man. Six, seven in the morning the bars open."

"What was different about her?" Ryan asked him. "You said she looked different."

Tunafish frowned, picturing her. "Yeah, well, not different. It was like she look sick. You know?"

Ryan didn't say much on the way back to where his car was parked on Beaubien. He thought about the girl named Lee, forming a picture of her in his mind, the blond hair and the beads and the glass of wine. In the picture she came across as a hooker, a flashy broad in a miniskirt and boots, somebody that would go around with a guy like Bobby Lear. Finding Lee would probably be next.

And if he couldn't find her, then the guy that was mentioned, Virgil something. He said to Dick Speed, "What's the guy's name, was in on the robbery with Leary, Virgil?"

"Virgil Royal."

"I didn't get that part of it."

"They held up the Wyandotte Savings and Loan. Virgil did time, Leary got off."

"Yeah, I understand that."

"What don't you get?"

"Why Virgil's looking for him. Because he got sent away and Leary didn't?"

"I think there's more to it than that," Speed said. "I think Leary made a deal and laid the job on Virgil, but I'm not sure. I wasn't in on that one, I'll have to look it up."

"And Mr. Perez," Ryan said. "Don't forget Mr. Perez."

Dick Speed phoned him that evening. "How'd you make out?"

Ryan was sitting on his fake-leather black couch,

his shoes off and his feet on a pillow on the foot-locker coffee table.

"I didn't plan it right," Ryan said. "I parked near Wayne University and walked south looking in the bars, every bar on Cass down to Temple, then another four or five blocks to be sure."

"Yeah?"

"I saw a lot of hookers getting their afternoon eye-opener and going to the grocery store, but I didn't run into anybody named Lee."

"Who said she was a hooker?"

"No, that's the way I see her. You know. Then I had to walk all the way back to get my car. How'd you do?" Ryan said. He was thinking of Mr. Perez.

"Well, there's a little more to it than I thought," Dick Speed said. "See, everybody *thinks* Leary laid the job on Virgil and that's why Virgil's pissed off. But that's not it. Virgil thinks Bobby Lear kept the money from the job and spent it while he was in the can. About eighteen grand."

"You mean you arrested them, but you didn't recover the money?"

"Well, actually, Bobby got about seventeen hundred from the cashiers that was never recovered. He must've spent it by now. But see, we had Virgil in the Wayne County Jail at that time waiting trial. So when the prosecutor's office is talking to him they pretend to let it slip that Bobby got about seventeen grand, not seventeen hundred, and stashed it someplace. See, Virgil *wants* to believe it, he's dying to—even if he read in the paper no money was taken—because he not only doesn't trust him, just associating with Bobby you never know, the guy's fucking wacko. Sometime he's liable to stick a gun in your mouth, you just don't know with a guy like that. The people here say that's, basically, what's on Virgil's mind, if he's thinking about anything."

"Jesus," Ryan said. "You actually do things like that?"

"Yeah, well, if we can't get to Bobby through channels, you know, and put him away, then we motivate Virgil and maybe he can do it. You think anybody's going to piss and moan over Bobby Lear?"

"*I* will," Ryan said. "Christ, I need him alive . . . at least for a while. How about Mr. Perez? You find out anything?"

"Not yet. I didn't have time this afternoon. Tomorrow, if that's soon enough."

"Listen, there's no hurry. It was just a thought," Ryan said. "The guy's probably a virgin and says the rosary every night before he goes to bed. But I wouldn't mind being sure."

6

THE GIRL WITH THE STRINGY BLOND HAIR over her shoulders and the trading beads and the black turtleneck and Levi's and the half-filled water glass of domestic wine in front of her on the bar said, "Do you like sex?"

Ryan hesitated. He said, "Sure."

The girl said, "You like to travel?"

Ryan said, "Yeah, I guess so."

The girl said, "Then why don't you fuck off?"

She was drunk—two o'clock in the afternoon—but didn't show it, sitting on the bar stool with her denim legs crossed. Maybe when she got up, if she ever did. She looked washed out and needed some sun, or makeup. Her blond hair was dirty, dull, flat to her head and showed dark roots. She was still a good-looking girl, in her late twenties or maybe thirty. She drank her Sauterne and smoked cigarettes and stayed somewhere inside herself.

"You do know him though, huh?"

"Who?"

"Bobby Lear."

"Never heard of him."

"You just said a minute ago, I asked you, you said—you called him something."

"I called him a cocksucker."

"So you don't think too highly of him. But you do know him," Ryan said. "Didn't you use to go around with him? I don't know, maybe you still do. That's what somebody told me."

"Who?"

"This guy that knows him."

"Who? Hoo, hoo. I sound like a fucking owl."

Ryan was patient. He knew he had no choice; he was talking to a drunk. He could resign himself to it, sip his Tab, or get up and leave.

An old man, a bum, had come out as Ryan approached the place—the Good Times Bar—walked across the sidewalk, leaned against the trunk lid of a car, and begun throwing up in the gutter. The old man was back inside, sitting at the bar with a bottle of beer. A black guy, in a maroon outfit, was at the end of the bar, near the door. The black guy was stylish, like a pro athlete, and didn't look as though he belonged here. Everyone else was drab, their clothes, their expressions. There were a few others, a man at the bar with a hacking cough, two men and a woman at a table. The woman had a high, irritating laugh. Everybody having a good time at the Good Times Bar, with its stale beer smell and afternoon sunlight showing through the venetian blinds. It was the first sunny day in a week, not a trace of smoke haze, and Ryan was sitting in a Cass Avenue bar drinking a can of Tab.

The girl, Lee, was on the fourth double Sauterne that Ryan had counted, the third one he had paid for. She would finish one with six good sips and two cigarettes. When the level was two-thirds of the way down the glass she'd be thinking of the next one.

"I've been looking for you for two days," Ryan said. "You know that? I started down there a few blocks, near Wayne, went in every bar on Cass. Then today, I came in here, I saw you and I had a hunch, I don't know why. I said to the bartender, hey, isn't that Lee down there?"

"I don't know you," she said.

"You know Bobby Lear, though. Robert Leary, Jr. What do you call him?"

"Shithead."

"You seen him lately?"

She finished the wine and brought the glass down hard on the bar.

"Innkeeper!"

The bartender with the bony shoulders took his hand off his thigh and his foot down from something behind the bar and came toward them.

"Same way?"

Ryan nodded. He let the bartender take her glass

and walk away before he said, "Lee . . . you're not worried I might be a cop, are you?" Ryan waited as she got out a cigarette. He held a match for her. "Believe me, I'm not a cop. . . . You want to know what I am?"

"I know what you are," the girl said. "I don't know who—hoo, hoo—but I know *what* you are. You're a fucking pervert, aren't you? You carry that raincoat—that's how you tell—bright sunny day, you got a raincoat."

"I didn't know when I left home it was going to be nice."

"Bullshit. You take your wang out and put the raincoat on, you see a little kid, little girl, you say, 'Hi, honey' "—her voice turned oily— " 'want to see the big snake I got in here?' "

"Except on cold days," Ryan said, "I describe myself."

She turned and looked at him with sleepy eyes. "You want to show it to me? Go ahead, take it out. Nobody gives a shit, it's a very friendly place. Art? You don't care if he takes his wang out, do you?"

"If it makes him happy," the bartender said. He put down the wine and can of Tab and took a dollar and a quarter from Ryan's change on the bar.

"I'll show it to you some other time," Ryan said. "Okay? Right now I got to find this guy and I don't seem to be getting anywhere."

"Hi, honey"—with the oily voice again—"you want to see my snake?"

"It's sleeping, gone nigh'-nigh'."

"Wake him up. Come on, I want to see what you've got."

"How about Leary's wife, Denise?" Ryan said. "You know her?"

The girl stopped, about to say something, and looked up at his face, staring at him.

"Do you know her?"

"Not very well."

"Do you know where she lives?" He waited.

But the girl's face turned away and she went back into herself. He watched her, after a moment, take another sip of wine.

"You want to get there, what're you fooling around with wine for?"

She didn't answer him.

"I used to drink mostly bourbon, over crushed ice, fill up a lowball glass. I also drank beer, wine, gin, vodka, Cuba Libres, Diet-Rite and scotch, and rye with red pop, but I preferred bourbon. Early Times. I knew a guy who drank only Fresca and chartreuse. I took a sip one time, I said to him, 'Jesus, this is the worst drink I ever tasted in my life.' He said, 'I know it is. It's so bad you can't drink very many of them.' A real alcoholic, though, can drink anything, right? . . . What time you start in the morning?"

Without looking at him the girl said, "Fuck off."

There was a silence. He watched her raise the glass.

"Okay, then, how much you drink a day?"

"I don't know," the girl said. "What do you think would be about right?"

"If you're not working, have the time, I'd say a gallon, gallon and a half. Depends what time you start."

"Early," the girl said.

"Right after you throw up?"

"Before," the girl said, looking directly at him now. "Before I get out of bed. Then I might throw up or I might piss in the bed, whichever comes first. You want to come home with me? You're so fucking interested, I'll show you what I did this morning."

"I've seen it," Ryan said. "I've been there. And you know what? I don't ever want to go back."

The girl turned to her glass of wine, subdued. She stared at it for a while before saying, "I'm not ready for you yet."

"Why put it off? Because you're having so much fun?"

"I'm not *ready*."

"You're close enough," Ryan said. "Every day you put it off you're going to hit harder when you quit. Maybe you want to crash and burn first, end up in detox. It's your choice, I'm not going to argue with you, try and convince you of anything. But listen"—he took one of his business cards out of his wallet and placed it on the bar next to her glass—"you've got to have a very good reason to want to kill yourself. Have you got one?"

The girl, staring at her glass, didn't answer. Ryan got up from the bar and left.

The black guy in the maroon suit stroked the corners of his bandit mustache. He picked up a wide-brimmed, Stetson-looking hat from the bar and went down to where the girl was hunched over the glass of wine. The tall, good-looking black guy lifted a hip onto the stool next to her.

He said, "Hey, Lee, what's happening?"

She looked at him sleepily, uninterested, and turned back to the bar.

"That man bothering you?"

"He wanted to show me his thing."

"Hey, no shit. He do it?"

The girl didn't answer him.

"He was looking for Bobby, wasn't he? . . . Lee?"

"Hey, Virgil," the girl said then. "You like sex?"

"What kind?"

"What?"

"I said what kind of sex you talking about? With a woman?"

"I don't know," the girl said. She seemed to have lost interest. "Forget it."

* * *

"Where's the key?" Rita said.

"In my coat pocket. Over there on the chair."

"You sure you want Chinese?"

"That's fine with me," Ryan said. "You better get another bottle of wine, too. I think that's about it."

Her glass, half full of rosé, was on the footlocker coffee table.

"It's not that I don't like your cooking, Ryan. I'm just in the mood for Chinese."

"You need some money? Here—"

"No, I've got it. Wait'll you're rich." Rita got the car keys from his sport coat and went out.

That was one of the good things about her, he didn't have to wait on her or always buy. She was used to working and knew what things cost. She'd run out and get the Chinese—eager to do it—because he was expecting a call and didn't want to take a chance with the answering service, have to call back and find out Dick Speed had left. He was anxious to hear from him.

A lot was going on. But he also had to rest once in a while and get his mind somewhere else.

He looked at Rita's glass on the footlocker and thought of the girl in the Good Times Bar. He'd picked Rita up at five, served a couple of writs, it was ten after seven now. They'd been here a half hour, Rita hadn't finished the glass yet. The girl in

the bar, Lee, she'd have knocked off two doubles
and be reaching for the third. Rita didn't have a
problem. Maybe in twenty years, but she'd have to
work at it, get into the morning routine. Vodka sitting on the toilet tank while you took a shower,
something to hold you till the bars opened at seven.
He couldn't see Rita doing that.

She was all right. She tried a little too hard—like
someone who didn't have an ear or a sense of timing trying to be funny—but there was a lot of girl
there in Rita.

He was a little horny, was what he was.

When Rita got back he'd pour her some more
rosé and sit close to her on the fake-leather couch,
not serious at first but saying funny things as he
started to fool around. What he said wasn't that
funny, but Rita always laughed and let him do whatever he wanted. He told her she had centerfold
breasts. Actually she had heavy white peasant
breasts with big brown nipples. She had a round
belly and the trace of a Florida tan line below the
navel. He was horny all right. Her pubic hair grew
wild and scraggly and reminded him of Che Gue-
vara's beard. She said, Why do you keep looking at
it? He said, Why do you think little boys like pictures of bare-naked ladies? They were all the same,
basically, and they were all different. That was
amazing and what made them so interesting and fun
to look at. They were all different. The phone rang.

Dick Speed said, "Am I interrupting anything?"

"Not yet," Ryan said. "What'd you find out?"

"I just want to say, your new friends are certainly interesting people. Take Mr. Francis X. Perez. Sixty-eight to seventy-two, he served four and a half years at Angola."

"That's a prison down there?"

"You bet it is. Louisiana."

Ryan felt pretty smart for a moment. "Embezzlement, or some kind of con, right?"

"Wrong. Accessory to murder. He was convicted of paying a man by the name of Raymond Gidre, a part-time employee, to shoot another man in the chest five times. Raymond Gidre was brought to trial, but they had to settle for second degree, I don't know why, and he got off with eight years hard time . . . released, let's see . . . just a couple of weeks ago. You know him, too? Raymond Gidre?"

"No, I never heard of him. But how'd they get him as an accessory? Perez."

"He was doing some kind of business with the guy who was killed and they tied Perez in with Gidre, checks or something, and I think the three of them were seen together. It sounded circumstantial. In fact, it looks to me like hearsay, but they convicted them. Perez appealed and lost it."

"Can I get the details from you?"

"What I have. Would you like to tell me what's going on?"

"I told you. Perez hired me to find Robert Leary. And the stock part of it. I've told you everything I know."

"Buddy, you want some advice. Get back to serving papers as fast as you can."

"I *am*," Ryan said, "as soon as I find the guy. I'm not involved in this. I give him an address and I'm done, I don't even have to talk to Leary."

"But you have to talk to Perez," Dick Speed said, "you're dealing with the man."

"I'm working for him. How does that look on my résumé? Shit, I don't like it at all, but I could be right next to fifteen grand."

"Okay, but remember," Dick Speed said, "nobody hands you money for nothing, unless you're giving a lot more than you think."

"Wait a minute," Ryan said, "I want to write that down."

They would talk and not say anything for a few minutes, exchange a few words and lapse into silence, and Ryan would concentrate on picking at his egg roll and chop suey.

When he looked at Rita again he said, "You know how long it takes me to make fifteen thousand? About eight or nine months. I've got a chance, I could make it in one day."

"What're you arguing with *me* for?" Rita said.

"You're going to do what you want."

"I'm not arguing."

"Then you're talking to yourself. What do you want me to say, go ahead? I've already told you what I think."

"What about if I give it a week? If I don't find the guy within one week, I forget the whole thing."

"Darling boy, I'm not your wife. Are you asking me for permission?"

"I'm laying it out," Ryan said, "so I can look at it."

"Why?" Rita said. "You've already made up your mind."

Maybe she was smarter than he thought. Or maybe he was dumber. What was he doing? Rationalizing. Like finding an excuse to have a drink. In this case it wasn't a drink, it was fifteen thousand. Maybe he did want permission, someone to tell him it was all right. Then if he messed up, got into something over his head, it wouldn't be entirely his fault. Someone else had said sure, go ahead. But it wasn't that way at all, was it? Rita was right, he had already made up his mind. So why keep talking about it? Do it. It was his decision, his responsibility for whatever happened to him.

There.

"Will you do me a favor?"

"If I can," Rita said.

"Call the *News* and the *Free Press* tomorrow. I want to put a message in the personals for the day after."

"Sure. What do you want to say?"

"I'll have to think about it, the right words." He looked at her now and grinned. He could relax again, for a while. He said, "How about if we went in there and laid down, took a little rest? Aren't you tired?"

Rita stared at him, her expression softening. "Now the little boy comes back. You're a hard guy to know, Ryan."

Rita left a little before midnight.

At two-fifteen in the morning, Ryan's phone rang again.

"I'm fucking up," the girl said, her voice sounding faint, far away from the phone. "I'm really fucking up good and I don't want to. I don't want to be here. I don't want to be inside me, but I can't get out. I don't know how."

"Where are you?"

"I'm so tired. Do you understand what I mean?"

"I know," Ryan said.

"I'm so fucking tired of thinking and being in here and I can't—goddamn it, I can't get *out*."

"Lee? Where are you?"

"I'm—the place's closed, I have to go home. Listen, I'm sorry. Let's forget the whole thing."

"Give me your address," Ryan said. He listened closely as she mumbled something and he said, "What? Give it to me again." He reached for his notebook and wrote down the street and number on Cass. An apartment upstairs. Two-oh-four. Probably within a block or two of the bar.

"Go right home, okay? Go to bed. But listen, Lee? Leave the door unlocked."

"I told him, I don't give a shit what happens to him. I don't give a shit if he *exists* even. The son of a bitch."

Ryan waited. "Who're you talking about?"

"Christ, Bobby. Who do you think?"

"Was he with you?"

"I mean it. I don't give a shit what happens to him. And do you know what?"

"What?"

"I never did. He wants me to—"

Ryan waited again. "What does he want you to do?"

"I told him he can go fuck himself."

"Lee, go on home now, okay? . . . You hear me?"

"I hear."

"Good," Ryan said. "I'll be there in twenty minutes."

7

THE VOICE ON THE PHONE SAID TO VIRGIL ROYAL, "You still in the subcontracting business?"

Virgil recognized the voice. "Yeah—but I got something on right now."

"I know what you got on. Thing I don't see is what you living on. Some lady feeding you?"

"I'm scratching," Virgil said. "I don't want this one to get away."

"Somebody's gonna tell you when he come out on the street. What you worried about?"

"Man's got people anxious to see him beside me. Got to get to him first or wait in line. But yeah, I could use something. How much we talking about?"

"I can go fifteen hundred for some fast action. Like today."

"You too busy?"

"Yeah, shit," the voice said, a tired, slow tone. "I got one, man won't sit still. It's taking some time. This other one, somebody wants right away. Reason I'm calling you this early. You want it, I can give you what you need."

"Who we talking about?" Virgil said.

"Name of Lonnie—used to work for Sportree? You know him?"

"Lonnie? With the high heels and shit? He's a doll baby."

"Talking doll," the voice said. "The policemen play with him and he talks to them. You want it?"

"Yeah, I guess so. Lemme see, I need some working capital, get me a driver. Only thing I got right now's this twelve-gauge Hi-Standard I was saving for somebody."

"Flite-King?"

"I don't know. Six-shot pump action. One thirty-four ninety-five."

"Yeah, it's all right. It's a big motherfucker."

"I already cut it down," Virgil said.

"I can give you a nice clean piece, still got the factory oil on it," the voice said. "If you want it. I never tell a man his business."

"I don't know. I been wanting to try the twelve-gauge before I shoot for the prize."

"Yeah, see what way it pulls."

"I'll be over pretty soon," Virgil said. "Let you know."

* * *

An hour and forty minutes later, Virgil called his brother-in-law from Sportree's Lounge on West Eight Mile. He told him he wanted to see him. His brother-in-law said, Man, way out there? His brother-in-law sounded half asleep. Virgil said it wasn't far, take him about fifteen minutes. His brother-in-law said he had some things he had to do. Virgil said patiently, "Hey, Tunafish? One more once. I'm at Sportree's and I want to see you. I want to give you some money. . . . That's what I said. Right now it's two hundred and fifty dollars. But you know what? It's gonna go down ten every minute you aren't here past eleven o'clock. You understand what I'm saying? . . . Then quit talking, man. Run."

Virgil came out of the phone booth grinning, seeing Tunafish throwing his clothes on, flying out of the house and jumping in the car—if Lavera hadn't driven to work. Then he'd have to borrow a car. Or pick one up. Virgil looked at the clock that was over the cash register, between the bar mirrors. Tunafish would get here about five after and he'd pay him two hundred. Which he'd already decided was about right.

See, there was the hard way to do things and there was the easy way. The hard way looked good at the time; in fact, it looked like the only way. But it upset your stomach and could break your knuckles. It produced blind spots that could mess you up and cause pain, not to mention losing your ass. The easy way required thinking and remaining cool. Not standing-around cool, but authentic genuine cool. Cool when you wanted to smash something or break down a door. No, hold it right there. Think on how to do it the easy way. Then turn the knob gently and the door opens.

Virgil learned patience at Jackson. Not the first time he was there, on the assault with a deadly weapon conviction—when he was still trying to do it the hard way, pushing and shoving, getting caught with tin shivs and spending a total of nine months in solitary—but the second time, the Wyandotte Savings and Loan armed robbery conviction. He learned patience thinking about Bobby Lear as he stamped out license plates—*Michigan, the Great Lake State*—and how he was going to get the motherfucker as soon as they turned him loose.

His lawyer had said Bobby didn't have any Wyandotte money, maybe a few bucks was all, and anybody who said he had a sizable amount was blowing smoke up Virgil's ass. There wasn't any talk that Bobby Lear was on the street spending money. He always had money, but he wasn't throwing any around, was he? Virgil didn't talk about it much at Jackson. He kept it in his head. Bobby Lear either had the money, hidden somewhere, or he didn't. Either way, it didn't matter.

When Virgil got out he would go see the man—
"Hey, Bobby, how you doing?" and all that shit—
and ask him where the money was. If Bobby said,
"I'm glad you mention that, I been saving your
piece of it . . ." Then it better be close to eight, nine
thousand, half what they said was taken. If it happened like that he would say thank you before
shooting the man in the head. If the man gave him
five seconds of bullshit he'd do it right then and not
have to listen to any more. It was the only way to
protect yourself from the man.

He didn't care for Bobby. Just looking at him and
feeling something, he didn't care for him. He also
didn't care for the way Bobby ran out and left him
humming Joe Williams in the Wyandotte vault all
by himself while the blue and whites were slipping
up to the curb. Bobby and Wendell Haines made it
out, with or without the cash from the cashiers' windows, leaving him dumb and alone in the vault. Virgil heard they got away clean. He sat in the Wayne
County jail between arraignment, examination, and
trial and didn't say a word. Then he learned Wendell
Haines was found shot dead in his room. That
wasn't hard to see. Either Bobby decided he didn't
want to split with Wendell or he was afraid Wendell
would get picked up, cop, and turn him in.

So then it was Virgil's turn, when he got out and
went to see Bobby, knowing what a sweet man he
was, what would Bobby do? Would he say, Hey,

baby, and put his arm around him, and buy him his dinner? Shit. Bobby'd sandbag him on sight. Or talk nice and get him relaxed first, it was the same thing. Bobby Lear killed people. That's why Virgil learned to be cool at Jackson.

The trouble was, by the time he got out and had bought the twelve-gauge Hi-Standard, Bobby Lear had been busted again and sent to a state hospital and Virgil had to use some more of the patience he'd learned and wait for him to get out. Then wait for him to show himself. Then use a little more of his running-out patience following Bobby's wine-head woman around.

Five minutes to eleven in the morning in an empty cocktail lounge and Bad George Benson coming out of the hi-fi system, Virgil was still waiting.

Tunafish came out of the sunlight into night darkness, looked over at the reflection of the bar mirrors and the empty stools, then at the booths on the other side of the lounge, and walked over that way. He knew it was Virgil because of his hat. Nobody had a hat like Virgil Royal's.

It had been a cowboy hat one time and was seasoned now and had a look of its own, with a brim that was almost flat except for a nice free-form curve to it, slightly up on one side, and a downsloping dent in the narrow-blocked crown. The hat was part of Virgil, and the way he wore it—with his bandit mustache and usually sunglasses—down a little on his left eye, almost straight but down, you knew you had better not touch it.

Virgil said, "Two hundred and ten dollars."

Tunafish, sliding into the booth, looked at his watch. "Hey, shit. Two hundred and . . . twenty."

"Two hundred and twenty, then," Virgil said. "You want something to drink?"

"I ain't had no breakfast yet."

"You want some coffee, milk?"

"*You* don't have nothing." Tunafish wanted to keep his voice calm, like Virgil's, but it was Virgil's calm that made him jumpy and suspicious. Virgil was different since he got out, quieter, like he knew a secret.

"I must have got you out of bed," Virgil said. He took a fold of bills from his shirt pocket, beneath the maroon jacket, and peeled off two hundreds and two tens. "Here. So you feel better."

Tunafish took the bills, all of them brand-new. He felt good, folding them and sticking them in his pants.

"What am I supposed to do now?"

"How you and Lavera doing?"

"Fine. We making it."

"Long as she working, huh?"

"I bring home money," Tunafish said. "You think I don't?" Virgil's tone was getting to him again. Virgil didn't seem to notice, though. He was looking away, like he was thinking about something else.

"I don't get no complaints from her."

Virgil's hat came back to face him. Virgil's expression was calm.

"You remember a boy name of Lonnie? Used to work for Sportree?"

Tunafish straightened, looking across the empty lounge. "Yeah, he was a bartender, at night. But he don't work here no more."

"I said used to. You know where he work now?"

Tunafish had an idea he'd short-cut Virgil, show him something. He said, "Lonnie don't know Bobby Lear. They was some dudes in a place talking about him one time, Bobby. I remember Lonnie say he don't know him."

Virgil waited, in no hurry. "What did I ask you?"

"What?"

"I said you know where he work?"

"Shit, Lonnie? He's dealing. What he always done. He was working here he was dealing."

"He's a good friend of yours, huh?"

"Pretty good."

"You see him much?"

"Yeah, you know. I see him around different places, sometimes the methadone center."

"How you doing with your habit?"

"I'm making it."

Virgil grinned. "Lavera stays right on your ass, don't she? She was a little girl she was always serious, like a little mama."

"She not worried no more," Tunafish said. "Lonnie, shit, he still doing both, couple of dimes *and* the meth. Fucked up good but he don't know it."

"What's he dealing?"

"Lonnie? Mostly he deal grass. Get this low-grade weed and sell it to the people out the V.A. hospital, tell them it's Tia-wanna gold, some bullshit name he make up. The stuff, man grow it in Pontiac." Tunafish started to grin, seeing Virgil grinning. "Assholes out the V.A., they go oooh, aaah, Tia-wanna *gold*, hey, shit, man, get us some more this stuff. Lonnie shake his head, he say he don't know but he try."

Virgil slid out of the booth, still grinning a little. "You want something now?"

"You gonna have one?"

"Yeah, something. I don't know yet."

"Give me aaaaah . . . vodka orange juice," Tunafish said.

He watched Virgil go over to the bar and wait for the bartender, down at the end, to notice him. The man had changed. Standing there waiting. Talking to the bartender now. Four years ago he would have called the bartender over here to the booth. It looked like Virgil because of the hat, but it didn't look like him, coming back, carrying two orange vodka drinks.

"I'd like you to call up Lonnie," Virgil said, seated again, looking right at him.

Tunafish didn't move. It was coming now, and for some reason he hadn't expected it to be about Lonnie. He thought that had been warming-up talk, bullshit talk, and Lonnie had happened into it.

"Tell him you want to see him," Virgil said. "Say you got a deal on some good weed he'd like to have."

"I don't know his number," Tunafish said. He was holding on to his drink. "Or he's got a phone or where the man lives. I *don't*."

"I give you two hundreds and two tens," Virgil said. "His phone number's on one of the hundreds." Virgil kept looking at him.

Tunafish was trying to think and act calm at the same time. He didn't want to ask any questions if he didn't have to.

"He might not be home."

"I bet right now he is," Virgil said. "Still in the bed with his little girl. What's her name? Marcella Lindsey. Two eight three two Edison. Upstairs. Tell him you be over six, six-thirty, if he wants a sample. None of that Tia-wanna shit, top-grade stuff. If he don't want to see it, you show it to somebody else."

Tunafish was listening carefully, nodding. He still hadn't moved.

"Go on, call him. Tell him that," Virgil said. Tunafish got up from the booth. "Hey—he say he can't see you, then you say you call him back later. Dig?"

Virgil watched him go over to the wall phone, taking the folded bills out to look at the number—narrow hunched shoulders and round afro shape, skinny kid in a leather coat too big for him. His head moving a little with the George Benson sound coming out of the hi-fi. Showing how he could set his friend up for his brother-in-law and not ask why. Knowing, whatever the reason, it had to be. Yeah, Tunafish knew what was happening. He didn't know all of it yet, but he knew enough.

Tunafish came back and slid into the booth.

"Say he can't make it at six, he has to be someplace."

Virgil grinned and relaxed against the cushion. Tunafish waited, but Virgil didn't say anything.

"When do I call him back?"

"Uh-uh, all I wanted to know, was he going to make his appointment."

" 'Pointment for what?"

"The beauty parlor," Virgil said. "Get his superfly hair fixed up. Every Friday, six-thirty, Lonnie comes in after the ladies have gone."

"Ladies' beauty parlor, huh," Tunafish said. "Man, he never told nobody that."

"Place called the Hairhouse, in Pontiac," Virgil said. "Little white boy name of Sal does his hair, Lonnie gives him a couple of baggies."

"You knew all that, what'd I call him for?"

"Make sure Lonnie's going to be there this evening," Virgil said. "Isn't having his period or something."

"Hey, shit." Tunafish shook his head, grinning, feeling pretty good now because his part of it was over. "Lonnie going to the beauty parlor. Got his red silk suit on, his red golf gloves he wears, his red high-heel shoes. I can see him."

"You might," Virgil said, "since you gonna be there. Come on, what you think I paid you for, making a phone call? Man, you my driver."

Virgil felt good the way things were going. Seeing his patience being rewarded. This afternoon seeing the ofay man who drove the light-blue Pontiac—in the bar talking to Lee—same man who wanted Bobby Lear and had showed up at the bus station and stood there by the men's room, looking around like he didn't know what he was doing. After this was done he'd go back to the Good Times and talk to Lee some more about the ofay man.

Virgil was feeling so good, maybe he'd give his brother-in-law another hundred.

He liked the dry cleaner's panel truck Tunafish

was driving. Nobody'd be looking for it till tomorrow. He liked the rain that had begun to come down in a cold drizzle about five. He could wear the raincoat and look natural walking down the street. Around the corner and partway down a block of store windows to the place with the orange drapes and the cute sign that said:

THE HAIRHOUSE
Mr. Sal

Virgil left his good hat in the panel truck with Tunafish and put on a tan crocheted cap that came down snug over his forehead. His right hand, extended through the slit opening in the pocket, held the twelve-gauge Hi-Standard pointing down his leg beneath the raincoat. About six pounds of gun with the barrel and most of the stock cut off. A little bell jingled when he opened the door.

Nobody heard him. Nobody was in the part where the empty desk and the couches were. Or in the section with the stools and the lit-up vanity mirrors. They were in the back part by the hair dryers: a short little dark-haired man in an open white swordfighter shirt and Lonnie in his red silk pants and a towel over his shoulders, bare skin beneath. Virgil walked toward them.

And a hairnet—Lonnie had on a hairnet holding the waves of his superfly in place.

Tight little red silk can sticking out, hand on his hip and gold chains and ornaments against his bare chicken-breast chest. Maybe the beauty-parlor man played with his titties. The beauty-parlor man looked like a little guinea or a Greek. They were both talking and giggling, Lonnie ducking down to get under a hair dryer. The beauty-parlor man was adjusting it, lowering the polished chrome thing down over Lonnie's finger waves.

Lonnie looked up and saw Virgil. He stopped talking. The little beauty-parlor man saw Lonnie's expression and turned around. It was quiet in the place. Both of them seemed helpless and afraid, like they might hold each other for protection. Maybe Lonnie knew him, maybe not. It didn't matter.

A funny thing happened.

Virgil was pulling down the zipper of the rain-coat with his left hand. The little guinea or Greek beauty-parlor man seemed to realize something then. He said, "Oh, my God, it's a holdup."

Virgil hadn't thought of that. He didn't have to say anything. The beauty-parlor man was telling him he had already emptied the cash register in front. The day's receipts were in that little room, the closet, and he'd go in and get them if Virgil wanted. All right? Honest to gosh, but it was mostly checks. He didn't want checks, did he? Virgil said no, he didn't want checks. The beauty-parlor man went into the closet room. He came back out right away putting a stack of bills in an envelope that said *Hairhouse* in the corner and handed it to Virgil. Virgil said thank you.

He had to put the envelope in the left-side pocket. His hand came out and finished unzipping the raincoat, pulling the skirt aside. The heavy stubby front end of the twelve-gauge appeared.

"And thank you, honey," Virgil said to the boy sitting there bare-chested with his chains and his hairnet and his mouth open. Virgil gave Lonnie a double-O twelve-gauge charge from ten feet away, pumped the gun hard with his left hand and hit him again, whatever part of him it was going out of the chair ass over hair dryer, making a terrible noise and shattering a full-length mirror, wiping it from the wall, as the beauty-parlor man began to scream, backing away.

Virgil stared at him, frowning at the painful sound, until he lowered the blunt end of the shotgun and zipped the raincoat over it. The beauty-parlor man stopped screaming. Virgil continued to frown, though now it was more an expression of concern.

He said, "Man, get hold of yourself." And walked out.

8

THIS END OF THE HALLWAY WAS DARK. On the wall, near the door, was a light fixture shaped like dripping candlesticks, but there were no bulbs in it. Ryan had to strike a match to read the room number. Two-oh-four.

He listened a moment before trying the door. The knob was loose, it jiggled, but wouldn't turn either way. He knocked lightly on the door panel and waited.

"Lee? . . . You in there?"

He had driven past the Good Times Bar and the place was empty. If she wasn't here . . .

He knocked again, giving it a little more but still holding back, and waited again. There was no sound. Silence. Then a creaking sound. But not from inside the apartment.

The figure approached from the far end of the hall where a dull orange glow showed the stairwell: a dark figure wearing a hat, coming into the darkness toward him.

"You locked out?" Virgil said.

A black guy who was bigger than he was—three o'clock in the morning in a dark hallway. Ryan did not have to decide anything. If the guy was armed he could have anything he wanted. The nice tone didn't mean a thing.

"There's supposed to be somebody in there," Ryan said. "She's expecting me, but I think she might've passed out."

"Let me see," Virgil said.

Ryan stepped out of the way. Virgil moved in. He tried the knob, then took a handful of keys on a ring from his jacket pocket. Ryan thought at first he had a passkey. No, he was feeling through the keys, trying different ones in the lock.

"Are you the manager?"

"I seen you, I wondered if you locked out." Like he happened to be standing in the hall, three o'clock in the morning.

"You live here?" Ryan asked him.

Virgil didn't answer. He said, "Think I got it. Yeah . . ." He pushed the door open gently, took a moment to look in, and stepped out of the way.

"Your friend laying on the bed."

A dim light from somewhere showed the girl's legs, still in the Levi's, at one end of the narrow daybed. Ryan tried to move quietly across the linoleum floor. He could hear her breathing now, lying on her back in a twisted, uncomfortable-looking position, her hips turned as though she had tried to roll over and had given up. The place smelled musty. The only light, a bare fifty-watt bulb, hung from the ceiling in the kitchenette part of the room. The faucet was dripping in the sink. There were dirty dishes, a milk carton, an open loaf of bread on the counter. A jar of peanut butter with the top off. Three half-gallon wine bottles, empty, on the floor. The only window in the room, next to the bed, showed a bare, dark-wood frame, no curtains. A shade with brown stains was pulled below the sill. He could see her in here during the day, on a good day, the room dim, silent, the shade drawn against the sunlight and whatever was outside that frightened her. Alone with her wine bottle, feeling secure as long as there was wine in it, sitting in the rocking chair smoking cigarettes and forgetting them and burning stains in the wooden table.

She could use three weeks at Brighton Hospital. If she had the money, or Blue Cross. She probably didn't have either one. It would cost about nine hundred. He had almost three thousand in the bank drawing 5½ percent. How much did he want to help her?

Ryan went into the bathroom, felt for the light switch, and turned it on. They all looked alike. The rust stain in the washbasin. The dirty towel on the floor, from some hotel. The hissing toilet tank. A comb with matted strands of hair. One toothbrush. One twisted tube of toothpaste. He looked in the medicine cabinet. No prescriptions, no tranquilizers. Good. An almost empty bottle of Excedrin. He'd check the refrigerator before he left.

He had forgotten about the black guy and didn't look for him in the room or by the open door. But as he knelt down next to the daybed, looking at the girl, he was aware of the rocking chair creaking with a faint, steady sound.

The black guy was sitting there watching him, the hat slanting down over one eye.

He turned to the girl again and brushed the hair away from her cheek. Her eyes were open and she was looking at him.

"You all right?"

"Fine." Her eyes closed and opened again. She was a long way from fine, whatever that meant to her.

"I want to ask you a couple of questions before you go to sleep," Ryan said. "You have any Valium? Anything like that?"

"I have some . . . Librium, I think."

"Where? It's not in the bathroom."

"I don't know." Her voice was drowsy; she barely moved her mouth.

"Come on, Lee? Where do you keep it?"

"I don't know. Someplace."

"Don't take any," Ryan said. "You hear me? You'll probably wake up, you won't be able to sleep, but don't take any pills, any kind, except the Excedrin's all right. Lee?" He touched her shoulder and waited for her eyes to open. "You have any family here? How about your mother and dad, where're they?"

"No, I don't have—they don't live around here. They're home."

"Where's home, Lee?"

"Christ, you tell me. Home . . . shit, I don't know."

"How about friends?"

"What?"

"You know some people, don't you? You have friends?"

"Fuck no, I don't have any fucking friends. My friends disappeared." She seemed awake now.

"You know people who live here, don't you? In Detroit, around here somewhere?"

But she wasn't awake. She was here and she was spinning around somewhere in her mind. Ryan remembered it, like falling backward and looking up at nothing, feeling a dizziness. He could hear the faint sound of the rocking chair creaking.

"Lee, try to think of somebody. People you used to know."

"I don't know any—no, hey, I know Art."

"Who's Art?"

"He's a prick. No, he's all right, he can't help it."

"Who's Art, Lee?"

"The *inn*keeper. Don't you know Art? Arty? Don't call him that, though. He'll fuck up your drink."

"How about Bobby Lear?" Ryan said. "You know him, don't you?"

There was a silence. The creaking sound of the rocker stopped, then started again, slowly.

"You said he called you. Lee, what'd he call you for? Tell me."

She laughed then. "Man, that's great. I said now you're asking *me*. Man, you got a lot of fucking nerve."

"What'd he want you to do?"

"He wanted *me* to help *him*. Jesus. I said Jesus, do you know where I am? Where you left me? I'm down in the bottom of a *hole*, that's where"—her voice rose—"and I can't see out!"

Ryan stroked her hair. Her forehead was cold, clammy. "You're going to be all right," he said. "Where is he, Lee? Where'd he call from?"

The creaking sound stopped again.

"I said what's it like, man—all that *man* shit— I'm tired, you know, I'm tired of all that cool shit."

"What'd you say to him?"

"I said what's it like, have it fucking turned around for a change?" She started to push up. "I think I'm going to be sick."

"Here." Ryan held her. Her head drooped, nodding, staring at the floor. He felt her pull away and let her sink back to the bed.

"Save it till morning," she said. "No, what I need—you don't happen to have a chill bottle of Pully, Poo-yee, shit, or even a warm bottle nigger strawberry pop wine. God, I don't care. *Something.*"

Ryan waited. She let her breath out slowly, her head settling against the pillow.

"Where is he, Lee?"

"He's at a place, the Mont . . . something. It's down, you know, it's down there by—the Mont-*calm.* That's the name of it."

"A hotel?"

"Yeah, for whores and people like—I can't, I don't want to see him, Jesus, please."

"You want to take your clothes off? Get under the covers?"

"Leave me alone."

"Lee, I'll be back in the morning. Don't leave here, okay? And don't have anything to drink. Promise me. If you feel the urge like you got to have something, call me. Anytime you wake up and feel it, call, okay? You got my number." What else? He knelt there looking at her, trying to think. He'd stop by a drugstore in the morning and get some B-12 tablets, load her up with it, stay close, and help her through the bad time. Check the refrigerator. Check her purse for the Librium. He felt like a cigarette. What else? Ryan was aware of the silence then. He looked around at the empty rocking chair.

Virgil was at the end of the hall, his hat shadowed on the wall in the raw orange light over the stairway.

"Wait a second."

Ryan got to him as he started down the stairs.

"You know that girl in there?"

Virgil looked up at him past the stair railing. "Do I know her?"

"Do you know who she is?"

Virgil seemed puzzled. "Don't you?"

"Lee somebody. That's all."

"Say you don't know who she is?"

"I was talking to her this afternoon, the first time," Ryan said. "We got on drinking, I saw she had a problem."

"Yeah, she got a problem all right." Virgil squinted at Ryan then, suspicious. "You honest to shit don't know who she is?"

Ryan tightened up a little. "If I knew, for Christ's sake, I wouldn't be asking you."

"That's Bobby Lear's wife," Virgil said.

Ryan stared at him. "But her name—that's not his wife's name. Lee?"

"I don't know about her name," Virgil said, "but that's Bobby's wife." In the orange light he looked up at Ryan with an amused expression, almost a grin. "Shit, you don't know *anything*, do you?"

Virgil started down the stairs.

"Wait a minute," Ryan said. "Do you know him? I want to talk to him."

"I do too," Virgil said, his hat disappearing into shadow. The sound of the man's steps, receding, came back to Ryan from the stairwell. The guy looked familiar. Like seeing somebody who played for the Lions in regular clothes. A black athlete, the outfit. The hat.

That's what he had seen, the hat sitting on a bar. A colored guy with a cowboy hat. Not a cowboy hat, but like one. The guy sitting there had been wearing a maroon outfit, maybe like a leisure suit. He thought of Jay Walt. No, the maroon outfit had looked good on the black guy. Light-colored shirt with the collar out. And a tight strand of beads showing. The guy sitting near the end of the bar this afternoon when he left the place.

She had called from there an hour ago.

The guy could've still been sitting there. If it was the same guy. No, but he could've come back and been there when she phoned. And heard what she said. And then waited for him to come.

Why?

Because he's the one who's looking for Bobby Lear. Hanging around the man's wife, waiting. Sitting in the rocker while he talked to her and hearing her say it. The Montcalm.

Shit, handing it to him.

Ryan went back into the apartment and found the Librium, two capsules, in the girl's purse and put them in his pocket. He'd give them back to her tomorrow, if she wasn't drinking. And bring some milk and a can of juice and a couple of eggs, which she'd gag on and refuse to eat. He looked through the room again to make sure there wasn't another jug of wine hidden somewhere. Then looked at her, asleep, at peace for a little while. Mrs. Denise Leann Leary . . .

Leann. Lee. It had never occurred to him to look at the wife's name and fool with it and see what else she might be called. He wondered if she had always been called Lee. When she was a little girl. Before she knew what wine tasted like. She had probably never looked this bad in her life. Her face puffy, blemished, her hair a mess. He didn't remember the color of her eyes. Dark eyebrows, a nice nose and mouth. She could clean up and be a winner, if she wanted to. And he could stand here looking at her all night, what was left of it, and it wouldn't do either of them any good.

Driving home, he planned his day.

Get up at eight, stop by a drugstore for some B-12 and be back at the girl's place a little after nine. Try to get her squared away, in the right frame of mind and something in her stomach. Or if she was in too much pain, with her nerves screaming at her, see about getting her into a hospital. Then stop by the Montcalm Hotel and ask for a Robert Leary, Jr. No, Leary would be using another name. All right, he'd start knocking on doors, and if a man in his mid-thirties appeared, if he opened the door, he'd say how you doing? If you're Robert Leary, Jr., we've got a whole lot of money for you, buddy. See if the real Robert Leary, Jr., could resist something like that. He'd have to make sure Leary was there. It wouldn't do Mr. Perez any good to have just the address.

He was getting close now, but God, it was a lot of work. He was tired of thinking. He was tired of driving, being in the car. Tired of waiting around. But more tired of thinking than anything else.

It was after four by the time Ryan got to bed.

When the phone rang at ten to seven he opened his eyes and immediately thought of the girl, Lee, crying for a drink.

But it was Dick Speed's voice with a pleasant good morning and how would he like to come down to the morgue and meet somebody.

9

IT WAS NEARLY EIGHT by the time Ryan got downtown.

The Wayne County Morgue—the exterior of the building as well as the lobby with its long polished-wood counter—reminded him of a bank. A uniformed police officer was waiting and seemed to know who he was. He said, "Dick's inside there, in the autopsy room."

Ryan was thinking he wasn't ready for this. It was too sudden, with no time to prepare. Unless he'd be looking through a window. They probably wouldn't let him in the room. Or it would be like an operation and he wouldn't be able to see what was going on anyway.

They passed through a door into an anteroom. An attendant with a clipboard moved aside. A middle-aged man and woman, facing the door as Ryan entered, were staring up at the wall. Neither moved. Ryan looked around as he edged past them.

There was a television monitor mounted high on the wall, angled down. On the screen was a black-and-white picture of a young woman's face, her eyes closed.

Going through a fire door into a narrow hallway, Ryan said, "What was going on there?"

The uniformed cop said over his shoulder, "Identifying a body. It's not as much of a shock that way."

"She seemed young," Ryan said. "The girl."

He was aware of an odor now. It seemed familiar. It wasn't antiseptic, which he expected, but the opposite. He thought of it as a wet smell, something old and damp. But a human smell. It was awful and it was getting heavier.

There should have been a sign that said *Warning, here it comes,* or something.

He wasn't at all ready for the first body he saw, turning a corner, walking close past a metal table, and realizing, Jesus, it was a woman. There was her thing. An old black woman with white hair. Purple-brown skin that didn't look like skin, peeling, decomposing to tan marble. Attached to her big toe, facing up, was a tag that bore a case number, a name and address, written in blue ink. She was right there, her body, but she didn't seem real.

None of the bodies did, and he wasn't aware of them immediately as human bodies. They were in the open, exposed, in the examining room and the connecting halls and alcoves. They weren't pulled solemnly out of a wall, covered with a sheet. They lay naked on metal tray tables waiting, as though with a purpose, waiting to be put to use. Waiting to dress a theatrical scene or a store window. Coming on them suddenly, they were props. Plastic figures fashioned in detail with fingernails and pubic hair, pale breasts made of rubber, tags on their toes and brown paper bags between lower legs, stuffed with clothing. Some were composed, at rest, with arms extended; the hands of a young black man at his penis, as if about to relieve himself. And some were contorted in shapes of anguish, limbs bent awkwardly, hands raised, clutching something that was no longer there, with pink traces of blood smeared on plastic skin. Ryan, at first, tried not to look closely at the wounds, at the slashes and punctures, and moved his gaze quickly from the sudden shocking wounds, the stump of a leg, a face torn away. But he would look again, gradually, taking it a little at a time and deciding he felt all right and wasn't going to be sick. He could look, because what had been a person inside, making the body human, was no longer there.

A television camera on a raised platform aimed its lens on the sleeping girl Ryan had seen on the monitor. There were no traces of blood that had been wiped away, no marks or blemishes on her body, except for a small tattoo above her left breast, a heart and a name that Ryan couldn't read. As he stared at her, the uniformed cop said, "Suicide. Apparent. She took forty-five Darvon." Ryan nodded, aware of the odor, not wanting to breathe it in. It was familiar, but he couldn't think of what it was. Something he remembered from when he was a kid.

"You ready?" the uniformed cop said.

"Yeah, I'm sorry. Where we going?"

"Down the autopsy room."

Ryan followed him to the basement and along a hallway past a deep-freeze room where, the cop said, they stored bodies that weren't claimed right away. Also the badly decomposed ones: firm 'em up before they were autopsied. Ryan felt like he was getting the tour. He was interested, but he was more anxious to know why he was here. "Come on down the morgue and see your friend," Dick Speed had said over the phone. Playing games. It didn't matter. Ryan knew who it was going to be.

Dick Speed was in the doorway of the autopsy room smoking a cigarette. When he saw Ryan, he waved for him and led the way to one side of the room where the cement floor was raised a few feet and set apart by a low metal railing. Following him, Ryan looked around.

He counted four autopsy tables equipped with sinks and hoses. Two men in white coats were working at a body tray pushed up to the second table.

Ryan could see thin yellowish legs and the brown paper bag and the identifying tag, but he couldn't see the rest of the body or the face. The two white coats were in the way, on this side of the table with their backs to him. One of them was hunched in close to the table and Ryan could hear the high-pitched whine of a power tool.

Jesus.

"You can see better up here," Dick Speed said.

"Who is it?"

"Unless you want to get down close. How you feel?"

"I'm fine," Ryan said. He was—no queasy feeling or saliva in his mouth—and felt pretty good about it. Then he wasn't so sure.

One of the white coats moved around to the other side of the autopsy table and Ryan was looking at the whole body, cut open from breastbone to groin and seeing the man's insides, his vital organs and a slab of ribs, lying in a pile on the table.

Like dressing a deer.

"That's the medical examiner," Dick Speed said. "The other guy with the power saw's an assistant. Something like this, we know it's a homicide, but we want a complete autopsy to be sure. Defendant's lawyer gets in court, he says, 'Yeah, it might've been gunshot, but who says it was fatal? Or how do you know he wasn't already dead?' That kind of shit."

The opened body seemed less human than the ones upstairs. It was a carcass with no face, or a face without features, a store mannequin. Ryan stared at the man's head and realized he was looking at the bare skull. The skin and hair had been peeled, pulled down, and lay inside-up over the man's face. That's why he seemed featureless. The attendant with the power saw had been cutting into the man's skull. He removed a wedge-shaped section. The brain was exposed for a few moments before the attendant pulled it out of the skull and placed it on the autopsy table.

"Who is it?"

"See," Dick Speed said, "the medical examiner, if he's got any doubt at all what killed the guy, he takes samples from the stomach, the liver, drains out some pee-pee, takes a piece of the brain—where you going?"

Ryan went down the steps and over to the foot of the tray table, not looking at the man's open body, keeping his gaze down and seeing only the yellowed, slightly bent legs and the bare feet pointing at him, like the man was stretching them out and in a moment the feet would relax to a normal position. Ryan didn't want to touch him. He was careful reaching for the tag and turning it over to read the words written in blue ink.

Unknown Man No. 89.

Behind him, Dick Speed said, "Now positively

identified by his prints as Robert Leary, Jr., age thirty-five. Also known as Bobby Lear."

"You know who it is," Ryan said. "How come the number?"

"Before we know who it is, we got to call him something."

Ryan, staring at the tag, let his gaze move up the yellowed legs, past the man's darker-shaded organ and thick pubic hair to the violent red opening. The assistant was doing something, scooping Robert Leary's stomach and internal organs into a clear plastic bag. He dropped the bag into the open cavity, working it in to make it fit, and laid the slab of ribs on top.

Unknown Man No. 89.

He might as well keep that, Ryan was thinking. He wasn't worth anything as Robert Leary, Jr. Not to anybody.

"Found dead at the Montcalm Hotel," Ryan said.

"Room 312," Dick Speed said. "You were getting close, weren't you? How'd you find out?"

"His wife. Turns out she's the wine drinker with the blond hair."

"Where's she live?" Ryan told him, and Dick Speed said, "We'll have to get hold of her for the disposition. Not to mention asking a few questions."

"She was in the bag last night," Ryan said. "She didn't want to see him, have anything to do with him."

"That's something in itself, isn't it?" Speed said. "Married to the guy, but doesn't want to see him. So maybe she gets somebody else to see him."

Ryan watched the autopsy assistant lacing Robert Leary together, using a hook and what looked like heavy cord.

"How was he killed?"

"With a shotgun. Dead center, twice. Also, yesterday evening out in Pontiac," Speed said, "you remember the faggy-looking guy was with Tunafish? At the methadone clinic. Lonnie, the drug snitch with the hair and the shoes. Same thing, with a shotgun. Twice."

"So you think it's the same guy."

"I'd bet on it," Speed said. "Get a match of the buckshot, the gauge, we'll know."

The autopsy assistant was at the opposite end of the tray table now. He replaced the skull section and—as Ryan watched—carefully pulled the hair and scalp up over the skull, revealing the face a little at a time, a man appearing, features forming, as though the assistant were fitting the lifeless skull with a Robert Leary mask.

Ryan stared at the face, the mustache, the closed eyes, the round cap of coarse black hair.

He said, "Jesus . . . look. The guy's *black*."

"He's black all right," Speed said. "That's what colored guys are, they're black."

"Jesus," Ryan said.

"You didn't know that? You're looking for a guy, you don't know what *color* he is?"

"I don't know why," Ryan said. "I guess I should've, the people he hung around with, at least some of them. But the thing is—you see, his wife is *white*."

Dick Speed waited. "Yeah?"

"I mean she's *white*."

"You mean very white, uh?" Dick Speed said. "Is that it?"

Ryan wasn't sure what he meant.

It was nearly ten by the time he got to her apartment, with the vitamins and the milk and stuff. He'd see how she was, talk to her, and then give Dick a call.

The place was really bad. The hallway dingy with dirt and soot, the linoleum worn out, peeling. He knocked on her door twice and waited, listening in the silence. She was probably still asleep. He hoped so, as he turned the knob quietly and walked in.

The daybed was empty. The bathroom door was open. The light was still on in the kitchenette.

Denise Leann Leary was gone.

10

"SNOWING," MR. PEREZ SAID. "Nearly the middle of April, it's still snowing."

"It's just flurries," Ryan said. "That kind of snow, it doesn't stick to the ground at all. It's a wet snow."

"I remember, coming in from the airport there was still some snow, very dirty-looking snow, patches of it along the highway, with all the rain you've had." Mr. Perez stood in the alcove of the floor-to-ceiling window looking out at the gray mass of sky and the light snow swirling in the wind. "You certainly have a long winter," he said.

"Or you can look at it as kind of an asshole spring," Ryan said. He didn't believe it—sitting here talking about the weather. "It's great for the skiers, though. Up north, I heard on the radio, they've still got a fifteen- to twenty-inch base," Ryan said—if the guy really wanted to talk about it.

Maybe he was finished. Mr. Perez came away from the window and sank into his favorite chair—

the Spanish governor of a colony, member of an old, titled family, who'd been sent out here and was pissed off about it, but kept it locked up inside. Ryan was here to give his report.

He was sitting on the couch this time instead of a straight chair, figuring they would have quite a bit to discuss. It was one-thirty in the afternoon. Near the door was a room-service table pushed out of the way. So Mr. Perez had eaten his noon dinner. Everything on the menu, it looked like, the way the table was cluttered with dishes, empty wineglasses, those silver dish covers and messed-up napkins. The man had a noon dinner, he had a dinner. He still seemed too skinny to be a big eater. Or else the white shirt, the collar, was a couple sizes too large.

"You find out he's colored," Mr. Perez said. "How does that change anything?"

"Didn't you think he was white?"

Mr. Perez nodded. "Yeah, I guess I did, judging from his name. It wasn't Amos Washington or . . . Thurgood Marshall, one of those. But now Mr. Leary's deceased and we know he has a wife. What's her name?"

"Denise. Denise Leann. But she goes by Lee."

"And you talked to her."

"Yeah, but not knowing, as I mentioned, she was his wife. The way I got it, she was like an ex-girlfriend."

"An ex-something, huh? Well, now we contact

the wife, who we'll presume is his legal heir, and deal with her. You say she's gone. But she doesn't have any reason to hide, does she?"

"Not that I know of."

"And you know what she looks like."

"Uh-huh."

"So you shouldn't have any trouble locating her. Do you see a problem?"

"There's a couple of things," Ryan said. "More than a couple. Something I didn't tell you. He's black, but the wife, Lee, is white."

"Up here, I'm not too surprised," Mr. Perez said.

"The other thing, she's an alcoholic."

Mr. Perez thought about that a moment.

"I like alcoholics. I've had a few. They're very easy to deal with, very cooperative. What kind of an alcoholic is she?"

"What do you mean, what kind? What does she drink?"

"I mean, how far along is she? Does she work? Or does she sit home and hide bottles around the house?"

"I don't think she works. No, she couldn't. But it's not that kind of a setup either, hiding bottles. They're right there on the sink."

"See," Mr. Perez said, "a white woman marries somebody like Robert Leary, what we've learned about him, she's pretty hard up, scraping bottom. A woman like that, her nose stuck in the bottle, no income, she's going to take anything she can get."

Ryan kept quiet. He'd listen and let the man tell him about alcoholics, what they were like.

"We make an offer, this kind of deal, the alcoholic woman isn't going to see money, unh-unh. She's going to see visions of gin bottles dancing in her head. She'll sign the agreement in blood if she has to."

"She's a wine drinker," Ryan said.

"Cheap dago red, huh?"

"Chilled Sauterne."

He could see the dirty glass on the bar and the empty half-gallon jugs in her kitchen. He realized he was trying to upgrade her and he didn't know why.

"The other thing, or one more to add to it," Ryan said, "the police are looking for her, too."

Mr. Perez raised his eyebrows. "They suspect she might've killed him?"

"Well, they'll question her, there's no doubt about that," Ryan said. "As my friend was saying, it's a homicide and they'll give it the full treatment. It doesn't matter, the fact they're glad the guy's dead. Somebody killed him and it's their job to find out who."

"You have any ideas about that? You seemed to've been getting in there pretty close," Mr. Perez said.

"Well, I ran into a guy, yes, and I know he found

out where Leary was staying. The same night it happened, in fact. This guy, I don't know what his name is, knows Leary's wife. I told the police about it already, gave them a half-assed description of the guy—his clothes, his hat, you know—but I don't know what's going to come of that. What I started to say—they're looking for his wife, yes, but mainly so she can claim the body, get it out of the way."

"And you say they don't know where she is."

"No, but I think it's only a matter of time," Ryan said. "They go looking for somebody, the cops, they find them. They've already checked the hospitals. She hasn't been admitted anywhere."

"Checked the *hos*pitals?" Mr. Perez said. "Check the bars, you say she's an alcoholic."

"Well, see, she's in pretty bad shape."

Ryan heard the toilet flush and paused. He looked over at the closed door that led to the bedroom. Mr. Perez waited, not offering an explanation.

A woman, Ryan thought. He wondered if she'd come out. He said, "I think his wife might've finally realized she was in trouble and it could kill her if she kept drinking. Her calling me like that was a good sign."

"So maybe she'll call you again," Mr. Perez said. "Save you some work."

"That'd be fine. But now I've got a feeling she's still drinking. She had a couple this morning to straighten her out and they went down so good she

kept going. So then she might've gotten another
room somewhere. She could call me, sometime, but
I'll probably have to wait till she bottoms out
again." Ryan shook his head. "It's very tough, trying to quit like that."

He saw Mr. Perez's gaze move past him. Ryan
glanced over at the doorway to the bedroom.

A stringy, heavy-boned farmer-looking guy had
opened the door and was coming out, his head
down, buckling his belt.

Ryan looked back at Mr. Perez, who was watching the man with a relaxed, pleasant expression.
Mr. Perez said, "I hope you had a good one, Raymond. You were in there a half hour."

"Traveling," the man said. "It throws me off my
schedule. I sure don't like to go on the airplane."

"Raymond Gidre," Mr. Perez said. "Shake hands
with Mr. Ryan, fella I was telling you about."

"Yes-sir, it's a pleasure to meet you." Raymond
Gidre smiled cordially, reaching for Ryan's hand as
he rose. The man seemed eager, flashing perfect
dentures in a weathered face that had been recently
shaved and bore traces of talcum powder. His curly
black hair, combed back severely, plastered down,
glistened with tonic that Ryan could smell and re-
called from barbershops years before. Lucky Tiger.
The man had a small-town-barbershop look about
him. Like he'd just come out of one. He wore a
short-sleeved sport shirt. Ryan noticed the tattoo

on his right forearm—something black and red—
but didn't want to stare at it. He shook Raymond
Gidre's hand and nodded and said he was glad to
meet him, held for a moment by the dentures and
the pale eyes smiling. Just a good-natured back-
country boy—stringy and hard after a half-dozen
years on a Louisiana prison farm.

"Raymond here's visiting from a place near New
Iberia, Louisiana," Mr. Perez said. "Avery Island,
huh, Raymond? Where the hot sauce comes from."

"Home of Tabasco," Raymond said. "Yes-sir,"
walking over to the room-service table. He poked
through the napkins and silver lids, found a hard
roll, and bit into it, still poking around. "You didn't
eat your snapbeans."

"Finish 'em up," Mr. Perez said, and looked at
Ryan again. "Raymond works for me on and off in
special capacities, you might say. For instance, if we
see you need some help, Raymond's the boy for it."

Ryan nodded as though he knew what Mr.
Perez was talking about, then decided he might as
well ask.

"What kind of help?"

"Well, if you were to need protection of one kind
or another, somebody to see you don't get hurt. I
wouldn't want that to happen."

"I wouldn't either," Ryan said. "But what would
I need protection from? I'm looking for the wife
now. The bad guy's dead."

"That's true," Mr. Perez said, "but somebody killed the bad guy, didn't he? Somebody, you said yourself, found out where he was staying. By the way, this man you talked to last night, was he colored?"

Ryan nodded.

Mr. Perez looked past him, across the room. "Got a colored boy, Raymond, might want to give us trouble."

"It's all the same to me," Raymond said, eating from a plate of green beans, "I'm not prejudice."

What the hell was going on? Ryan felt himself starting to get a little worked up. Perez talked to him very seriously, then would say something to his hired hand and almost break out in a giggle.

"I don't understand something," Ryan said. "We don't know who the guy is, the black guy I met. We don't know if he was the one that killed Leary. I mean, we can't even begin to assume something like that. Or, okay, let's say even if he *did*, what's it got to do with me? That I'd need protection? I'm looking for the *wife*."

"You said you put a notice in the paper—"

"I also put another one in," Ryan said, "that's due to run tomorrow."

"Let me finish," Mr. Perez said. "All right?" He waited a moment, staring at Ryan with his solemn expression. "You put a notice in the paper and two people called you up. Is that correct?"

Now he was standing on the carpet, in the principal's office. "That's right," Ryan said.

"You thought one of the two might have been Leary, but not both of them."

"That's right," Ryan said.

"You suspected somebody was looking for him."

"I *knew* that. And it's obvious somebody found him. The guy's dead." Ryan paused a moment. Mr. Perez's tone might be a little pissy, but maybe he was sincere, at least meant well. "I see," Ryan said. "You think if it was the guy I met in the apartment, he might be afraid I'll identify him."

"That type of thing," Mr. Perez said. "I didn't have anything that specific in mind, of course, when I telephoned Raymond and asked him if he'd like to visit the Motor City. I felt we were mixing with ugly people, getting ready to do business with one of them; so it wouldn't hurt to have some protection. Mr. Leary's dead, but there are still some ugly people around, aren't there?"

"You might be right," Ryan said.

"I have to be, least most of the time. Now—anything else on your mind?"

Ryan realized he was being dismissed. "No, I guess that's it." He got up and walked over to where his raincoat was draped over the back of a chair. "I'll follow up on the girl." What else would he be doing? He wanted to say something, calm and matter-of-fact, and that was all he could think of.

"I'm going to be out of town a few days," Mr. Perez said. "But Raymond'll be here. Not right *here*, but he'll let you know where he's staying. Let's get it done and we'll all go someplace where it's warm. How's that sound?"

It sounded to Ryan like the principal talking again, patting him on the head. He didn't like the feeling that came with the man's patronizing tone. The man probably didn't realize what he sounded like, thinking he was putting one over on the clucks—the dumb process server—with his easygoing one-of-the-boys delivery. Ryan had suspected it the first time they met, getting the feel of the man. Now he was sure of it. Hiding inside the gentleman from Baton Rouge was a pretty cold and heartless son of a bitch.

Ryan's second insertion in the personal columns of the *News* and *Free Press* appeared the day after Robert Leary was found shot to death and his wife disappeared. Ryan had almost called the papers to cancel the insertions if he could, then changed his mind. The notice said:

BOBBY LEAR
MONEY
waiting with your
name on it. Contact
Box 5388

* * *

Virgil Royal read the notice and said, Shit.

He should have waited to see what the man wanted with Bobby, though it had felt good, what he'd done . . . walking into the Montcalm Hotel whore joint with his raincoat on and knit cap down over his head. He didn't have to scare the night clerk any, because the night clerk didn't give a shit, he was mostly drunk and looked like he had been mostly drunk and wearing the same shirt and pants twenty years. He took the ten-dollar bill, Virgil almost seeing him translating it into two fifths and a six-pack, and said, "I believe the party you're looking for's in 312. Light-skinned gentleman—"

"Where is that, in the front? Three-twelve?"

The night clerk had to stop and think. "It's on the left, toward the back."

Bet to it—on the side with the fire escape, by the parking lot. Virgil was counting on it for his cute idea to work—room with a fire escape out the window. It wouldn't be all luck. Virgil would bet the shotgun under his raincoat Bobby's room had two ways to get out.

He took the elevator up to the fourth floor, walked down the hall and knocked on 412.

A woman's voice, irritated, said, "What do you want?"

"Nothing," Virgil said.

He took the stairs up to the fifth floor and knocked on 512. No answer. He knocked a couple more times before taking out his ring of keys and finding one that fit. Entering the room, he felt his patience paying off again—thinking, doing it the easy way—seeing the window in the darkness, the square of outside light and the rungs of the fire escape. Virgil took off his shoes. He went down the fire escape two floors with the shotgun in his hand, edged up to the window of 312, then past the drawn shade to the railing, reached out, and laid the sawed-off Hi-Standard twelve-gauge on the sill of the frosted-glass bathroom window.

It seemed like it was taking a lot of time, but that's the way it was, being patient. He could've poked the shotgun through the glass and blown Bobby out of bed. He'd decided, though, he'd rather talk to the man first, ask him a question. Not while he was holding a shotgun on him. No, the way to do it, while Bobby had a gun and felt he was the boss.

Virgil remembered almost changing his mind, standing there at 312. Then he was knocking and it was too late to back out. Close to the door, he said, "Hey, Bobby? It's me, Virgil," keeping his voice low.

It didn't take too long after that.

Once Bobby Lear was sure it was only Virgil, nobody backing him up, he had to play his Bobby Lear part: take the chain off and let him in, holding a nickel-plated .38 he could trim his mustache in, not pointed right at Virgil, holding it loose once Virgil's raincoat was off and he'd given him a quick feel for metal objects.

Bobby asked him how he was doing. Virgil told him fine, there was nothing like going to bed at ten and eating home-cooked prison chow to make a person fit, was there? Bobby said that was the truth. Virgil asked him whatever happened to Wendell Haines and Bobby said Wendell had died. Virgil said he heard something like that, but who was it shot him? Bobby said it beat the shit out of him. Probably the police. Virgil said how come he was living in the Montcalm Hotel, on account of all the cute ladies? Bobby said that was it. Five floors of pussy. Virgil said, You hiding from somebody? Bobby said, It look like I am? Virgil said, Uh-huh. Bobby said, From who? Virgil said, From me. That got him to the question.

"Something I been waking up at night wondering," Virgil said. "How much we get from the Wyandotte Savings?"

Bobby seemed loose, leaning with his arm along the top of the dresser and the nickel-plated .38 hanging limp in his hand. He had his pants on, his shirt hanging open, no shoes or socks. Very loose. But Virgil knew his eyes, the way he was staring. The man was here talking, but thinking about something else, making up his mind. Like a little kid's open expression.

"We didn't get nothing," Bobby said.

Virgil nodded, very slowly. "That's what I was afraid you were going to say. Nothing from the cashier windows?"

"Nothing," Bobby said. "No time."

"I heard seventeen big big ones."

"You heard shit."

"Told to me by honest gentlemen work for the prosecuting attorney."

"Told to you by your mama it still shit."

"Well, no use talking about it, is there?"

"Let me ask you something," Bobby said. "You put that in the paper to me? Call this number?"

"No, I wondered you might think it was me," Virgil said. "It somebody else looking for you."

"How you know about it?"

"I saw it, same as you did. I saw the man that put it in."

"What's he want?"

"Man looking for you—I thought maybe you owed him money, too."

"You telling me I owe you money? On the Wyandotte?"

Got him up, now push him a little.

"You owe me some*thing*," Virgil said. "Or I owe you something. One or the other."

"Shit," Bobby said. "I think somebody give me the wrong information. You the one, Virgil, should be staying here. You all fucked up in your head, acting strange."

"Wait right there," Virgil said.

Bobby straightened up. "Where you going?"

Virgil was moving toward the bathroom. "Make wee-wee. That all right?"

"Don't touch the coat."

"Hey, it's cool," Virgil said. "Take it easy." He went into the bathroom, turned on the light and swung the door almost closed. There was nothing more to talk about. Bobby knew it. Bobby would have a load in the chamber of the nickel plate and he might have already decided on his move. You couldn't tell about Bobby. He could try it right now or in a week, or wake up a month from now in the mood. That's why Virgil eased open the frosted-glass window and got the twelve-gauge from the sill.

Nothing cute now, the cute part was over. He'd like to take the time to see Bobby's face, but not with the man holding his shiny gun.

Virgil used his foot to bring the bathroom door in, out of the way. He stepped into the opening and gave Bobby a load dead-center that pinned him against the dresser and gave Virgil time to pump and bust him again, the sound coming out in a hard heavy *wham-wham* double-O explosion that Virgil figured, grinning about it later, must have rocked some whores out of bed. Virgil picked up the nickel-plated .38, wiped it clean on Bobby's pants, and took it with him.

But he should have waited. As good as it felt hitting Bobby, it didn't pay anything in prize money. He should have waited to see what this other money was about.

Bobby Lear. Money waiting with your name on it.

Then look at it another way. Dead or not, Bobby still owed him something. If he couldn't collect from Bobby, then how about from his wife?

Virgil sat down and closed his eyes to meditate, think it out.

Something was going on between the wife and the ofay man who'd been looking for Bobby. Name of Ryan. Virgil had the name and the man's phone number on a piece of paper in his wallet. He'd remember the name, anyway. Standing close to the drunk old man who'd called the number for him—sour-smelling old shitface bum who told him, drinking the two doubles, how he loved colored people, saying they were like little children to him—standing close, smelling the man, he'd heard Ryan say the name and repeat it and then spell it. Virgil knew he'd remember the name because it was the same as the name of a stripper he had seen at the Gaiety when he was a boy, Sunny Ryan, and she was the first white lady he had ever wanted to fuck. It was funny how you remembered things.

Now the wife and the man name of Ryan both knew from the paper Bobby was dead. But something else was still alive that had to do with money. That part was hard to understand. If the man knew Bobby was dead, how come he put the second one in the papers? *Money waiting.* Or maybe he didn't know Bobby was dead when he put it in. But wouldn't the money still be waiting? If the money was for Bobby, would his wife get it now? Maybe. If it was like money left to him.

The only thing to do, Virgil decided in his patience, was go see Bobby's wife. Buy her some wine and ask her what she knew about it. If she didn't know anything, then call up the man and sound real nice and arrange to meet him. Ask him the question. What's this money with Bobby's name on it? And if it sounded like the man was blowing smoke, pick him up and shake it out of him.

It turned out to be easier than Virgil Royal thought it would. He went out looking for Bobby's wife and at the first stop ran into the man name of Ryan.

11

THE MANAGER LOOKED AS THOUGH he hadn't smiled in a long time and had forgotten how. It was a shame, too, Ryan was thinking, because he had a wonderful job taking care of the Mayflower, the actual carved-in-stone name of the apartment building on Selden, in the heart of the Cass Corridor, where he could sit in his window and watch muggings in broad daylight and the whores go by and the people from Harlan County and East Tennessee on their way to the grocery store for some greens and cornmeal. The manager said he hadn't seen her. She was still living in the apartment for all he knew.

Ryan gave him a five-dollar bill, saying for the inconvenience. The manager stood there in his brown coat sweater, hands pushed down in the sagging pockets, watching while Ryan looked around.

Ryan's problem, this was the logical place to begin, but he didn't know what he was looking for. He should at least appear to have a purpose, like he knew what he was doing. He wished the manager would go away. What would anybody want to steal? The only thing he sort of liked was a dinner plate from Stuckey's that had Lyndon and Lady Bird Johnson's portrait on it, in color. It wasn't bad.

The dresser and closet were empty. The daybed had been stripped. The kitchen had been straightened up in sort of a half-assed way, the counter and sink cleared but the empty bottles still on the floor.

The business card he had given her—SEARCH AND SERVE ASSOCIATES—was in the bathroom, lying on the lid of the toilet tank.

What did that mean? The medicine cabinet was empty. Okay, she'd taken her toothbrush and comb, that kind of stuff, and put them in her purse and saw his card in there and took it out. Because she was thinking about calling him again. Or because she had no use for it. He came out of the bathroom.

The manager said, "You find what you're looking for?"

"Not yet," Ryan said. He was looking at the black guy standing in the doorway, recognizing only the familiar shape of the hat, the nice curve to the brim, the hat sitting lightly on the man's head, down a little, almost touching his wire-frame sunglasses. A tan leisure outfit today, dark-navy shirt open and pale-blue neck beads. It looked good on him. Ryan was thinking if he put it on, though, he'd feel like a showboat—look at me trying to look cool.

Virgil said to the manager, "Go on downstairs. We need you, we let you know."

The manager might have been a tough little guy at one time who didn't take any shit and maybe something that hadn't withered yet stirred inside him. He said, "Who the hell you talking to? You come in here—I don't know you. I don't know him either. What business you got coming in here?"

"Hey, Papa?" Virgil said. "Leave us. You understand what I'm saying?"

"If you want to look around," Ryan said, "it costs five bucks."

"Get the tour, huh?" Virgil took out a roll of bills and peeled one off for the manager. "Find out all the famous people got laid here. Thanks, Papa."

The manager grumbled something. Virgil didn't move from the doorway and the manager had to edge sideways to get past him. Virgil was looking at Ryan with his easy, pleasant expression, almost smiling.

He said, "I'm Virgil Royal."

"I know," Ryan said. "From Wyandotte Savings and Loan by way of 4000 Cooper Street, Jackson, Michigan."

"Hey, shit." Virgil was grinning now. "How you know that?"

"No sense in keeping secrets from each other," Ryan said. "A policeman told me."

Virgil hesitated a moment. "Yeah, looking for Bobby, finding out this and that. But you're not a cop. What're you?"

"Confused," Ryan said. "I know I saw you the other night. Did I talk to you on the phone? Last Friday?"

"No, was a man I had call you."

"Yeah, well, I didn't know if you were the first one or the second one."

"Other one must've been Bobby. Talk real slow? Like he gonna fall asleep?"

"I don't remember," Ryan said. "I never did get to meet him, so I'm not sure it was him."

"Little too late," Virgil said. "Now you back looking for his wife. Where's she gone?"

"I don't know. She didn't leave me a note."

Virgil's gaze moved over the room. "She didn't leave much of anything, did she? Moved out." The sunglasses came back to rest on Ryan. "Now she gets the money, huh?"

Ryan didn't answer, getting some words together.

"Tell me about the money, say it's got Bobby's name on it. Somebody leave it to him?"

"Something like that," Ryan said. "It's a legal matter."

"You a lawyer?"

"Process server. You want a divorce, I'm the one hands the papers to your wife."

"I don't want a divorce," Virgil said, "I want some money Bobby owes me."

"You talk to him about it?"

"Man, you getting sneaky now. When did I last see Bobby Lear? Other night? After I saw you? Where was I between three and six A.M. and all that shit."

"The police talk to you about it?"

"Not yet. They do, I have to tell them I was at my sister and brother-in-law's. Got there at three-something, slept till noon. What else?"

Ryan shrugged. "You're talking, I'm not."

"No, I'm asking," Virgil said, "what this money deal is. See, now that the man's dead, I should get the money from his—what you call it—his estate. Right?"

"I don't know," Ryan said. "I told you, I'm not a lawyer."

"Yeah, but you not serving papers either," Virgil said. "You into something else. What's it about?"

"Let me put it this way," Ryan said. "I've got no reason to sympathize with you or tell you anything about what I'm doing, because it's none of your fucking business. Okay?"

"Hey, shit, come on," Virgil said, "talking like that. It's to our mutual interest, man. You gonna be looking for the lady, so am I. We *both* in it. We can help each other."

"You mean all three of us," Ryan said. "You and I and the Detroit Police Department."

"That's all right, it's cool. Sure, let them do their job. Somebody's gonna find her and then I'm gonna talk to her. So why don't you tell me what it's about now, case I'm wasting my time."

"I'll tell you one thing," Ryan said.

"What's that?"

"You wear that hat."

Virgil gave him a little nod. "Yeah—thank you."

"See, she doesn't know what the deal is yet," Ryan said, "and nobody seems to know where she is, anyway, so why don't you just be patient for a while. What's the hurry?"

"Yeah, you right. It messes up your stomach," Virgil said. "Can cause your knuckles to get broken. No sense in having that, is there?"

"It's dumb," Ryan said, "getting worked up, instead of being patient and letting it happen. You know what I mean? It works out or it doesn't."

"I can dig it," Virgil said. "I know, patience can help you through all kinds of anxieties and concerns, including deep shit and solitary confinement."

"That must be awful, solitary. I don't think I could do it."

"If you don't fight it," Virgil said.

"Well"—Ryan looked toward the kitchen—"I could make some instant coffee—since neither of us seems to know where the fuck we're going, anyway."

"Yeah." Virgil nodded. "That'd be fine. Something else I been meaning to ask you. Your name's Ryan, huh?"

"That's right."

"You got any relation name of Sunny Ryan?"

12

SHE WASN'T IN KEN'S, the Gold Dollar, the Good Times, the Temple, the Hotel Ansonia, the Royal Palm, the Willis Show Bar, or Anderson's Garden.

Ryan checked the bars for a couple of days, thinking she might've felt safer with the drunks, the familiar atmosphere, and was still in the neighborhood. The trouble was, she could stay in a room drinking and seldom come out. She must have money, some, anyway. And if she did, she could have taken off. She could be anywhere.

He called his answering service several times a day—in case she remembered his number and phoned, which wasn't likely—and listened to the answering service girl recite the messages. Call Virgil Royal, and the number. Call Raymond Giddy? Gidre. Rhymes with hid-me. Staying at the Eldorado Motel on Woodward, and the number. Call Rita. Call Jay Walt. Call five, six, seven lawyers with papers waiting to be served. The list of lawyers kept growing. The others kept trying.

Ryan went back to the county clerk's files and checked the marriage license again.

Denise Leann Watson. Occupation: student. Birthplace: Bad Axe, Michigan.

He didn't notice it the first time he checked. *Bad Axe.* He'd worked in that area of the Thumb twelve years ago, in the sugar beet and cucumber fields. He might've seen her on the street in Bad Axe or Port Austin, the majorette with the blond ponytail and the perky ass, twirling for the consolidated high school marching band. Or in the backseat of a car at the drive-in, drinking Boone's Farm.

Father's name: Joseph L. Watson.

Ryan talked to Mrs. Watson on the phone. He could feel her withdraw and lock up when he said he was inquiring about Denise. Was she there? Mrs. Watson said she had not heard from Denise since Christmas. She did not see her then and did not care either, because Denise was not going to hurt her anymore. Ryan asked if, by any chance, Denise had gone to Wayne—picturing the psych or sociology major who'd got lost in the inner city and messed up. No, she'd gone to Michigan State and then to Detroit Arts and Crafts. Ryan thanked her.

He called the art school and found out Denise had studied there four years ago. Graphic design.

So he visited art studios in the Cass Corridor area—storefronts painted over in bright colors, a corner building that looked like the Alamo, painted white, and had been a Hi-Speed gas station. He talked to artists who looked like mechanics. The one who remembered a Denise Watson was building a sculpture out of hubcaps, welding them together. He turned off his torch, put his goggles up, and said, Denise. She did whales. She did wailing fucking whales, man. Denise's whales, man, she drew whales, she painted whales, she fucking *carved* whales better than the Eskimos.

Ryan called Dick Speed.

Nothing on Denise Leary yet. Sure they were still looking—a guy is killed and his wife disappears? Her name was at the top of the all-points. For questioning.

"How about Virgil Royal?"

"Yeah, we talked to him," Dick Speed said. "We talked to his sister, we talked to his brother-in-law. They say he spent the night with them. We talked to Virgil again. We had the night clerk at the Montcalm Hotel happen to pass through the office. He said he didn't know, maybe, they all looked alike to him. He said the guy had on a raincoat and a knit cap, maybe a beard. You remember Tunafish?"

"Sure."

"That's Virgil's brother-in-law."

"It's getting like everybody knows everybody," Ryan said.

"How about birds of a feather?" Dick Speed

said. "If they're not screwing each other's sister, they strike up meaningful relationships at Jackson. They're all in the life together."

"You believe Tunafish? I mean since he's supposed to be on your side?"

"Tunafish, he gives us a little straight stuff and a lot of bullshit. With something like this—well, if you had a brother-in-law was a hard-time con who might've blown away a couple of people with a shotgun—would you get him sore at you?"

"So what do you do now?"

"Stay on it. Talk to people. Like the hairdresser out in Pontiac. He gave us the same description, raincoat, knit cap, but no beard. So we don't think much of the beard the night clerk might've seen. The hairdresser looked through the family album. 'Mmmmmm, no. No . . . no . . . no. That's cute, the earring. I know a fella wears his mother's wedding ring in his ear.' We say, How about *this* mother? And point to a nice full-face and profile of Virgil. He says, 'Mmmmmm . . . mmmmm. Well, there *is* a likeness . . . no . . . well, maybe. No, I can't say posi*tive*ly, so I'd better not say.' We parade Virgil through the office, Virgil looking around like he's never been here before—isn't that interesting, a calendar, and a window, and all those mug shots on the wall—he probably *knows* half the fucking guys up there. The hairdresser, he'd glance at Virgil and look away, like he didn't want to be impolite and get caught staring at him. To make a long story, no positive I.D. Virgil's on the street."

"He keeps calling me," Ryan said. "He wants to talk to the wife."

Dick Speed said, "Who doesn't? The broad's sitting somewhere, she doesn't know how popular she is."

There was a story about the disappearance of Denise Leary on page 3 of the *Free Press* and a graduation shot of her out of the Michigan State *Spartan*. It became a *before* in the before-and-after pictures of her Ryan kept in his mind. Her blond hair was shorter then, dipping close to her eye in a soft curve, and she was smiling. It was the first time he had seen her smile.

The news story said she was being sought for questioning in the slaying of her husband. Ryan wondered where they dug up words like that. *Slaying*. He didn't see anything in the news story he didn't already know.

Ryan stopped by the Eldorado Motel to see Raymond and find out what Mr. Perez was doing. The Eldorado was a midtown motel on Woodward Avenue. Ryan couldn't figure out who would stay there. He asked Raymond how it was going.

Raymond Gidre said he had never seen so many

niggers in all his life. He said he'd walked from the motel down to the river and all he'd seen was niggers.

Ryan asked him if he liked to walk, since it was about three miles.

Raymond said if he'd known it, he wouldn't have. He had walked over to the General Motors Building, but there wasn't nothing to see there. He liked the Fisher Building, though, the way they lit up the gold top at night. He said the street lights on Woodward were funny. They were kind of pink.

Ryan said he'd never noticed.

Raymond said near two weeks, he hadn't found a good place to eat other than a nigger joint he happened to go into. They had collards and okra. Nobody seemed to have heard of red beans and rice. Raymond couldn't believe it. He told Ryan he understood one thing now. At the Saint Charles Hotel in New Orleans, before they tore it down, and different places, the Monteleone, he'd wondered why a person couldn't get a shoeshine no more. It was simple once he saw why. All the niggers had come up to De-troit.

Ryan asked him if he'd heard from Mr. Perez.

Yeah, Mr. Perez had been to Chicago and Fort Wayne and was down to Indianapolis now.

Same kind of business?

You bet. It was what Mr. Perez did. He never sat around much, he was always on the go.

Ryan asked Raymond what he did for Mr. Perez.

Raymond said oh, he looked up people, he drove Mr. Perez on trips, he went with him sometimes to see people. Otherwise he fooled around, worked some at the Jungle Gardens and Bird City, then'd go on down to New Orleans for a while. Shit, Canal Street was about five times wider than Ryan's Woodward Avenue.

Ryan tried to think of things for Raymond to do. He asked him if he'd been to Belle Isle, in the Detroit River.

Raymond said shit, there was nothing there worth seeing. Some statues, the aquarium—gaw fish were little bitty things. Ryan should see the gaw fish they caught down at Barataria and Grand Isle, man, big ones like Ryan never seen. Ryan said, Oh, you mean *gar* fish. And Raymond said, That's what I said.

Raymond was freshly powdered, with his hair wetted down. He looked like he'd shaved with a hunting knife. He said most of the time, shit, he'd get dressed and sit here, waiting for somebody to call. When was something going to happen?

Ryan said well, if it didn't happen soon, he'd give Raymond a treat and drive him past the Ford plant.

Raymond looked at him, not quite sure, scratching at his forearm where the tattoo showed like an old bruise through the hair. The tattoo was a faded black and red scroll within a flower that said *In Memory of Mother*.

She could have gone anywhere.

Ryan didn't like to think of it that way, even after three weeks without a word.

She did go somewhere.

That was better. It gave him something to picture, even if the picture was usually a bar in the afternoon. He always saw it the same way: a cheap, dim lounge with glass-brick windows or venetian blinds holding out the sunlight.

What were her thoughts when she woke up that morning?

What were her options? Keep drinking or quit. Kill herself or quit. *Want* to quit. Or play the I'll-quit-tomorrow game. He could picture that easily enough: the girl saying she was going to do it herself, without help, resenting help. First, though, a few glasses to get through the hard part. Then a few more, and then, with the glow, a change of attitude: she was all right, it wasn't a serious problem, Christ no, she had a lot on her mind and the wine soothed her nervous system and melted anxieties. She could quit anytime she wanted. Maybe she wouldn't do it all at once, though, in one day. That would be like driving along fast and slamming on the brakes. You could go through the windshield. Better to slow down gradually, ease to a stop, and not get hurt.

Or keep going and not touch the brake at all, finish it.

But she had called him. She had said she didn't want to be inside herself.

She wasn't a name in a county clerk's file or a picture in the newspaper, she was a person and he was aware of her as a person. He should have stayed and been sitting there when she woke up and said to her okay, here's what you have to do. Here's what you're *going* to do, and don't give me any shit about doing it any other way, because there isn't any other way. That close, looking at her. A person inside somebody she didn't want to be. She had told him that. And he had let her get away.

Maybe not far, if she didn't have much money. If she didn't work and if Bobby had been in jail or in a state hospital, where would she get money? Unless she got a job.

Ryan dialed Dick Speed's number, looking out the window at another overcast day, possible showers. Maybe it was the weather that made him feel depressed. At least it helped. He wanted to be doing something. He hoped he didn't have to leave word and then wait for Dick to call back. Or go out and have to check with the answering service and take all day to get hold of him. Dick Speed answered, and Ryan felt a little lift.

"I was wondering, if Denise Leary was working, wouldn't she have to give them her social security number and there'd be a record of it in Washington?"

"I guess so," Dick Speed said, "but it wouldn't do us any good. They won't release that kind of information, not even on a murder warrant. You're thinking, though. Keep it up."

Keep thinking. That's all he'd been doing, trying to put himself in Denise Leary's place. He realized he wasn't just thinking about her in relation to the money, the fifteen thousand he'd get. He was thinking about her as a person. She had called for help and he had let her down. He could say it wasn't his fault, she changed her mind. But the feeling, the concern, stayed with him. He wondered if it was a feeling of guilt. Either that or a strong compulsion to kick himself in the ass.

The phone rang.

Dick Speed said, "Guess what? I was talking to a guy in the Seventh Squad, they're handling it. They found out a Denise Watson applied for a driver's license three days ago in Pontiac."

"How do they know?"

"They checked with Lansing, both her married and maiden name. She gave an address on the application, 1523 Huron Street, Pontiac. The Oakland County Sheriff's Department's on it now."

"What'll they do?"

"Make sure she's there first, then get back to us."

Ryan felt the lift again, the second one that morning, and higher this time. It woke up his confidence and kept him up and eager all the way out Woodward to Pontiac, making it from his apartment in a quick twenty minutes. He found Huron Street and followed the numbers and the lift began to descend. The 1500 block was all commercial. Fifteen twenty-three was a red, white, and blue building with a sign that said *Uncle Ben's Pancake House.*

Ryan saw the manager. The manager said he had just talked to the police. Who was this girl, anyway? What'd she do? She certainly hadn't ever worked for Uncle Ben.

Maybe not, but for some reason she had used the address. She was around, somewhere.

That was on a Monday.

13

WEDNESDAY AFTERNOON, Ryan was sitting in a bar on Saginaw Street in Pontiac. It was about four-thirty, a nice sunny day. Ryan was about an hour away from being drunk.

The bartender said, "Same way?"

"Yeah, do it again."

"That was a bourbon mist?"

"Early Times over crushed ice."

The bartender gave him the look that meant *That's what I said.* He didn't say it. Shit no, the guy was made of wood, he didn't say anything. You had to drag things out of him. Ryan watched the bartender make the drink. He was neat and methodical and slow. He used a chrome shot glass to measure the whiskey and poured it carefully over the crushed ice.

"You don't do it by sight, huh?" Ryan said. "Pour it right from the bottle, give it that turn with the wrist, little extra hit? You know what I mean?"

"You want a double?" the bartender asked him.

"Yeah, I guess so. If I can't talk you into anything."

The bartender got the bottle from the backbar again and picked up the chrome shot glass.

It was too bad. Ryan felt confident and alert, not the least bit down, the way he'd felt the last week or so. He felt like talking to somebody, doing something. Not with Rita, though. He wanted something to happen. It was too quiet in here. It wasn't a friendly place where you heard people talking and laughing. The bartender didn't give a shit. He wasn't paid to talk. Maybe listen, if you held him against the bar and threatened to punch him out.

He placed a fresh napkin and the mist in front of Ryan. Ryan said, "What I started to tell you before."

"Sir?"

"About the time I was serving papers to the rock group."

Either the bartender didn't remember or it didn't matter. He stood with his hands behind him, at parade rest.

"They were being sued by some hotel where they wrecked the place," Ryan said. "I was backstage, see, but I couldn't get near them, all the security cops and groupies and different people. I can't remember their name. It was something like Norfolk and Western. It sounded like a railroad."

"Excuse me," the bartender said. He moved off to serve a customer.

Fuck you, Ryan thought. He drank the bourbon and sat without moving, staring at his reflection in the rose-tinted mirror.

What was he doing sitting here? He could go home right now, take a nap, have dinner, feel a little shitty this evening, get a good night's sleep, and feel about 75 percent okay in the morning. But if he kept going until the bars closed at two he'd be on his way. Open his eyes in the morning and hope there was still some vodka in the cupboard. Or else get dressed and go out and find a seven o'clock opener, a workingman's bar. Then serve a few papers, get that done. Have lunch, a few beers. Go through the motions of looking for Denise Leary, who wasn't anywhere around Pontiac, Drayton Plains, Clarkston, or Keego Harbor. Rochester was next, maybe Rochester. And finally, by late afternoon, feeling a drunk's idea of normal as he started on the bourbon and sailed with it through the evening, becoming more talkative, confident, funny, interesting . . .

"I'll have another one."

"Same way?"

"No, I'll have a double bourbon mist this time."

The bartender gave him the look again. He made the drink, placed it in front of Ryan, and picked up the two empties.

"I saw I couldn't get near the group backstage," Ryan said, "so I waited till they went on and started playing and I walked right out there, in all the lights and the crowd screaming, walked right up to the lead guitar."

"Excuse me," the bartender said. He walked off with the empty glasses.

So interesting the bartender could hardly wait to hear the rest. He was aware of what he was doing. He asked himself, why do you want to fuck up? He had said to the girl, Because it's so much fun?

It didn't make sense. How could he sit here drinking? Like running out in front of cars on the expressway and saying he might not get hit. Since Monday afternoon . . .

Tired, getting the down feeling again, sitting in a bar on M-59 having a Coke. Feeling down—was that the excuse? The bartender had said, "You want something else?" Meaning, You ready to pay? and he had said, "Yeah, give me another one," and paused and said, "With a bourbon this time." Not thinking about it and getting an excuse ready first, but coming right out with it. He could come up with all kinds of excuses if he had to.

Because he was depressed.

Because he deserved a drink.

Because he couldn't keep walking into bars and ordering Cokes. It didn't seem natural.

Because he was tired and depressed was the best. He needed a drink to pick him up.

Then the next rationalization. He could have

one or two and not go berserk, for Christ's sake. That was a lot of shit about one drink and you're off again. He had had one drink Monday afternoon. No trouble.

He had had eight drinks Monday evening. Okay, that was it, the urge had been satisfied.

He had had two Bloody Marys at lunch Tuesday in Clarkston. He had had four vodkas and tonic during the afternoon. Eight, maybe ten bourbons that evening. And he'd bought the pint of vodka and had one with root beer before going to bed. He had seen an outdoor sign on the highway advertising Smirnoff and root beer. It was a Charlie something.

Then, this morning, a couple of vodkas and orange juice. At lunch in Drayton Plains he'd decided to pass on the Bloody Marys and had two beers with his chili. Then another bowl, it was so good, and another couple of beers. Then, two bars before this one, four bourbons. Two, three more here with the friendly bartender. That was thirteen drinks and it was only a quarter to five.

His wife or somebody had told him once, his problem was he didn't count his drinks. Okay, he was counting them. He could continue to drink socially till midnight and bring the total to thirty without any trouble. A good two whole fifths' worth of booze. But why stop at midnight? He wouldn't; he'd keep going.

He didn't have to, though. Right now he was at the border. With a relatively clear head he could say, "Good-bye brains," and start pouring them down. Or he could quit right now. Except it would seem like stopping right in the middle, before he'd taken advantage of getting drunk, before he'd had any fun. Maybe a couple more days. Relax and let it happen. Look into some of the interesting afternoon lady drinkers he'd seen, the housewives with their gimlets and stingers and Black Russians. Tell them about serving the papers to the rock group and how he'd got his picture in the *Free Press*. Tell that one a few more times. Show the housewives what a funny guy he was. Score in a motel on Telegraph with a fifth of vodka, pop out of the machine. Or cold duck, because the housewife thought cold duck was romantic.

By tomorrow afternoon he wouldn't be thinking about it, he'd be doing it. Half in the bag trying to do it, sweating, and nothing happening. Or quit right now. Four years ago he was ready to quit on September 28, but he had put it off a few days because October 1 would be easier to remember as the day he quit and joined AA. He had quit six or seven times since then and wasn't sure of the last date. It didn't matter. He had been clean three and a half years and now, for some reason, he was sitting in a bar drinking. Deciding if he should keep going.

Actually considering it, knowing the pain he would experience when he finally stopped cold and withdrew. It wasn't a hangover pain; that was simple, you could numb it with aspirin. The pain in withdrawal was the extreme feeling of anxiety that Ryan remembered well—a raw, hypersensitive feeling, like a sunburned nervous system—wanting to either take a drink or go out the window. With Ryan it would last a couple of days while he paced and filled himself with liquids and ate B-12 tablets like peanuts.

The question, was it worth it? Of course not? But that didn't seem to matter, because it didn't have anything to do with now.

Why he was drinking didn't matter either. Because he was Irish or basically insecure? He was drinking. He could admit he was powerless over it once he got going, and he was still drinking. Sitting quietly in a bar, looking at his options and his reflection. He looked good, tan in the tinted bar mirror. His memory wasn't too sharp, though. He wasn't sure of the exact date, April 25 or 26. May 1 was a little too far off. The thing to do was call one of his friends in AA, admit he was fucking up and needed help, a kick in the ass. Or he could go to a meeting tonight. He hadn't been to a meeting in about four months, and maybe that was his problem. Find one in the area. Call the main office and find out where to go in Pontiac. Go home and take a shower and a quick nap first, have something to eat. Pay and get out of here.

Or have just one more.

14

"I WOKE UP LAST NIGHT AND LOOKED AT THE CEILING,"
the woman across from Ryan said. "And you know
what? It wasn't spinning around. I got up to go to
the bathroom and I found it without bumping into
furniture or knocking anything over. It was right
where it was supposed to be. Sometimes I used to
wake up in the morning on the floor and I'd say a
prayer, before opening my eyes, that I'd know
where I was."

The table leader said, "I know what you mean.
The first six months to a year in the program, I'd
still wake up in the morning expecting to be hung
over. I was amazed I actually felt normal."

The meeting was in a windowless basement
room of Saint Joseph Mercy Hospital, Pontiac.
Cinder-block wall, fluorescent lights, lunchroom
tables and folding chairs, the coffeemaker, the Sty-
rofoam cups, the cookies. It could be an AA meeting anywhere, with groups of eight to twelve
people at the five tables.

Another of the women was saying that sometimes she'd wake up in a motel room and there'd
be a man with her she'd never seen before in her
life and she'd scream at him, "What're you doing
here! Get out!" The poor guy would be baffled—
after the beautiful evening they'd had that she
didn't remember.

There were four women and seven men at the
table, including Ryan. He wasn't sure if he was going to say anything when the table leader got to
him. He might pass, say he just wanted to listen this
evening. He wondered if there might be a trace of
whiskey on his breath. He asked himself then,
Would it matter? Like someone might point to him
and they'd throw him out of the program. Amazing, two days of drinking and the guilt feelings
were back. He had stayed away from meetings too
long. He knew it, but he didn't feel part of it
tonight. At least not yet.

A man two chairs away from him said, "Thank
you. I'm Paul, I'm an alcoholic, and I'm very glad
to be here. You know, there's a big difference between admitting you're an alcoholic and accepting
the fact. That's why I like to sit at a First Step table
every so often. Not only to listen, but to keep re-
minding myself that I'm powerless over alcohol. I
wasn't like Ed there, who mentioned binge drinking, go off for a couple of weeks and then

straighten out, stay sober awhile. Shit, I was drunk *all* the time."

What were you? Ryan was thinking, a moderate drunk? A neat drunk. He had always hung up his clothes at night and only wet his pants once.

A woman about forty-five said that Saturday night finally did it when she came home drunk and had a fight with her fourteen-year-old daughter: the unbelievable language she used, screaming at the child, Mommy in one of her finest scenes. The next morning she wanted to die. But she called a friend in the program and went to a meeting that night. She had come to meetings Sunday, Monday, Tuesday, and she was here tonight and was going to keep coming.

The guy next to Ryan leaned close to him, reaching for the ashtray, and said, "What does she want, a fucking medal? She doesn't have any choice."

When the guy's turn came to speak to the table, he said, "I wasn't an alcoholic, like the rest of you drunks. Hell no. In a two-year period I got fired from three jobs, my wife divorced me, I was arrested twice for drunk driving, I smashed up the garage and five cars, but I wasn't an alcoholic. I was a heavy social drinker." There was laughter and some nodding heads. Ryan smiled.

Everyone at the table had been there.

"Cats slept in my car," a woman said. "It had so many holes in it from smashups."

Ryan remembered scraping the side of his sister's house pulling into the drive, ruining the flower bed. He remembered picking up the strip of molding and throwing it in the car while his brother-in-law ran his hand gently over the brick wall, like the scrape mark was a wound.

"I wouldn't, the way I was, I wouldn't go any-where unless I was sure I could get a drink," the woman was saying now. "I'd be at a school PTA meeting, I'd say excuse me, like I was going to the bathroom. I'd go out to my car. I always kept a cou-ple of six-packs in the trunk."

In a cooler, Ryan remembered. Unless it was winter. Open the trunk like it was a refrigerator. Drive with the can between your legs. He looked at his watch.

Nine o'clock. Another half hour. The room was close and he could feel himself perspiring. All the hot coffee and cigarettes. The ashtrays around the table were full. Walk into a room like this any-where, and if everybody was drinking coffee and smoking cigarettes it was an AA meeting.

A man was saying that two years ago, when he and his wife were in Europe, they'd taken a boat trip down the Rhine. He didn't see much, though. The only thing he looked for along the river was liquor stores.

The table leader said to Ryan, "I'm sorry, I don't

know your name. Would you like to say a few words?"

Ryan had lighted a cigarette, getting ready, knowing his turn was coming. He said, "Thank you." He paused. The people at the table waited.

"I was going to pass," Ryan said then, "or make something up . . . but I might as well tell you where I am. I've been in the program three and a half years." He paused. "I'm Jack, and I'm an alcoholic. I got drunk yesterday and the day before, and I thought I'd probably keep going a few more days. Why I started drinking again, I don't know. Maybe because my car needs new shock absorbers. Or it was King Farouk's birthday. The reason doesn't matter, does it? I slipped—no, I didn't slip, I intentionally got drunk—because I've stayed away from meetings too long, four months, and I started relying on myself instead of the program. I forgot, I guess, that when you give up one way of life, drinking, you have to substitute something else for it. Otherwise all you've done, you've quit drinking, but you've still got the same old resentments and hang-ups inside. You're sober but you're miserable, hard to get along with. You're what's called a dry drunk. Sober, but that's all. Well, I've been very happy the last couple of years. Not only because I've been sober and feel better physically, but because the program has changed my attitude." He paused. "A friend of mine has a sign on the wall at his office, it says *No More Bullshit*. And that's the way I feel, or want to get back to feeling again. I know I can be myself. I don't have to play a role, put up a front, pretend to be something I'm not. I even listen to what people say now. I can argue without getting mad. If the other person gets mad, that's his problem. I don't feel the need to convince everybody I'm right. Somebody said here tonight, 'I like myself now, and it's good to be able to say that.' I had fun drinking, I'll admit it. At least, I had fun for about ten or twelve years and, fortunately, I didn't get in too much trouble or hit bottom and sleep in the weeds. But once I realized I was thinking about the next drink while I still had one in front of me—once I started making up excuses to drink and got drunk every time I went out—I was in more trouble than I realized. You know what happens after that, drinking not to feel good but just to feel normal, to get your nerves under control. What I'm saying, I'd be awfully dumb to go back to that when I can feel good and be myself— that's the important thing—without drinking. I don't know where we got the idea we need to drink to bring ourselves out."

Ryan paused again, not sure where he was going.

"I'm glad I'm here and can tell you what I feel," he said then, "instead of sitting in a bar thinking.

The best thing we can do, besides staying out of bars, is try to stay out of our heads."

It was a good feeling, coming out instead of beating himself down. He picked up his empty coffee cup, and the guy's cup next to him, and went over to the urn and filled them up. When he sat down again, a girl at the end of the table was speaking.

She was saying she thought the sign was a great idea. *No More Bullshit*. Because that's what the program, to her, seemed to be all about. The idea, quit pretending and be yourself . . . a way to self-awareness that everybody, not just alcoholics, seems to be more interested in today. That's what had surprised her most about the program, the positive aspect of it. Not simply abstaining from alcohol, but as Jack said, substituting something positive for it, a totally different way of life, not inner-directed anymore, but outgoing.

The girl stopped.

Ryan was sipping his coffee.

"I'm sorry," she said then. "I started talking—I forgot to say I'm Denise, and I'm an alcoholic."

Ryan lit another cigarette and leaned forward with his elbows on the table, watching her. It couldn't be the same girl. But now the voice was familiar.

"I have the feeling everything I say you've heard before," Denise said, "but I guess that's part of it too. We can empathize, put ourselves in each other's places."

The nose was the same. Her face was different, it seemed narrower, smaller. Her blond hair was much shorter. It fell in a nice curve close to one eye, and she'd brush it away with the tips of her fingers.

"I reached the point finally, I guess I did think about killing myself, but even then I put off thinking how I would do it, whether to go off the bridge or turn the gas on or what. I'd think about it tomorrow, after I finished the half gallon of wine."

The empty Gallo bottles on the kitchen floor. The girl lying on the daybed with her hair in her face. Hair and lint on the dark turtleneck. Ryan remembered it. The greasy blue jeans and pale white unprotected feet. Moving her foot and not knowing someone was there watching it move. The girl at the table would be about the same age, twenty-eight. She wore a navy-blue sweater with the collar of a print blouse showing. She looked fresh, clean.

"It was a feeling that I wanted to get out of myself. Do you know what I mean? Every once in a while I'd see myself, what I'd become, and I'd say, 'What am I doing here? This isn't me.' I couldn't stop *thinking*. Do you know what I mean? Going around in circles, afraid of not particular things but *every*thing."

The voice on the phone had said to him, "I don't want to be here. I don't want to be inside me, but I can't get out."

"I had some help. Right at the end, when I didn't know what to do. I remember someone tried to help me."

She was looking this way, but her gaze might be directed past him, or at the table leader a couple of chairs over. Ryan wasn't sure.

"But I guess my pride screwed things up. I had to do it myself, so I ran away. Which is a pretty good trick, running away from yourself. Then I got the idea I was going to go home, the little girl wanting her mommy. But I didn't do that either, thank God, which was probably a good thing. If I'd gotten the lectures and all the shoulds and shouldn'ts, and Mother taking my screwing-up as a personal affront, trying to hurt her—I didn't need somebody like that, who wouldn't even begin to understand the problem. My mother's idea of drinking—well, never mind."

Good, Ryan thought. It would've been a bad move.

"Somehow I got to a meeting. It was at Holy Trinity in Detroit, you know, in Corktown, and there was a real mixture of people there. I remember a black woman who kept referring to her higher power as God Honey. That was my first meeting. I'd find a meeting every night somewhere, and finally I came out here." Denise paused. "I got a job, I start Monday. I'm living in Rochester in a very nice place and—the amazing thing, it seems like such a long time ago, and yet it's only been three or four weeks. I'm still a little fuzzy about periods of time."

Three and a half weeks, Ryan thought. Twenty-five days.

"I just hope it lasts, the good feeling." She paused again and looked at the table leader. "Thank you."

After the meeting they stood in lingering groups talking. Most of them seemed to know one another. Ryan got a half cup of coffee and waited. She was standing with the man from their table named Paul and the woman who used to wake up in motel rooms. Paul finally left them. They glanced over this way, then came toward him, both of them smiling. She was a good-looking girl, neat and trim, Ryan's idea of the perfect size. The other one, he couldn't imagine her waking up in a motel room with anyone.

"It's Jack, isn't it?"

"Right. Denise and . . ."

"This is Irene. I was just telling her—you said this was your first time, but I know I've seen you somewhere. Do you ever go to the Teamsters' Hall on Sunday?"

"No, I've heard about it, but I've never been there."

"It's a good meeting. Eleven o'clock Sunday morning."

"I'll have to go sometime. Yeah, I've been in the program three and a half years, but this is my first time here. Usually I used to go to Beaumont."

He was letting it get away. He wanted to ask her a question to be absolutely sure, but Irene stood there smiling at him. It had to be the same girl, now with trusting eyes, a pleasant expression, looking at him and sensing something but not remembering. He wouldn't have recognized her on the street.

"It was a good meeting, wasn't it?" She seemed eager to keep going.

"Yeah, I enjoyed it. I guess I always do. Everybody's straight, it's the one place people tell you honestly what they think."

"*No More Bullshit*," Denise said. "I love that. I think I'll paint it on my wall."

"The guy I mentioned has it," Ryan said, "is with an advertising agency. I don't know if it helps him or not. Maybe."

Denise smiled again. "Are you in that business?"

"No, I'm a process server."

She nodded and seemed to be thinking about something.

"You know what that is?"

"I've been served, evicted, and repossessed. I know exactly what it is. Not lately, though."

"Not in the past three or four weeks anyway, huh?"

It went past her or she didn't hear him. She was looking at the people beginning to leave.

"I told Paul and some of the others I'd meet them for a bite," Denise said. "Would you like to join us?"

"Fine. I've got a car."

"I came with Irene. Why don't you follow us over, unless you know where it is."

"Where are we going?"

"I'm sorry, I thought all AAs went to Uncle Ben's after meetings. It's the pancake house on Huron."

"Maybe he sick," Tunafish said.

"Got sick all of a sudden," Virgil said. "Park his car and walk in the hospital, say he's sick."

"Then he visiting somebody."

"That's where we're at," Virgil said. "Who? Bobby's woman? Maybe so. She was in bad shape."

"Ask him," Tunafish said. "You know the man."

"The man ain't talking much. He don't call me back. But all of a sudden he got this interest in Pontiac, going to the bars, going home, come back out here. He know something he ain't telling."

They sat in Virgil's white Grand Prix in the visitors' parking lot, Saint Joseph Mercy Hospital. If Virgil were to pop on his headlights, the beam would show part of Ryan's light-blue Pontiac Catalina. Tunafish was cold. He held himself tightly with his hands in the pockets of his leather coat. He didn't know what he was doing here, keeping Virgil company. Virgil was smoking a joint, the new quiet Virgil. He had smoked hash all the time and was never this quiet before. He spoke so slow Tunafish wasn't sure he'd ever finish what he started to say, the joint putting spaces between his words. Virgil kept his window open a few inches. That's why Tunafish was cold, feeling the damp night air.

He wished he knew what he was doing here. He didn't like to ask, but he didn't like the way it had been going lately, Virgil calling him, getting him pulled into some shit going on about Bobby Lear and Bobby's wife. People asking about her, looking for her. He didn't like not knowing who this man Ryan was. The man seemed familiar, like he'd seen him someplace, and he kept thinking of the man as a cop, even though Virgil told him he wasn't. Tunafish wanted to know things, but he didn't want to know too much, in case anybody was to sit him down and ask him questions. He got a little excited and sat up straighter when he saw Ryan come out and get in his car.

They followed him through Pontiac, around

Wide Track Boulevard and out Huron to Uncle Ben's Pancake House, the second time tonight.

"Man's ape shit about pancakes," Tunafish said.

Virgil didn't say anything. He watched Ryan wait in front of the place, by the door, until two women and a man walked up to him. They went inside. Some more people came and went in about the same time, everybody all of a sudden hungry for pancakes. Ryan had planned to meet some of them here, Virgil was sure of that. But who were they? When had Ryan talked to them? Uncle Ben's, another place to check on, though it didn't look as good as the hospital.

"What you're doing," Virgil said to Tunafish, "you're learning how to do it. How to sit and wait for the man. The other thing is to write down every place the man goes, and what time."

"I don't have no car," Tunafish said.

"We talk to Lavera, she let you use the car," Virgil said. "If we have to rent it from her."

"I follow him around, huh? Wait for him while he eats?"

"I'm going to the hospital tomorrow, see if Bobby's woman's staying there. If she is, you don't have to do nothing else. If she ain't, you follow the man where he goes."

Tunafish wanted to ask Virgil what Virgil would be doing, but he didn't. He worked down into his leather coat to keep warm and sat there most of a half hour.

Virgil watched Ryan come out with one of the women. Skinny little thing, blond hair—he couldn't see much else. Ryan helped her on with her raincoat and they stood talking, facing each other, neither of them moving. It looked to Virgil like the man had something going. But the other woman came out and the two of them walked off together. Ryan remained where he was, watching them. He watched them drive off and still he didn't move right away.

"Something's going on," Virgil said, spacing the words. "I'm looking at it. But I don't know what it is."

15

RYAN GOT UP TO ANSWER THE PHONE Monday morning. It wasn't quite seven.

He had been lying in bed thinking. He should have called Mr. Perez Friday or Saturday. Sunday had been all right to let go by. But he had to tell Mr. Perez something today. Either say it was hopeless and he was quitting, or give Mr. Perez Denise's address and stop worrying about her. Those were his options. He had to make a decision and quit thinking.

But when Mr. Perez said, "How you this morning?" Ryan started thinking again, trying to talk and sound pleasant.

"I didn't get back to you last week."

"Yes, I know you didn't." Mr. Perez sounded patient, as though he didn't mind.

"I wanted to," Ryan said. "I was pretty much on the go all day."

There was a silence.

"What I think I hear," Mr. Perez said, "are words. What're you trying to tell me?"

"I'm saying there's only one way to find out if she's around, and that's to keep at it." Ryan managed a good straightforward sound.

There was a silence again. Ryan waited.

"I hope," Mr. Perez said, "you're not making plans of your own."

"I don't know what you mean."

"Feel you don't need me, can handle this yourself."

"Well, I don't see how I could do that."

"I don't either," Mr. Perez said, "but you still might be considering it, thinking maybe she knows about the stock, heard the name of it one time."

"She hasn't even claimed his body."

"I mean, if you were to bring it up, poke at her memory a little bit. If you've got something like that in mind," Mr. Perez said, "I'd suggest you forget it. After all the work and effort I go to compiling a list, it wouldn't be fair of you to steal one of my names, would it?"

"No, it wouldn't," Ryan said. He hadn't even thought of the possibility before.

"It not only wouldn't be fair, it would be poor judgment on your part. If you understand me."

"I'm working for you," Ryan said. "I'm not interested in your business. I don't know anything about stock, I wouldn't know how to go about any-thing like this."

"It *is* tricky," Mr. Perez said. "You'd be much happier in what you're doing."

"No, I'm not for getting into anything over my head," Ryan said. But why hadn't he at least thought of it? "You don't have to worry about that."

"I'm not going to," Mr. Perez said. "I'm not go-ing to worry one bit."

"You want to give me a few more days, then? See if I can find her?"

"Yeah, you may as well. I've dug up the names of a couple more lost souls that might live in the area, so you keep at what you're doing," Mr. Perez said. "I'll be here waiting."

And watching. He didn't say it, but that's what Ryan felt. Mr. Perez on one side. Virgil Royal some-where on the other. While he stood in the middle with Denise Leary, playing games.

Monday evening Ryan drove to Rochester to pick up Denise. She was living in a colonial complex of red-brick apartment buildings. He didn't go in. She came out when he buzzed, and they went to a meeting at Saint Andrew's Episcopal in Drayton Plains.

At the table Denise told about a new experience she'd discovered and was enjoying. Eating breakfast in the morning. Cereal, eggs, toast, the whole thing. Unbelievable. Instead of throwing up and having a few glasses of wine and trying to remember what had happened the night before. She told them today was her first day on a new job, checkout girl at a supermarket. She was amazed how friendly and willing to talk most people were. She said she had a strange feeling, as though four or five years had been taken out of her life and she was starting over. Each day was new and interesting, whether anything interesting happened or not. She said, "God, I sound like Little Mary Sunshine, don't I? But I can't help it, it's how I feel. I hope I don't get used to it or find out it's a phase you go through." She looked at Ryan across the table from her. "I like feeling good. I like being excited again about little things and wondering what's going to happen next, without being afraid."

Outside, after the meeting, Ryan said, "Aren't you a little tired of Uncle Ben's? It's so bright in there."

"I'm tired of drinking coffee more than anything," Denise said. "Is that all right to say?"

"What we should do, go to a nice dim lounge with a cocktail piano. Order Shirley Temples on the rocks."

"Or go back to my house," Denise said. "If you like red pop or tea."

"I'd even drink coffee at your place," Ryan said.

Tunafish wished he knew what the fuck the man was doing. One night he goes to the hospital. Look at this, Virgil. Next two nights he goes to church, different churches. Saturday night, nothing. He doesn't even go out. Then on Sunday he doesn't go to church, he goes to a building says LOCAL 614. Monday night he goes to church again.

Tunafish wrote it down in the notebook he'd show to Virgil. Time to move. He gave the man a good lead and followed his taillights east toward Rochester.

There were killer whales in Puget Sound and a sperm chasing a school of salmon in the Strait of Juan de Fuca.

Ryan could make out the shapes, dark shadows in the misty blue. The specks of silver and yellow must be the salmon.

"They're both oils," Denise said, "from memory. Not very good, either. I mean the technique or the memory. I've got to loosen up more, I'm stiff."

"You like whales, huh?"

"I love whales."

Ryan hadn't thought much about whales, but he said, "I can see where they'd be good to paint."

"During one summer I trailed a herd of gray whales from Vancouver Island down the coast to Ensenada, in Baja. I must've made a hundred and fifty sketches."

"You still have them?"

"No. Some are at home, if my mother kept them. The rest were lost, thrown away." She was staring at the two unframed canvases propped against the wall. "These are the first things I've done in about three years."

She moved away now, going into the kitchen that was separated from the living room by a bar-high counter with two stools. She called it part of the hot-setup contemporary decor. The place, she'd found out, was full of young swingies who turned their hi-fis up in the evening and invited each other in for cocktails and sangría at their studio bars. She had gone to one party and sipped coffee and the swingies had lost interest. It had been fun watching, though, she said. Like amateur night.

Ryan looked around the room again before going over to the counter. The place was freshly painted white and didn't feel lived in. There wasn't any worn-out furniture, things that had been handed down or bought at garage sales. There was beige carpeting and an Indian-looking rug. There were no curtains: a limp plant hung in the window.

What dominated the room was a drawing board tilted up, with a straight chair, and a table littered with tubes of paint and brushes, a few ceramic pots, coffee mugs, and a full ashtray. There was an aluminum floor lamp that looked new, and a pair of director's chairs with bright-yellow canvas. Most of the wall area was bare and stark white except for a number of black-and-white sketches of whales above the drawing board, stuck to the wall with pieces of masking tape. There were the two blue-looking finished canvases and a word, *Kujira*, painted on the wall in thin, flowing black letters that seemed more a delicate design than a word. Ryan didn't know what to say when they came in and Denise turned on the floor lamp and he stood looking around. He said, "Did you do all this?" He studied the oils, not knowing what they were until she told him whales. The design on the wall, *Kujira*, was the Japanese word for whale, and the technique, the flowing, stiff-armed brushstrokes of ink, was called *sumi*. Denise said she was thinking about doing *No More Bullshit* in *sumi*. Ryan said it was a nice place. Clean. Denise said it was funny, she never thought of a place that way, being clean or dirty.

Leaning on the counter, he watched her as she put a kettle on to boil and dropped tea bags into blue ceramic cups.

"You mentioned, I think it was at that Saint

Joseph meeting, you almost went home. Where's that, your home?" He had to think before he spoke and not refer to anything about her he had learned on his own.

"Bad Axe," Denise said. "You know where it is?"

"Everybody knows where Bad Axe is. Why didn't you go there?" He was interested. He was also groping, looking for a way to ease into telling her what was going on. Relieve his own mind without disturbing hers. Maybe if they got talking about real feelings and were honest with each other . . .

"I almost did," Denise said, "I guess, wanting to feel protected. But when I'm home, I'm not ever really me, I'm somebody or whatever my mother expects me to be. You know what I mean? I have to pretend I'm still her little girl and, oh gee, is it nice to be home, it's so good to see you, Mom, and all that shit. I love her, I really do, but I can't be honest with her and tell her how I feel. She wouldn't understand. She's full of shoulds and shouldn'ts and she's not going to change now. So I thought, why get into all that? I've got enough of a problem getting myself straight without worrying about offending good old Mom. In her own way, she's as unreal and fucked-up as I am. But she doesn't know it and that makes a difference."

Denise looked at him as she turned and placed

the mugs of tea on the counter. "That's a habit I'm going to have to break."

"What is?"

"Talking dirty. I always said 'fuck' a lot when I was drinking."

"It's okay as long as you smile."

"The past year, I don't remember having much to smile about." She looked at him again. "Does that sound like 'poor me'?"

"Maybe a little," Ryan said, "even if it's true." He wanted to lead her along, get her to talk about herself. "How come you didn't paint?"

"I was too busy drinking."

"I asked you one time," Ryan said and stopped. "No, I guess I didn't."

"What?"

"When you started drinking."

"At State, I guess. I went to East Lansing, did the wine and pot thing. I guess I drank quite a bit, but I didn't worry about it then. Everybody got high or stoned, one way or another."

"Then you went to—what, art school?"

"Detroit Arts and Crafts. Did I tell you that?"

"Yeah, I guess. Or else I just assumed you studied somewhere."

"It has a different name now," Denise said, "like the Creative Center or something, and a new building. I went there three years, got very involved in fine art, mostly oils and acrylics. Then,

well, I was living in the art center area, you know?
around Wayne and the art museum, the main
library—"

Ryan nodded. About ten blocks from where he
had found her in the Cass Avenue bar, the Good
Times.

"—and I felt I was into real life, there was so much
going on around there. Sort of a Left Bank atmosphere with the art and the freaky students at Wayne
and the inner-city stuff, the hookers and pimps in
their wild outfits, all sort of mixed together. At the
time I thought, wow, beautiful. Or bizarro, if it was
a little kinky. That was one of the words. Or something would berserk you out, like a wine and pot
party in a sauna. You see, I was very arty and open-
minded, I mean as a life-style, not just on weekends
playing dress-up. I was going around with a couple
of black guys most of the time. . . ." She paused.

Ryan waited.

"Yeah? You trying to find out if I'm prejudiced?"

"No, I was thinking, if I'd ever told my mother,
God. Maybe that's what I should do sometime, say,
okay, here's your little girl, and unload everything
I've done. If she survives, fine. If she doesn't . . ."

"What?"

"Well, it would be her problem, wouldn't it?"

"I don't think you'd be unloading," Ryan said.
"I think you'd be dumping on her, paying her back.
You don't have to do that."

"No, I guess not. I keep looking for reasons, how I got here."

"We can save guilt and resentment," Ryan said, "if you want to keep it light."

"And my Higher Power, God Honey," Denise said. "I'm having a little trouble with that, too. I've got a long way to go, but already I *feel* good. I say it at a meeting and try to describe it, the feeling, but I don't tell everything I feel. I don't want to name names and put anybody on the spot." She was looking directly at him now. Her eyes were brown. She was in there feeling good things about him, letting him know.

"I don't think anybody tells everything," Ryan said, "at a meeting."

"Can I tell you?"

"If you want to."

"Maybe I'd better wait," she said. "Everything's working out, then I begin to worry maybe it's a false high. I get up there and find out it isn't real but an induced feeling, or else something happens."

"Were you on drugs," Ryan asked her, "when you were doing the arty thing?"

"No, downers once in a while when my nerves were bad, but that was part of the drinking. I smoked, there was always grass, but I never cared much for the smell. What I liked to do best was drink."

"The two, you mentioned a couple of black guys, did they get you going?"

"No, I didn't need help, I sort of went that way naturally. They didn't care. Then—well, I started drinking more and more until I was at it most of the day. It was what I did in life."

"Was there a reason? I mean at first, were you depressed or just out for a good time?"

"Both, I suppose. I used it either way." She hesitated and looked thoughtful as she fooled with her tea bag. "I got into a bad situation. I was married . . ."

Ryan waited. He wasn't sure if he wanted her to go on.

". . . in fact, I still am. We're separated now, we haven't been together in—I haven't seen him in months. I don't even know where he is." She paused, holding her tea bag, and looked at Ryan. "Bobby was black, too."

Ryan hesitated because she was waiting for him and he didn't know what to say. He said, "Yeah?" And then he said, "Leary. It doesn't sound like a name, you know, a colored guy would have." Ryan froze, realizing his mistake. She had told him her name was Denise Watson. Not Leary.

But she was looking at the tea bag again, lifting it and letting it settle. "We weren't together much. He was in and out of . . . mental hospitals most of the time. That's not why I drank, I was drinking before that, but I guess it was a good poor-me excuse. Right?"

"It sounds as good as any," Ryan said.

"Why we got married—I don't know, maybe as you said before, to pay back my mother, if you want to get into all that, look for a subconscious reason. I don't know, maybe I was punishing myself or I saw it as a challenge and thought I could save him from . . . the way he was, the kind of person. Or, shit, I was attracted to him physically, the cool, hard dude—I mean, talk about cool, Christ—he scared me to death. I wanted to paint him, too." She paused, thoughtful again. "But I never did. Now—I hope I never see him, but I suppose I'll have to. I want to get a divorce started and out of the way and I think that, getting it off my mind, will help a lot." She looked up at Ryan. "Maybe you'll serve the papers. Wouldn't that be something?"

"If you file in Oakland County . . ."

He didn't know what he was starting to say. She hadn't asked a question that required an answer; he could duck around it. But he was sitting three feet away from her across the counter, looking at her face, her eyes. . . .

"I do some work out here," Ryan said, "and in Detroit, Wayne County. I like to move around."

"Do you ever get into any weird situations," she

asked him, "where the people don't want to be served?"

You bet he did, like serving a rock and roll band in front of thousands of screaming fans, walking right out on the stage. . . .

There, they were off of it.

They talked about Ryan for a while, about serving papers and how he got into it, and about working in the cucumber fields north of Bad Axe. They talked about Denise's new job at the A&P and almost got into it again.

She told him she was using her maiden name, Denise Watson, because it was on her social security card. Trying to steer away, Ryan said, You like it, huh, the job? She said it was a new experience. It was funny to hear people calling her by her first name again, Denise. She hadn't been called that in years. Ryan said he thought it was a nice name. And hoped that would end it.

She told him, then, she had done something dumb: applied for a driver's license in Pontiac and put down the Pancake House as her address. She hadn't found the apartment yet, she was staying at a motel, didn't have a permanent address; and going to the Pancake House after meetings she had felt good there, comfortable.

"Have you gotten the license yet?"

"I'm afraid to ask if it came."

"Why?"

"Well, why did I use their address? I'd have to explain all that. They might think I'm doing something, you know, illegal."

"You are."

"Not intentionally. I think the best thing, I'll apply for another one and do it right."

"Let's see what I can do first," Ryan said, now protective, wanting to help her, wanting to tell her, right now, who he was, but still holding back.

What was he doing? Playing with her, drawing out information, then ducking when his poor sensitive guilty awareness felt she might tell him too much. Then playing safe with a little how's-work chitchat. Then feeling sorry for her—no, not sorry—feeling close to her and wanting to touch her because she was a winner, a good-looking winner with nice clean-looking hair and eyes that held his while he sat there hiding everything, afraid to tell her. A soft, smiling expression in her eyes. . . .

Afraid of what? Well, afraid she might not understand, get the wrong idea and start drinking again. Trusting somebody and seeing it blow up. Afraid of what she'd think of him, sneaking around, playing games. She'd ask why, and the wrong answer would be there before he could explain it.

For the money.

That's what she'd naturally think, that he'd

slipped in snug and close so he'd be here when the money came in.

Picture it, when she found out he knew all the time. Her eyes holding his. . . .

Try convincing her eyes the money didn't have anything to do with it. He'd been looking for her, yes, he'd admit that. But he hadn't gone to the meeting to find her. That was an accident. She could be someone else, he'd still be here. . . .

But why go into all that if he didn't have to? At least not yet. He'd tell her sooner or later, naturally, but not just yet, okay?

The manager of the Pancake House didn't remember Ryan. He said, "Yeah, it came yesterday as a matter of fact. I called the Pontiac Police, and they said call the Sheriff's Department. I called them and they said they'd send somebody over."

"Oh, here," Ryan said. He took out his wallet and showed the manager his official Oakland County Constable star.

"I thought you'd be here yesterday," the manager said. He lifted the change drawer in the cash register and handed Ryan the Department of State window envelope addressed to Denise Watson.

"Thanks a lot," Ryan said.

16

"I'M TICKLED TO DEATH I'M TALKING TO YOU," Mr. Perez said. He was hunched over the papers and folders that covered the desk, smiling into the telephone.

Ryan, on the couch, was trying to listen while Raymond Gidre was telling him how he got along with niggers, how he didn't bother them and they didn't bother him.

"I know it must be a surprise, yes indeed." He was giving it his Nice Mr. Perez tone. "I'm just happy I was able to locate you. . . . No, I'm pretty sure. Miz Robert Leary, Jr., is that correct?"

"Matter of fact I had a good friend was a nigger," Raymond Gidre said to Ryan, across the coffee table. "Boy name of Old Jim, we called him. Me and Old Jim'd go crabbin' down to Grand Isle."

"No, I'm afraid, Miz Leary, I can't tell you much more than I have on the telephone. What I'd like to do is come out and see you, explain this in detail. . . . No, it's a property. . . . No, not necessarily,

Miz Leary. Tell me something. When would be convenient for you?"

"You ever go crabbin'?"

Ryan said yes, to shut him up. Raymond told him about it anyway, how you put the meat in the crab net, rotten meat if you had some, and how the sides of the net collapsed when it was laying on the bottom, then, see, the sides raised up again when you lifted out the net.

"Yes, ma'am, I can come out this evening, or I can meet you somewhere if you'd rather. Whatever's convenient."

"Drop them suckers in the boiling water, watch 'em turn red. First, though, you want to put in your bay leaf and your Tabasco, also some thyme."

"That'd be fine, Miz Leary. It was nice talking to you and I'm looking forward to seeing you. . . . Yes, ma'am, five o'clock. Bye-bye."

"I generally eat five, six. Shit, they go down good."

"What's that, Raymond?" Mr. Perez was off the phone.

"Gulf crabs."

"What'd she say?" Ryan asked.

Mr. Perez was grinning at Raymond. "Now you talking. Leave this meat and potato country and get back to cooking."

"How'd she sound?" Ryan said.

"Surprised . . . though not too excited." Mr. Perez got up and walked around to his bookcase bar next to the window. He began making himself a drink. "She seemed vague, like she just woke up."

"Well, I doubt she'd be expecting anybody even to call her," Ryan said. "You think?"

Mr. Perez came over with his drink. Raymond got up quickly and Mr. Perez sat down in his deep chair.

"You talked to her, did you?"

"I had to. Find out where she lives."

"How'd she sound? I'm wondering if the booze has made her soft in the head any."

"She's not drinking," Ryan said. "She quit."

"She tell you that?"

"She was sober. You could see she hadn't had anything in a while."

"How do you tell that?"

"Her appearance. She looks like a different person now," Ryan said. "It couldn't have just happened overnight."

Mr. Perez nodded, accepting that, but still curious. "You say you hung around this place, Uncle Ben's. She came in to get her driver's license and you started talking to her. How'd you go about that?"

"I went up to her, I asked her if she remembered me. She said no. I said, Aren't you Denise Watson? I told her I met her in a bar one time. We had a cup of coffee and talked a little."

"You tell her who you are?"

"I told her my name, I told her what I did. She seemed nervous then; but I didn't pull out any papers, so she relaxed."

"How'd you find out where she lives?"

"I asked her. Well, first I asked her if she'd like to go out sometime. She wouldn't say yes right away, but before I left she gave me her phone number and told me where she lives."

"In Pontiac?"

"No, it's in Rochester."

"Rochester doesn't mean shit to me."

"It's east of Pontiac," Ryan said. "The address is on the piece of paper I gave you. With the phone number."

"You go to her place?"

Ryan paused. "Yeah, I did, to check. Make sure it wasn't a phony address."

"But you didn't go in, huh, and visit?"

"No." Ryan shook his head. "I was wondering," he said then, "when you see her you don't have to mention my name, do you?"

"Why?"

"I mean, if she asks how you found out where she lives. Since she isn't in the book or anything."

"I ask you why," Mr. Perez said, "but you won't tell me."

"I just wondered, that's all. In case I ever see her again."

"I don't see any reason to bring you into it," Mr. Perez said. "Your part's done. 'Less she gets drunk and runs away again."

"I don't think you have to worry about that," Ryan said. "Once she finds out her husband's dead, I think she's gonna be more relieved than anything else."

"Feel you know her pretty well, huh?" Mr. Perez gave Ryan a little smile to show he understood. "How many cups of coffee you have with her?"

"A couple," Ryan said. He was being honest and literal and gave Mr. Perez a nice boyish grin in return.

"You interested in her?"

"Well, I got to admit she's a good-looking girl," Ryan said. "Is that what you mean?"

"Another week or so, when she gets her money," Mr. Perez said, "she's gonna be even better-looking, isn't she?"

"Well, I don't know about that," Ryan said.

Raymond was grinning now. "Wants to fuck him a rich lady for a change. Shit, I don't blame him."

"They're no worse or no better," Mr. Perez said, and looked at Ryan again. "I don't blame you, either. It's none of my business what you got in mind for Miz Leary, once we're done. As long as it's her you intend to fuck and not me."

"I hope I'm not offending you," said boyish Jack Ryan, "but I think if I had a choice . . ."

Mr. Perez smiled and Raymond Gidre laughed out loud and Ryan said he'd keep in touch and left. In the silence, then, Mr. Perez sipped his drink.

He said to Raymond, "You feel it?"

"Feel what?"

"That boy's gonna try and run with it," Mr. Perez said. "I don't think he knows it yet, but he's gonna try."

Mr. Perez visited Denise Leary on Tuesday, after she got home from work. He spent forty minutes with her while Raymond Gidre waited outside in the rented car. Raymond watched people coming and going in and out of the apartment complex and studied some of them very closely, but he did not see any niggers.

At seven-thirty Ryan called Mr. Perez at the hotel.

Mr. Perez told him it went about the way he'd expected. He'd left the agreement with her and would call in a day or two. There was nothing to do now but wait. Ryan tried to ask questions. How did she react? What'd she say? But Mr. Perez told him to save it, he was going out for his supper.

Ryan had decided not to bother Denise this evening, so he didn't call her until the next morning at eight. He'd ask her if he could pick her up after work, get something to eat and go to a meeting.

There was no answer.

At noon he drove out to the A&P in Rochester and found out Denise wasn't working today. She'd called in sick.

He called her several more times that afternoon and evening. On what he had decided was his last try, at ten o'clock, Denise answered the phone.

"Where've you been? I've been trying to get hold of you all day."

"Why?" She sounded all right. Calm.

He had to settle down. For all he was supposed to know, she could have been anywhere. "I was worried about you."

"Were you, really?"

"I stopped by the grocery store, they said you were home sick. I kept calling and there was no answer."

"That was nice of you," Denise said. "Can you come over?"

"Now?"

"Yeah, if you can. I've got an awful lot to tell you."

17

THE WHALES WERE DOWN FROM THE WALL, THE
sketches of the grays and humpbacks off California. In their place, in flowing black *sumi*, were the
words *No More . . .*

"Then what?" Ryan said.

He was in one of the director's chairs. Denise
came out of the kitchen with two glasses of red pop
and found room for them on the low table with all
the paint tubes and ceramic pots.

"I identified the body," she said. "Driving down,
I was pretty nervous, I didn't know what it would
be like. But the way they do it—they showed just
his face on a television screen—it wasn't bad at
all." She picked up the pottery ashtray heaped with
cigarette butts and went back to the kitchen with it.

"The police were there?"

"A detective, we went to his office. No, first I
called a mortuary and took care of that, then I went
to the police station."

"Do you have money? I mean for the burial?"

"He's going to be cremated," Denise said. She came back in with the ashtray, her eyes moving briefly to the wall. "I'm still working on my new motto."

"I see that. How were the police?"

"Polite, official," Denise said, sitting down in the other chair. "They asked questions—when I'd seen him last, that kind of thing. I can't believe it. I mean, the way I found out, a man I don't know. I didn't read a thing about it, I guess I didn't see the papers at all for about a week. Mr. Perez had a picture of me he'd cut out, an old one from when I was at State they must've got from my mother. I don't know where else."

"How're you feeling?"

"Fine." She was lighting a cigarette. "You mean nervous? I just can't believe he's dead. It's over and I don't have to do anything about it. I must live right, huh?"

"What did this Mr. Perez say?"

"He said something about a property or assets I'm entitled to, if I'll sign an agreement. But Bobby didn't own property, anything of real value."

"Maybe," Ryan said, "it isn't property the way you think of property, real estate. You said assets. It could be stock, something like that."

"He didn't own stock. I doubt if he even knew what it was."

"Somebody could've left it to him." Ryan was edging in. "His dad or somebody?"

Denise was staring at him, making up her mind about something.

"We're not talking about a normal, ordinary person," she said. "As far as I know, he didn't have a dad, or a mother. He was a street hustler, he was an addict, an armed robber. He was . . . he killed people."

"You knew that?" Ryan asked.

"I don't know, I suppose. I didn't want to know and I didn't ask about much. I drank. He was arrested, he was always being arrested, and if he was convicted they'd send him to a state hospital. He had a history of mental illness. He'd come out, I wouldn't see much of him. I guess he lost interest. Usually I'd hear he was living with somebody."

Ryan shook his head. He didn't know what to say. Denise was still looking at him.

"Did you read anything about him in the paper, that you remember? Bobby Leary?"

Ryan hesitated. "I don't know, I may have."

"The best way to describe him," Denise said, "picture a black heroin addict who killed people. But the reason we didn't hit it off, he was shorter than I am."

Ryan smiled. "Come a long way from Bad Axe, haven't you?"

"Almost full circle," Denise said. "But I'm sure as hell not going back."

"I heard a minister one time at a meeting," Ryan said. "He'd lost his congregation, they found out he was drinking and kicked him out, after about twenty years. He said if it hadn't happened he could have gone another twenty years being a minister, preaching, giving the sermons, and never look at himself and find out who he really is."

Denise said, "Is that me?"

"It's where you are," Ryan said. "You're not Mom's little girl anymore, or a drunk, or married to an addict who kills people. You're you, without a label."

"None of the other shows?"

"I don't see anything," Ryan said. "You could've been a nun before. What difference does it make?" He took a sip of red pop and let her think about it.

"Sometime, if you want," Denise said, "I'll tell you about him."

"Who?"

"Bobby."

"Sometime tell me about you," Ryan said. "If you want to. Right now, aren't you curious about this property, or whatever it is? What else did the guy say?"

"That's all. I'm entitled to something and he'll tell me what it is if I'll sign the agreement. It's in the kitchen. You want to see it?"

"That's all right. What does he take, a percentage?"

"He gets half."

"*Half?* For giving you something you own?"

"Well, he said I wouldn't know about it if it weren't for him and he went to a lot of trouble, but he said there wouldn't be any other charges or expenses taken out."

"He's generous with your money, isn't he? Did he say what the value of this asset is?"

"He said a considerable amount."

"Aren't you curious?"

"I think it's a come-on. I asked him if he was trying to sell me something."

"What'd he say?"

"He said no. What else would he say?" She drew on her cigarette and exhaled the smoke quickly, to say something. "I don't know what to do with Bobby's ashes. I have to decide."

"Where are they?"

"At the funeral home. They said I can have them buried in a cemetery plot or take them home—I can see that, Bobby sitting on the mantel in a Grecian urn. Or I can have the ashes scattered. That's another thought—rent a plane and have his ashes scattered over Jackson prison."

"I'd say you're taking your bereavement pretty well," Ryan said.

Denise looked at him calmly. "I'm glad he's dead. I could jump up and do a dance, but I can't get it into my head that it's true. I've never been this lucky before."

"And Mr. Perez comes along—things're looking up, uh? What're you going to do about that?"

"I told him I'd think it over."

"Did he seem anxious, try and get you to sign right away?"

"No, he was polite, courteous," Denise said. "Whatever it is, I guess to him it's still just a job."

"Besides the food and the lovely view of Canada over there in the rain," Mr. Perez said, "I'll tell you what else I don't like. I don't like sitting around waiting for a drunk woman who works in a grocery store to make up her mind."

Ryan didn't like sitting here listening to him.

If she hadn't signed the agreement yet and the deal was still up in the air, what good was he doing here? He could sit on the couch or go look out the window with Mr. Perez or watch Raymond hunched over the room-service table sucking his frog legs. They were always bitching about food, but one or the other always seemed to be eating or about to eat or had just finished.

"Three times I've called her," Mr. Perez said to the window. "Shit, twelve, fifteen times. I've called, three times I've talked to her, and she hasn't decided yet what she's going to do. I asked her, 'Are you talking to your lawyer? That's fine, I'd do the same.' She says no, she's been busy, hasn't had time to think about it. Busy doing what?"

It wasn't a question. Mr. Perez wasn't looking at either of them. Ryan answered it anyway. He said, "Maybe staying sober."

Mr. Perez turned from the window now and seemed to study Ryan.

"If she's having a hard time, concentrating on it," Ryan said. "Maybe that's what she means."

"Staying sober," Mr. Perez said.

"It could be more important to her than money," Ryan said.

Mr. Perez waited. "You tell me you haven't seen or spoken to her?"

Ryan shook his head. "No, sir." Mr. Perez could believe him or not. Screw Mr. Perez.

"I recall you said you told her you're a process server. Is that right?"

"When I got her address, yeah."

"She wouldn't be surprised, then, if you walked up and served her some papers."

"For what? You going to bring suit now?"

"No, I'm thinking I'm going to pull it out from under her," Mr. Perez said. "Three times I tried to talk to her, offering to give her half. All right, three times and she's out."

"She doesn't know what it's half of," Ryan said.

"So she won't be disappointed. I think it's time to get this thing done."

Ryan was paying close attention now. "Are you talking about screwing her out of everything?"

"She won't feel it," Mr. Perez said, "if we handle it properly. I was thinking, if you were to serve her a paper that looks like a writ or a summons of some kind, and she signs it—"

"The one getting served doesn't sign anything," Ryan said.

Mr. Perez was patient. "Does she know that? You come to her, you represent the court. You tell her to sign some papers that have to do with her husband, a certification of his death. Use some legal-sounding bullshit. One of the papers she signs—she sees just the bottom part—gives us her power of attorney to get the stock from the company and sell it." Mr. Perez nodded, thinking about it. "It's crude, I'll admit, but I don't see why we have to finesse it any. Raymond, what do you think?"

Gidre sucked the bone as he pulled the frog leg out of his mouth. "Sounds good to me."

Ryan said, "And she gets nothing. You never meant to give her any of it, did you?"

"No, the agreement I gave her specifies half—"

"What, she gets nothing because she won't sign right away?"

"Why don't you shut up for a little bit and let me talk," Mr. Perez said. "I'm not punishing her. I can't hurt her if she doesn't know she's being hurt, can I?"

Ryan didn't say anything. He was on edge now and didn't want it to show. He watched Mr. Perez come over and stand behind the deep chair, resting his hands on the high back.

"What occurs to me," Mr. Perez said, "is that we have a unique situation. A great deal of money, much more than usually's at stake, and a beneficiary who either doesn't believe me or doesn't give a shit about the asset she's entitled to. All right, we reach a point, if she doesn't want it—and I offered it to her, didn't I?—then *we'll* take it. We're not stealing from anybody, we're picking something up that's been discarded. That's if you need a rationale."

"Pick it up?" Ryan said. "You got to fake her out to get her signature."

"I'm not finished," Mr. Perez said. "If that's hard for you to chew on, then how about this?" He rested on his arms, leaning over the back of the chair and looking directly at Ryan. "Since we double the profit, we double your fee from ten percent to twenty. That's somewhere in the neighborhood of thirty thousand dollars for playing like you're serving some papers. Does it sound better now?"

Ryan didn't say anything.

Mr. Perez waited, giving him a little time. Finally

he said, "What is it you're thinking about, whether or not you want to do it? I'll tell you something, I'm not holding my breath. I can call your friend Jay Walt and he'll get the papers signed, won't he? What would he charge, about fifty bucks? You've put a lot of time in this, you've worked hard, and my feeling is you're entitled to a share. But as I watch you sitting there I begin to think, Wait a minute, what am I being so nice for? You work for me, but generally what I get are arguments and that's a bunch of shit when I'm paying you for what *I* want done. Isn't it? So what I'd like to hear you give me, without a speech or any more questions, is a simple yes or no."

"All right," Ryan said.

He took the elevator down to the lobby.

It was his own game he was playing, so he could make up the rules. *All right*, according to the game, wasn't yes or no, it was neutral, no more significant than a grunt, and meant nothing. It got him out of there and gave him a little more time. He could say to himself, in game-honesty, I haven't agreed. All I said was all right.

He could go in the Salamander Bar and think about it. The doorway was across the lobby. It would be a quiet place to relax and think—a clean, dimly lighted place. A hotel cocktail lounge in the afternoon.

It was almost two. Denise was off at four-thirty.

Get her to sign the agreement and take it to Mr. Perez. There, she signed it. Let's go ahead the way you originally planned, okay? Get it done. You can keep my ten percent. Really, I'd just as soon not have it or talk about it.

So he could say to himself, See? I didn't take anything. So I didn't take advantage of her, did I? Good boy. The game no one else knew about, going on in his head.

He took the escalator to the ground floor and walked outside and thought about Mr. Perez looking out the window bitching about the cold, wet April weather and traces of dirty snow. He began thinking about Florida. He hadn't had a vacation, a real one, in three years. Play the game on the beach, lying in the sun. Tell himself it had got too complicated. Christ, he didn't have to get involved in something like this. Take off. Never see any of them again.

It was just too goddamn involved. There was no way to do it without screwing somebody. There was no way to stay in the thing with even a questionable conscience, one you could talk to and bullshit a little.

He could tell the police Mr. Perez was extorting money. Whatever he was doing, whatever it was called, was illegal. Except he'd still be involved. He was a part of it. He could be facing Perez and Raymond Gidre in court, or, shit, he could be sitting with them.

Just take off.

Tell Denise first, everything, then take off.

No, that would be leaving her with it, getting her all fucked-up and running out.

So just leave.

You have an organized mind, he told himself. But you think too much. Look. Go to Florida and lie in the sun and drink a little beer, that's all, just beer, and find some secretaries on their vacation and smile a lot and get laid every night and forget it.

Or, go along with Mr. Perez. Take the thirty thousand and don't think about it and go to Florida, shit, go to some place in the Caribbean and do it right.

Who was it had taught him to look at options? Somebody at a meeting had said pre-think your options. Then when something happens you're ready, you don't panic and fuck up.

He got his car from the parking lot and drove north on the Lodge Freeway.

Do it and take the money.

Don't do it. Forget the whole thing.

Go to the police. Call Dick.

Tell Denise everything and leave.

Or—

Christ. He saw it coming. He had seen it in his mind before, glimpses of it, but not as clearly as he saw it now.

—tell Denise everything and don't leave. Turn the whole fucking thing around. Ace Mr. Perez.

How?

He was beginning to feel excited. Ace the son of a bitch. In his own words—pull it right out from under him.

How? He didn't know the name of the stock. He'd have to find that out first.

No, first tell Denise. Tell her everything.

She wouldn't believe him. Why would she? She'd have as much reason to trust Mr. Perez.

But why assume that? How did he know until he told her? What was all this assuming what people were going to think and do?

She'd believe him or she wouldn't. She'd go along or she wouldn't. He didn't have to try to convince her of anything. He'd say, Here it is. What do you want to do?

Simple?

Simple.

He had stopped playing the game with himself, and it was a good feeling.

Virgil lost Tunafish for a few days.

Tunafish was arrested and arraigned on charges of conspiring to commit extortion and great bodily harm and released on a $3,000 bond. He was out, awaiting the examination, but Lavera wouldn't let him have the car.

Virgil asked him what the fuck was wrong with

him? What was this jive five hundred dollars extortion shit? You want five hundred dollars, go to the liquor store.

Tunafish said it was a friend of his, Bonzie, had been doing it, calling ladies at home in the evening and telling them he had their daughter and they were to bring five hundred to room 307 of the Ramada Inn on Telegraph or else he was going to jump on the daughter's bones. Tunafish said he listened to Bonzie make some calls while they were smoking joints, and Bonzie was laughing and fucking it up. Nobody believed he was serious.

Virgil said a woman would have to be severely retarded in the head to believe shit like that and come with the money. What's the man doing, sitting in room 307? He say thank you very much, here's your little girl? Shit. What women? How'd he know them to call?

Tunafish said Bonzie was hanging out in the dormitory lounges at Oakland University, giving his cool-nigger shit to the little white chickies new there, making out some and finding out things. See maybe, Bonzie's idea, maybe there was some mothers *was* dumb enough to bring the money and not call the police, they was so scared. Bonzie wouldn't be in the room, he be outside. He see the woman *go* to the room and come back to her car. If he don't see any police around, he take the money from her. See, but nobody believed him. They call the police, but nobody brought any money. This time they made a call, this time they told the woman, Hey, we got your daughter here and we gonna drop her out the window on her *head*, Mama, you don't bring the money. The woman come? Virgil asked. The woman come with three Southfield police cars, Tunafish said, and picked up him and Bonzie in the parking lot. Tunafish wasn't worried, though. The woman said she recognized Bonzie's voice. Tunafish grinned and said, Yeah shit, but it was *me* that talked to her.

That's why Virgil Royal was back on duty, following Ryan to the churches, the hospital, the Pancake House—not having any idea what Ryan was doing—and each day out to the apartment in Rochester.

There was something about the woman Ryan was with all the time. The way she walked? Something. Virgil couldn't put his finger on it.

The third day back on the job, following Ryan at four-thirty in the afternoon and pretty sure he was going to Rochester, cutting over Big Beaver to I-75, Virgil stopped off at Abercrombie and Fitch in the Somerset Mall and lifted a pair of $400 Steiner binoculars. At six o'clock Ryan and the woman came out of the apartment building. Virgil, in his Grand Prix, maybe two hundred feet away, put the glasses on the woman and adjusted the focus and saw Lee Leary up close with short hair and glasses, close to Ryan and looking at him, but not the way she had looked at him in the bar. A week ago in front of the pancake place, the same one. The man had been with her all the time.

There was no reason to get angry and say things to the man. It was the woman, Bobby's woman, Virgil wanted to talk to.

The next morning he watched her come out of her place and walk down the drive and across Rochester Road and the big open parking area and go in the A&P. She didn't come out.

She didn't come out until a quarter to five in the afternoon. He saw her in there, working a check-out counter.

It was the next day, and Virgil went in at four-twenty. He looked over the wine shelves for a few minutes before picking up two half-gallon jugs of Gallo Chablis Blanc, walked over to the express check-out counter, and placed them on the conveyor.

As Denise took the first bottle to bring it past her and rang up the amount with her other hand, Virgil said, "This is your brand, isn't it?"

She looked up at him. "Pardon me?"

Virgil said, "How you doing, Lee?" Maybe she recognized him, staring at him; he wasn't sure. It didn't matter. He said, "Let's drink some wine this evening, have a talk."

18

VIRGIL OPENED THE DOOR. He stared solemnly at the look on Ryan's face.

"You the one been calling?"

Ryan came in past him. "Where is she?"

"I believe she making wee-wee." Virgil closed the door and watched Ryan as he looked toward the hallway at the bathroom door and back to the low table where the two glasses and the half-gallon bottle, almost empty, stood among the paint tubes and pots. A cigarette burned in the ashtray, its smoke rising in the light from the chrome lamp. There were no other lights; the kitchen and hall were dark.

"How much has she had?"

"That one, one before it," Virgil said. He put a leg over one of the bar stools and leaned against the counter. "She likes the sauce, don't she?"

The inscription on the wall had been finished. *No More Bullshit.* It seemed to be little more than a design of thin, curving lines, without meaning.

Ryan looked at Virgil. "You know what you're doing to her?"

"We talking," Virgil said. "Taking turns. I tell her something, she tell me something. You haven't talked to her like that, have you? Shit, she so surprised, I don't believe you told her *nothing*."

The toilet flushed.

"What I like to know," Virgil said, "how much is it the man wants to give her and where the man lives. This Mr. Per-ez? He the one you work for, huh?"

Denise came in from the hall. She looked at Ryan and past him to her glass on the low table and picked it up as she sat down. She looked at nothing then, at the wall opposite her that was stark white, bare.

"I called you," Ryan said. "I've been calling since about five."

Denise took a drink. She said, "Big fucking deal. You go to a meeting?"

"At Saint Joe's."

"How're the bleeding hearts?"

"Why don't you go to bed, okay? Get some sleep and then we'll talk."

"Why don't you fuck off?" Denise said.

A low sound, a laugh, came from Virgil. "Soon as she start drinking. I remember that from before. She used to sit still, not say anything. Then the sauce start working in her, man, she don't shut up."

"But why don't *you*?" Ryan said. "Why don't you get out of here?" It was an effort to say it quietly.

"Man, you the one crashing the party," Virgil said. "We having a nice time."

Ryan walked over to him. Virgil didn't move, leaning with his arm on the counter, his hand hanging limp.

"I don't want to hit you," Ryan said.

"Shit—"

"I mean it. There's no sense in us breaking up the place and making a lot of noise, maybe get her kicked out. But that's what I feel like doing," Ryan said, holding on to the quiet tone. "I feel like punching the shit out of you. Maybe you got something on you, a gun, something, I don't know. I'd be willing to take a chance. That's how strongly I feel about it. But if we get into that, what good would it do us? We got enough problems. Right?"

Virgil shook his head, grinning. "You go waaaay out and then come back around and all you've said to me is nothing."

"No, I said you better get out of here," Ryan said. "What you're doing, maybe you don't know it, you're killing somebody. I can't, I'm not gonna stand here and see it happen. I can't do it."

"Where's the man live? Mr. Per-ez."

"How about if we talk tomorrow?" Ryan said. "I'm not kidding you, if you don't get out of here

we're gonna be bouncing off the walls and somebody's gonna go through the window. Okay?"

"You don't do nothing else without me," Virgil
said.

Ryan shook his head. "Right, I'll call you, get
your permission. Now leave, okay?"

Virgil came off the stool slowly. Ryan let him
take his time.

"Is there any more wine?"

"That's it. What she's got," Virgil said.

"Okay, I'll see you." He wanted to push him, run
him through the door, but he stepped away and let
Virgil take his hat from the counter and put it on,
holding the crown lightly with one hand and setting
it on his head at the right angle with an easy motion,
where it belonged, and not having to adjust it.

"That's a good hat," Ryan said.

Virgil gave him a mild look. His eyes moved to
Denise. He said, "Take it easy, now," and walked out.

Ryan closed the door. Denise was pouring the
last of the wine into the ten-ounce glass, filling it
more than half. She put the bottle on the floor next
to her. Ryan waited in the silence. She wasn't going
to look his way. She was Lee again, but with short
hair and clean slacks and the navy-blue sweater.
Her glasses were on the drawing table. She seemed
determined not to look this way. She was getting
ready for him now, waiting for her cue.

Ryan walked over and sat down in the chair facing her. She was drunk but she didn't look bad: a little glassy-eyed. Her hair was combed. She seemed at ease, looking past him in thought, calmly ignoring him. Inside she was crouched, waiting.

Ryan said, "Well, here we are. You having a nice time?"

She didn't answer him.

"I'm gonna get the silent treatment, huh?"

"Fuck you," Denise said.

"Fuck you, too," Ryan said. "You dumb broad." He waited, watching her take a drink. "Can you hardly wait'll tomorrow, when you wake up? Be fun, uh? Listen, if you want, I'll tell them over at the A&P you're sick. They might want to know how long you'll be out. What do you think, a week? A month?"

"Jesus," Denise said, "is that how you do it? What do you call it? Twelfth Step work."

"To tell you the truth," Ryan said, "I've never done it before. You're my first one."

"You want to help me? Really?"

"Sure I do."

"Go across the street and get another one of these." She kicked at the empty bottle with her bare foot and missed and kicked at it again. "Get a couple."

"Why don't you go? You can walk."

"Oh, you'd let me?" She put on a slightly prissy tone.

"If I didn't," Ryan said, "then you'd have all the more reason to feel sorry for yourself. You already think it's my fault. If I don't let you out, then you'd know for sure I'm a heartless bastard, I don't care anything about you, I'm in this only for myself."

"You're a prick," Denise said. "Like all the rest."

"All the rest of what? Men? Jesus, you gonna give me that one? You poor little thing. Suck on your bottle."

"Asshole."

"What am I, parts of the anatomy? Prick, asshole. What else? How about knee? You fucking knee. Or shoulder. You rotten, miserable shoulder."

"You're really funny."

"I'm literal, if that's the word," Ryan said. "I don't have much imagination. I see something, I say what it is. I see you sitting there drinking wine. Maybe you think you've been getting a rotten deal and you want to pay me back, or you want to pay back your husband or your mother, I don't know. I don't know why you drink, but what I see, I see you killing yourself."

"And you don't want that to happen till I get the money. How much you gonna make, anyway?"

Ryan didn't say anything.

"Then you work on me some more," Denise said. "What do you have in mind? I mean, how do you get any of it out of me? Unless maybe we got married. Jesus, there must be an awful lot in this."

"A hundred and fifty thousand," Ryan said.

"You were going to get half, but the way they're thinking now, you don't get anything." As he said it, he felt better. But it was a little late and not doing much for Denise at all.

She was saying, "A hundred and fifty thousand *dollars?* Bobby owned something worth that much?"

"It's stock," Ryan said. "I don't know what kind, though. His dad put it in his name when he was born and it's been going up ever since." He watched her thinking about it. "That's a few bottles of wine, isn't it?"

She looked at him. "You really AA, or is that part of your bullshit?"

"I wasn't looking for you when I went to that meeting," Ryan said. "I needed to go. You said your name, I still wasn't sure. You remember talking to me in the bar?"

"Virgil mentioned it. I'm not sure." She started to rise, then sat back again and put her hands on the wooden chair arms to pull herself up. She went into the hallway and came out again, looking at the floor.

"I can't find my goddamn shoes."

"Where you going?"

"Out."

"Why don't you go to bed? I mean it."

"You mean shit." Denise went into the kitchen then and turned on the light. "There you are," she said to her sandals.

Ryan went over to the door and put on the chain lock. She came out, taking her purse from the counter, and stopped, looking at the door and then at Ryan. When she moved toward the door, Ryan stepped in front of her.

"Come on, what're you going to do, tie me up?"

"Think about tomorrow," Ryan said.

"Think about tomorrow. It sounds like a fucking soap opera. Get out of the way."

"If you go to bed now," Ryan said, "not have any more, you'll be in pretty good shape."

Maybe. She was having trouble with her balance. Her eyes, narrowed at him, were glazed. She was past thinking or listening or reasoning. If she told him she hated him or wanted to kill him, he'd believe it.

"I'm going out," Denise said. "You stop me and I'll have all the more reason. You said it, I didn't. All the more reason to feel sorry for myself. Right? You'll be responsible for it, you sneaky son of a bitch."

"I've changed my mind," Ryan said. "I don't give a shit what you feel, you're going to bed."

He grabbed her, pinning her arms to her body, and dragged her, twisting against him, into the bedroom.

Denise stopped fighting. She said, "All right, leave me alone." She stood by the double bed, weaving slightly.

"Get undressed," Ryan said.

Denise looked at him, closing one eye. "Now we're horny, huh? I've been wondering when it was coming. All the times you've been here, I was thinking, I don't know, maybe he doesn't have any balls. Is that your problem, Ryan? No balls, huh?"

He left the room as she spoke, crossed the small hallway to the bathroom, and looked in the medicine cabinet for aspirin. There was a small bottle of Excedrin. He had to go to the kitchen for a glass of water. When he came back to the bedroom, Denise had her slacks off and was pulling the navy-blue sweater over her head. Ryan looked at her compact little can in the white panties. Good thighs, slender; but very pale. She needed sunlight on her and clean air. Ryan thought of Florida again, the second time that day, this time seeing the two of them, tan, walking along a sundown empty beach.

"Fucking sweater," Denise said, inside the navy-blue folds. It was caught on her bracelet. She pulled the sweater free, dropping it, and was looking at him again. Ryan handed her two Excedrin tablets and the glass of water. She took them without a word and handed the glass back to him, staring again with her glazed expression.

"I'm gonna stay here tonight," Ryan said.

"Uh-huh." She was unbuttoning her blouse now, working down from the top.

"I'll be in the other room."

"You're not going to sleep with me?"

He moved to the bed and pulled the madras spread and sheet from the pillows. "No, but I'll tuck you in," Ryan said.

"Was that *tuck* you said?"

"Be nice, okay? Get in bed."

"How nice? Hey, Ryan . . ."

When he looked at her she opened her blouse to show her breasts for a moment and let the blouse fall closed again. They were small breasts, but good ones.

"What do you say, Ryan, you want to fuck?"

He walked around the foot of the bed to the door.

"Hey, I thought you were gonna tuck me in." She pulled the blouse off, hooked her thumbs in the waist of the panties, and pushed them down. When she tried to step out, she stumbled against the bed. Ryan watched her from the doorway.

Denise rolled onto the bed. She settled on her back, on top of the madras cover, her legs apart, the panties caught on one ankle. As she looked at him now, with a contrived expression, eyes half-closed, she raised up on her elbows and spread her legs a little more.

"Come on, Ryan honey. You and God Honey, you know everything, don't you? You prick. Come on, you sneaky little prick, let's see if you're any good." She moved her hips up and down, twice.

Ryan moved to the side of the bed. "Lift up your can."

"Like this?" She arched her back, raising her pelvis toward him. "You want some of that?"

Ryan pulled the spread and sheet to the foot of the bed and brought them back, letting the covers settle over her. He went out, closing the door. In the living room, as he sat down and reached for a cigarette, he heard her call him. Hey, Ryan, repeating it several times. He heard her call him a rotten motherfucker and heard her voice, sounds, but not the words clearly. Finally there was silence.

During the night he thought about Denise and would see her body again, the way she had showed it to him, her private nakedness that he had had to imagine before. He wasn't worried about Denise now. That was a funny thing; he had a good feeling about her. She wasn't down in a hole, depressed; she was mad, and that was something he felt he could handle. What he thought about most of the night, when he'd wake up sitting in the canvas chair with his feet on the edge of the low table, was Mr. Perez. Mr. Perez in his hotel suite. Mr. Perez speaking in his quiet, deceptive tone. Mr. Perez, shit, standing on this thing immobile, like a dead weight, and the bayou hillbilly helping him hold it down.

How did you go about pushing Mr. Perez, or faking him out? Leave him standing there with nothing.

*   *   *

In the morning, he heard Denise get up and go into the bathroom. She came out and went back to the bedroom. When she appeared she was wearing a raincoat, barefoot, her hands deep in the pockets of the coat.

"It's cold in here." Her voice was subdued: someone who had come out of a sickroom.

Ryan looked over. "How're you doing?"

"I can't find the Excedrin."

"Oh, it's in the kitchen. I'll get it."

He rose, pushing out of the chair and arching the stiffness from his neck. She was already in the kitchen, standing at the sink with the water running, her back to him as he came in.

"I'm sorry," she said.

"You mean, for trying to seduce me?"

"I remembered—when I woke up I remembered things I said . . . what I did. I'm very sorry."

"How do you feel otherwise?"

"Otherwise, shitty. I'll thank you for one thing," Denise said, "not letting me have any more last night. Beyond that, I'm not sure we have anything to talk about."

Ryan turned her around by the shoulders, seeing her eyes briefly, before she looked away.

"We have quite a bit to talk about, after you have some breakfast."

"Just coffee."

"All right, just coffee," Ryan said. "I'm not going to argue with you. I'm not going to try and force you to believe or do anything I say. But I'm going to ask you to listen to me. After that, if you want us to be friends again, fine. If you don't, okay, that's that. But you're not allowed to think of something else while I'm talking, or what you'd like to say, or interrupt with some smartass remark. All right?"

Denise shrugged. She didn't seem to care.

She didn't want Ryan to look at her. She was tired and felt sick. She stood at the counter smoking cigarettes and sipped the coffee getting cold, staring at it while he talked to her in a quiet tone. She liked the sound of his voice and at another time would want to believe him, but right now it didn't matter. She looked awful and felt awful and didn't want to be here.

Not today but tomorrow she could walk in her mother's house with a happy-daughter smile and say, "Hi, Mom, I'm home." Her mother would let Denise kiss her cheek. They would sit down in the kitchen to have a nice cup of coffee with real cream. She would think of all the things she could tell her mother to try to be close to her as a person and not simply a daughter. She could say, "Mom, I've been drunk for three years," saving Bobby Lear till later, and for a moment her mother would stare at her. Then her mother would say, "How could you do that to me?" Or she might say it was impossible because no one in the family drank. Or she might pretend not to have heard. Or she would be saved and protected by an act of God: the telephone or a neighbor at the door, and her mother would come back in the kitchen with a letter from Denise's brother, Don, who worked for National Cash Register in Dayton, and show her Polaroids of Don and Joanne and their three boys, Scott, Skip, and June Bug doing "soooo big" with his arms raised over his head.

She could give up and let herself melt into her mother's life and wear a dress on Sunday and sit with her mother's friends in the maple living room and compare Edison bills and watch TV, the new Oral Roberts who no longer healed people, and, in the evenings, watch *Name That Tune* and *Let's Make a Deal*. She would run into boys on the street she had known in high school. Her mother would say all the nice boys were married and had good positions with State Farm and John Deere and the bank or mixing prescriptions. Two of them would be on the County Board of Commissioners. Her mother would find one, though, who had not married. Harold something, a long German name that was on the Edison Company centennial farm plaque hanging in the new annex of the courthouse.

She could live with her mother and listen to her

complaints and make molded salads and never have to think again.

"Are you all right?" Ryan said.

"Fine."

"You don't look fine. You listening or trying to hide?"

She stood with her head down, staring at the counter. "I think I'll go back to bed," Denise said.

"I'll tell you something. This is the hardest thing I've ever done in my life," Ryan said. "I'm telling you everything, but I could be losing something I want very much." He waited.

She was aware of the silence and felt him watching her.

"What? The money?"

"Shit. You're not listening." Ryan waited again. "Well, it's up to you. Either you're not listening or you don't believe me."

She did believe him, because she wanted to believe him, but she needed assurance and protection and time; so she said, "Why should I?"

"You know why?" Ryan said. "Because I'm all you've got. You want the money, then you've got to trust somebody."

She looked up at him now. "I haven't said I want it."

As she started to look away Ryan reached across the counter and raised her face with his hand and held it a moment.

"And you haven't said you don't want it. God-damn it, wake up and listen to me!"

He saw her eyes come alive. When he took his hand away she continued to stare at him. Good. He held her gaze and told her quietly she had three ways to go. She could trust Mr. Perez. She could believe him and sign his papers and end up with nothing. And if she gave him any trouble, it was very likely he would have her killed. Mr. Perez wanted it all. Or she could trust Virgil Royal and ask him to help her, believing Virgil only wanted what was owed him. But if she got past Mr. Perez, Virgil would kill her for the whole prize. Either way, Mr. Perez or Virgil. They killed people or had them killed and didn't think much of it.

"Or you can trust me," Ryan said. "I want to help you get it, the whole hundred and fifty thousand if that's possible, because I owe you something. Look at it another way, I think I owe them something, too."

"And what would I owe you?" Denise said. Staring at him was not hard now. She was getting back her confidence.

"You don't owe me anything."

"Why not?"

He was uncomfortable again and it made him mad.

"I'm not looking for anything," Ryan said, "or trying to make a deal with you. I've been playing enough games, I want to get this thing done and feel good about it, about myself. You understand? You've been to enough meetings, you ought to know what I'm talking about."

Her eyes were watery, red-looking. He knew she was aware of herself, and the way she kept staring at him, not letting go, surprised him.

She said, "How would we do it?"

"I call Perez, tell him you're in the bag," Ryan said. "If he comes over with the papers, I can probably get them signed."

"Yeah, then what?"

"You can't even hold on to the pen. I tell him, leave the papers, I'll get you to sign when you start to come out of it."

Denise waited.

"If he's made out the power of attorney paper, that he sends to the company, then we'll know the name of the stock."

"He doesn't seem dumb," Denise said, "somebody that'd make a mistake."

Ryan shook his head. "No, he isn't dumb, but maybe he's overanxious."

Mr. Perez sounded calm on the phone, though, the son of a bitch. Polite and in control. He said he and Raymond would be right out.

*   *   *

Raymond was there with him in the hotel suite. Mr. Perez hung up the phone. He said, "You heard the saying, Don't ever shit a shitter?"

Raymond nodded. "I know it well."

"I don't believe our friend does," Mr. Perez said.

Ryan came back from the A&P with two half gallons and a fifth of Gallo Rhine. He put the fifth on the counter, opened the two half gallons and poured them into the sink.

"Don't look," Ryan said.

Denise didn't say anything. She turned to the paint table, picked up the full ashtray, and reached down for the empty wine jug on the floor.

"No, leave those," Ryan said. He put the two empty half gallons on the counter. "Dirty dishes, everything. You're not getting ready for company, you're on a drunk."

Denise watched him, holding her arms, cold. "Will I be in bed?"

"Not in it, on top of the covers, with the raincoat, and barefoot. That's a good touch, the raincoat."

"It's what I wear," Denise said.

Ryan smiled at her. "So it won't be too hard to fake, will it? Your eyes are great."

"Thanks," Denise said.

*　　*　　*

Ryan opened the door. Mr. Perez came in, followed by Raymond Gidre, who was wearing only a suit coat, his shoulders tightly hunched.

"Cold enough for you?" Ryan said.

"Jes-*us*," Raymond said.

Mr. Perez walked over to the counter, laid his attaché case down flat, and snapped it open.

"She called me this morning about five," Ryan said. "You can see what she's had."

"Like a couple of gallons," Raymond said. "Jesus, Mary, and Joseph, little skinny thing."

"Where is she?" Mr. Perez said. He had typewritten papers in his hand and was taking a pen out of his inside pocket, his gloves still on. He was wearing a gray hat, a gray herringbone topcoat with a black velvet collar, and the thin, tight-fitting gray gloves that looked like suede.

"She's in the bedroom," Ryan said. "You want to take your coat off?"

Guess not. Mr. Perez didn't bother to answer. He took the papers and pen and went through the hall area into the bedroom. Ryan followed him, seeing Denise lying on her side in the raincoat, her white feet drawn up, her eyes closed. Mr. Perez sat on the edge of the bed looking down at her.

"Miz Leary," Mr. Perez said, "how you feeling, dear?"

Denise made a sound or mumbled something, burrowing into the pillow, that Ryan couldn't hear.

"That's a shame, little girl taking sick. Honey, look at me. I got something for you."

"Go fuck yourself," Denise said, barely moving her mouth, eyes still closed.

Mr. Perez said, "Is that nice?"

"I guess she talks like that," Ryan said, "when she's been drinking. You should've heard her before."

Mr. Perez nudged her gently. "I'd just like you to sign these papers, little girl, then you can sleep long as you want."

Denise asked him, slurring the words just right, why he didn't fuck off and leave her alone and get his ass off the bed. Mr. Perez looked over his shoulder. As Raymond came in, Mr. Perez said, "Sit her up," losing some of his sweetness.

Between them they got her upright, leaning heavily against Raymond, her legs doubled under her beneath the raincoat. Raymond pulled the collar of the raincoat out a little, trying to look inside. Mr. Perez put the pen in her hand.

"Pull the table over."

Raymond grabbed the night table with one hand and gave it a jerk to bring it over in front of them, letting the lamp with the glass chimney fall and shatter to the floor. Denise opened her eyes.

"What're you doing? Hey, for Christ's sake—"

"There she is," Mr. Perez said. "Got your little eyes open?"

Ryan went over and began picking up the pieces of broken glass, listening to Mr. Perez's sweet words.

"That's a good girl, hold the pen. There. Now, see those papers? Right in front of you on the table. All you got to do is sign your name where you see the little Xs. Precious, you see them? Down there at the bottom. Write 'Denise L. Leary.' You don't have to worry having it notarized, I'll get that done for you." To Raymond he said, "Take her hand and put it there."

Raymond tried to. Denise pulled her hand away and let the pen drop to the floor.

"Get it, Raymond."

Ryan stood up, carefully holding the pieces of broken glass. As he started out, Mr. Perez was saying, "Now, let's try it again. Come on, sugar, you can do it. Hold the pen. That's it."

In the kitchen Ryan opened the cupboard beneath the sink and dropped the glass fragments into the trash basket.

"Goddamn it, sign the goddamn thing! Now!"

Ryan tensed. In the silence that followed, he let himself relax. He lit a cigarette, then took the tin paper and screw-top off the fifth of Gallo on the counter. He was in the living room when Mr. Perez and Raymond came out. Ryan looked at the papers in Mr. Perez's hand.

"She sign them?"

"She can't see to pee straight," Mr. Perez said.

"Goddamn drunken woman. There's nothing worse than a drunk woman."

Ryan stepped aside to let Mr. Perez walk over to his attaché case on the counter.

"Maybe when she sobers up a little," Ryan said.

"I swear, all I been doing on this one is waiting. Waiting to find her, waiting for her to make up her mind, waiting for her to sober up." He dropped the papers into the open case.

"I was thinking," Ryan said, "she starts to come around she's gonna want a drink, glass of wine. So let's say I give her about a half a glass. Then when she wants some more, dying for it, I say, Okay, but you got to sign some papers first. I think, the condition she's in, it'll work."

Mr. Perez turned a little to look at Ryan. "You're betting thirty thousand dollars it works. If it doesn't, I don't see I'll need you anymore."

Ryan shrugged, showing he was at ease. "It's okay with me. I never intended making a career out of this. Give me till about noon and I'll call you."

"Maybe it won't take that long," Mr. Perez said.

"Maybe, but I think a couple of hours the way she's sleeping," Ryan said. "Let her dry out a little, she'll wake up dying of thirst."

"Well, Raymond and I could wait around for that matter." Mr. Perez was playing with him now.

Ryan shrugged again, as though it didn't matter. "It's up to you," he said, "you want to sit around."

"Or I could leave Raymond."

"You decide what you're going to do," Ryan said. He was tense and had to move. He walked around into the kitchen and turned the burner on under the kettle. "You want some coffee?"

"No, I guess we'll leave it in your hands," Mr. Perez said, taking the papers out of the attaché case and laying them on the counter. "Two copies of the agreement, two giving us power of attorney. It won't hurt to get them both signed, and the copies." Mr. Perez picked up his case and started out. "You'll be sure and call me, now."

"The minute she signs," Ryan said. "You got my word."

Denise sat up as she heard the door close. She was scuffing her feet into her sandals when Ryan came in, looking at the papers.

"What does it say?"

"Wait—'We believe you are the legal owner of assets you are entitled to receive.'" He paused. "No, this is the agreement." He looked at the other typewritten form. "'I, Denise L. Leary, hereby appoint Francis X. Perez'—I love that, named after Saint Francis Xavier, the son of a bitch. This is it." Ryan looked through the form quickly, then read it slowly, every word, before shaking his head.

"What?" Denise said.

"No company or stock name. The spaces are

blank." He dropped the papers on the bed. Denise didn't pick them up or even look at them.

Ryan walked over to the window. He looked out at the wet asphalt of the parking area that was empty except for a few cars. His light-blue Catalina stood alone near the entrance. It was quiet in the bedroom.

"They didn't have to break my lamp."

Ryan was thinking, Get in the car and go.

There was silence.

"Look, I don't care," Denise said. "If I don't sign, then he doesn't get anything either, does he? So why don't we let it go at that? I'm tired and I really don't care one way or the other. Really. I'd just as soon forget the whole thing. Shit, everything."

There was silence again for at least a minute, maybe a little longer.

Ryan turned from the window. He said, "Pack a bag, a suitcase."

Denise looked up at him. "Why?"

"Come on, pack something and let's get out of here."

19

THEY WENT TO FLORIDA. Ryan was going to drive, but changed his mind heading south on 75 and made the turn to Detroit Metropolitan, got them seats on a Delta flight to Lauderdale and a Budget Rent a Car to Pompano Beach, a Pinto without air, and by seven o'clock that evening they were in an efficiency at the Vista Del Mar with groceries, new bathing outfits, thongs, and Coppertone, looking out at the Atlantic Ocean.

"There," Ryan said. "No more thinking for a week. Whoever mentions Perez or the stock or anything connected with it has to put five bucks in the kitty."

Denise looked around the room, from the picture window to the flowered rattan chairs to the twin beds, against opposite walls, that featured tailored beige spreads and bolsters that disguised them as sofas. Forty-five dollars a day including color TV and the ocean view. What more could you want? Ryan said.

Denise said, "What I'd like more than anything is a glass of wine."

Ryan went into the kitchen and dug into a grocery bag. He came back out with a bottle of Blue Nun and two jelly glasses.

"You mean it?" Denise said.

"If the corkscrew works," Ryan said. He took it out of his coat pocket.

Denise watched him twist it into the cork. "You're gonna have one, too?"

"So you won't have to drink alone," Ryan said. He got the cork out. Pouring the wine, he said, "It's not cold, though."

"I don't care." She took the glass he offered, with yellow daisies on it, and said, "Jesus, I don't believe it." Then took a drink and closed her eyes and opened them. "Jesus," she said again, and watched Ryan sip his wine. "Why're you doing this?"

"I guess—I don't know," he said. "I guess I want us to be like normal everyday people on a vacation. Not think—I don't mean get drunk and not think. I mean not worry about anything, relax, and have a good time. We can have the steak and a salad, I thought, instead of getting dressed and going out someplace."

"That sounds fine."

"I got a bottle of red, too, we can have with the steak."

"I didn't see you get the wine."

"No, well—we can have this before, then the red with dinner. You want to fix it, or you want me to?"

"No, I'll do it."

"You feel okay?"

"I feel fine. This morning, it seems like a long time ago," Denise said. "I was going to take a shower, unless you want to eat right away."

"No, go ahead," Ryan said. "We're not in any hurry. We're on our vacation."

They were polite, but it didn't seem forced. That was the idea, to be natural.

Ryan went outside with his wine. He turned on the orange light by the door, then turned it off again and sat down in a deck chair, propping his feet on the low wall that separated the patio area from the empty beach. It was a good time of the day: alone, feeling the breeze and listening to the ocean as it came in out of the darkness and broke and washed in forty yards away. He was here and she was in the shower and Mr. Perez was somewhere and out there were the Gulf Stream and Bimini, the Bahama Islands, and way out there in the darkness some of Denise's whales talking to each other, not giving a shit about Mr. Perez getting mad and tense as he telephoned and got no answers. Maybe he'd go out to Denise's again. Then what? Ryan could think about Mr. Perez without putting five bucks in the kitty, but he wished he could turn the man off in his mind. Kick the habit. He didn't know what he was doing with the wine. Playing a game. Helping her through a bad time. Having some with her so she wouldn't feel like a drunk. Making excuses. It didn't taste that good, yet. She was probably pouring herself another one. He almost got up, but he made himself sit there, looking out at the ocean, and smoked a cigarette, and then, after a few minutes, smoked another one.

"I was thinking about your whales," Ryan said. "What do whales do?"

"What do they *do?*" She held her knife and fork poised over the piece of sirloin on her plate and looked from the kitchen to the picture window in the other room. She looked clean and scrubbed in the faded green sweatshirt. Her tongue moved around inside her mouth. "They eat squid," she said finally. "They love squid. And they like to play around, talk to each other."

"Make love?"

"When the cows are in the mood."

"It's up to the girl, uh?"

"I guess so, unless the boy whale's really horny."

Ryan was feeling good—when he came in, he saw the wine in the Blue Nun bottle at the same level—but he didn't want her to think he was working up to something, talking about the whales making out. It was strange, last night she'd been naked, shoving her box at him; but now she was a different person and he was afraid to say the wrong thing.

They had finished the white while she broiled the steak. They were halfway through the Almadén red now. When her glass was down, she wouldn't pour her own. She'd wait for Ryan to pour it, and he'd feel or imagine her watching him fill their glasses, making sure he didn't take more for himself. He imagined it because it was something he used to do. He didn't look up to see if she was watching; he was afraid to.

When they finished eating, there were still two inches of wine left in the bottle. She picked up the bottle as she cleared the table and didn't seem to know what to do with it.

"You want to finish this?"

"No, I don't care for any more," Ryan said.

He watched her set the bottle on the table again. While she was doing the dishes, Ryan drying, he put the cork in the bottle and placed it on top of the refrigerator. There it was for whoever wanted it.

After, they took their shoes off and walked down to the flat smooth sand and stood watching the surf, feeling the shock of cold as the water rushed in and the sand alive beneath their feet as the water was drawn back into the sea. He was at ease with her outside, on the beach, and then sitting in deck chairs on the patio. Even when they were silent he was at ease and felt good.

But when they went in again and were alone in the room he was self-conscious and wondered what she was thinking, if she expected him to touch her and make the moves. The night before, she had said, "I've been wondering when it was coming—all the times you've been here." She had been drunk saying it; still, she had thought it and said it. He wanted to touch her and she probably expected him to. He didn't know why he felt dumb and awkward. If she didn't want to do it, she'd tell him. But it had to be natural.

She went in the bathroom and came out, and he went in and washed and brushed his teeth and combed his hair. When he came out, she was in bed. The slipcover had been taken off his bed and the light blanket and sheet turned down.

"Where'd you find the pillows?"

"In the closet."

He took off his shirt and pants. "Well, good night."

"Good night," she said. "Sleep well."

He got in bed and lay on his back staring at the ceiling with the good-looking girl lying in her bed fifteen feet away. An outside light from somewhere reflected on the ceiling.

Maybe she'd come over.

No, she was waiting for him. Go on, for Christ's sake. She was going to think he was a fag.

In the silence he could hear the surf, a good sound, far away.

She said, in the darkness, "Ryan?"

"Yeah?"

"You're a nice guy, you know it?"

"Thanks," Ryan said. "You're nice too." After a little while he rolled over on his side and rolled quietly a few more times in the hour it took him to go to sleep.

She had expected him to come over. She was ready and would have let him get in her bed. When he didn't, she was surprised, but not disappointed. There was time and she knew it would happen, not with one of them making the move, but letting it happen, perhaps when they least expected it.

He said to her, "You better be careful the first day."

She said, "No, I look like I burn, but I don't. I get tan pretty quick, a couple of days. How about you?"

"Yeah, I used to burn, but I don't anymore."

That kind of beach conversation and talk about

food—Do you like key lime pie? Do you like oysters?—and movies and movie stars and books they'd read, the one Denise was reading—"I know it's dumb and she's a terrible writer, but I love it"— lying in the Florida sun, rubbing each other's back with lotion, going in the water to cool off rather than swim, neither of them was a swimmer—nothing about Mr. Perez. What was he doing? Who gave a shit?—and going to sleep on the beach in the late afternoon, waking up in cool shade, the sun behind the wall of condominiums, going to the Oceanside Shopping Center with the feel of the sun and the sand still on them, natives in one day, to buy straw hats and beach towels that said *Pompano Beach, Florida*, and oranges and avocados, a half pound of pistachios. They ate ice-cream cones and watched the white Cadillacs of the retirees take fifteen minutes to make a right-hand turn. Ryan said, You know what you do when you're retired? You wait for the mail. First you wait for the paper and then the mail. Then you wait to get two thousand miles on your car so you can take it in for an oil change and a tune. He said, You see those Bermuda shorts the retired guys wear? You see how high they wear them up over their stomachs? Denise said, Yeah? Ryan said, What I want to know, where do they get zippers that long? Denise said, The same place the wives get the sequined sweaters they wear over their shoulders. Do you think the sleeves are real or fake? Ryan told her why didn't she ask one of them, a retiree wife? She did, too. She asked a woman in front of the Oceanside Market if the sleeves of her sweater were real or for show. The woman looked at her. They walked back to the Vista Del Mar, past the hot red Pinto parked in front. Washing your car every day is also big, Ryan said. The salt air. Denise said, Washing me isn't going to be any quick rinse. I'm dying to take a shower. Ryan said, You want some help? She laughed, she didn't really answer him. It was coming, though.

Denise took her shower first. She came out with a Pompano Beach, Florida, towel wrapped around her, drying her hair with a bathroom towel.

She said, "Your turn." A look passed between them.

Taking his shower, Ryan thought about the look and the girl in the room in the quiet early evening and felt himself becoming aroused. Drying himself in front of the mirror he liked his color, he liked the way he looked, the way his hair hung down uncombed and the shiny glow on his face. He rubbed in some Ice Blue Aqua Velva. He looked strong and healthy. He felt good.

When he came out, with the bathroom towel around his waist, he saw Denise still in the Pompano Beach, Florida, towel, rubbing her short blond hair. As she brought the towel down, he saw the look again, felt it, and knew she did too. She kept looking at him as he came over to her and put his hands on her arms, then let them slide around her, feeling her hands on his ribs, her hands slowly moving around him as they closed their eyes and kissed, moving their heads a little, getting it good and comfortable, feeling each other's mouth and parts of lips, holding and pressing gently, making it last and knowing there was a lot more to come. There was relief in it too, finally, the sound of relief when they breathed and came back to each other.

They smiled as they made love.

Boy, it was good, and Ryan told her he didn't believe it. He said, It's so good making love to somebody you love. Like the first time, only way better. Do you feel that? He could ask her because he knew she felt it. She smiled and said, Uh-huh, I feel it. He said, God, I don't know what to do. I want to do everything at once. Seeing the smile in her eyes, knowing they were both feeling the same thing, kissing and not being able to kiss each other enough, putting his hand on the patch of hair between her legs and feeling her girl hand on him, still kissing, their mouths moving, holy shit, it had never been like this before. He said, I've never been here before. I've never had a feeling like this. She said to him, Put it in me. He watched her eyes and heard the sound that came from her. They were there and he didn't know if he could stand it, aware of himself for only a moment before he was aware of both of them, trying to get closer, all the way, and somehow get lost within each other. They let go, straining to hold on tight, hearing sounds coming from inside them. He breathed and got his breath and they were kissing again, lying on their sides facing each other, kissing, breathing against each other's skin, faces, kissing, looking at each other, smiling tired effortless smiles.

When he was lying on his back, looking at the ceiling, she said, "Where are you?"

"I'm here."

"What're you thinking?"

"I was wondering, should we have the ham or the chicken? We could brown some onions and green pepper, put in some tomato sauce . . ." He felt her move and looked at her, propped up on an elbow. "Why? What were you thinking?"

"Nothing," Denise said. "I'm not going to tell you now. You're thinking about food."

"Come on, tell me."

"I love you," Denise said. "I absolutely adore you and I'm in love with you."

"Good."

"*Good?*"

"Yeah, because I'm in love with you."

"Do you know you said it? You said, making love to somebody you love."

"It's something, isn't it? We're all set, we're stuck with each other."

She lay back on the pillow and was silent. They could hear the surf and the wind gusting through the open window. She said, "But what if after a while . . ."

"What if after a while, what?" Ryan said. "Do you want to know everything that's going to happen to you, or you want to take it a day at a time and be surprised?"

She said, "Couldn't I know just a little of what's going to happen?"

"Maybe," Ryan said, "it depends. What's worrying you?"

She said after a moment, "I was married before."

"I know you were."

"I wondered if . . . you ever pictured me with him. The kind of person he was."

"I don't think of him as a person," Ryan said. "I think of him as a number."

"You do?" Puzzled. "What number?"

"Eighty-nine. That was the number he had in the morgue. Before he was identified."

"Oh. You saw him?"

"I saw him, but the only thing I remember about him's the number. The man who had it's gone."

They went out in the sun for five days and turned brown and felt better, both agreed, than they'd ever felt in their lives. Though sometimes when he was silent she would ask him if everything was all right. He'd say, Everything's fine. She believed him and it would be enough for several hours or until she felt the need to ask him again. She knew about living one day at a time and not worrying about things that might never happen. She felt comfortable and happy being with him, and when they made love she was sure of him beyond any doubt. But she would feel him leave her in his mind and wonder where he was, if he was sorry and had misgivings and was escaping, if he was only being nice to her because she needed someone. She would say to him, standing in the kitchen, "Hold me." Then it was good again. She could feel he loved her. He told her, often, he loved her. She would say, "But—" And he would say, "Why don't you just believe me and not think about it?" He would tell her every day to feel and try not to think so much. She said, "But what if I feel and I get scared of the feeling?" He said, "What's wrong with being scared?" He said, "You have to leave yourself open and take chances and that can be scary, you bet. But if you don't take chances, what do you win?"

You make molded salads and watch *Name That Tune*.

She could cross that one off, one less option to think about. And living alone was dumb. So why not bet on Ryan? If she felt good with him, natural, herself, and was happier than she'd ever been, what was the problem? As long as he would reassure her from time to time.

The fifth day the feeling of anxiety would not go away. They didn't talk or smile at each other as much or as naturally. He's had enough, Denise thought. He's bored. She asked him if he wanted to do something, go somewhere. He said, No, he didn't think so. She didn't ask him where he was or if everything was all right.

She said, "Your back's not going to get very tan."

She was lying on a towel on her stomach, her face turned to Ryan, sitting in a canvas chair with his straw hat tilted low on his eyes, staring at the ocean.

"My back gets whatever it can," Ryan said. "I don't like to lie down like that unless I'm gonna take a nap."

His tone was all right, but he was quiet, inside himself, deeper in there than he had been during the previous days. She had to think up things to say to him. Maybe put him on a little. She raised her face from the towel, looking at the sky.

"We've been lucky with the weather."

He didn't say anything.

"It's going to be eighty today, light showers expected tomorrow."

Ryan looked at her now. "Is that right?"

"One winter in Bad Axe the snow was so deep,"

Denise said, and stopped. "You want to know how deep the snow was?"

"How deep was it?" Ryan said.

"It was so deep outside you had to shit in a shotgun and shoot it up the chimney."

"That's pretty deep," Ryan said.

Denise lowered her face to the beach towel. "So are you."

Neither of them spoke for several minutes. Finally Ryan said, "Okay."

Denise didn't say anything right away. She watched him lean over and fish inside the straw bag for something. He brought out his wallet. Denise raised her head a little.

"Okay, what?"

Ryan took out a five-dollar bill, reached over, and let it fall on the end of the towel, by her face.

"Mr. Perez. Let's go get him."

"How?"

"I've got a couple of ideas."

"Is that what you've been thinking about?"

"Part of the time," Ryan said. "You want to go after your money? It's up to you."

She liked the line of the straw hat brim, low over his eyes as he looked at her. She liked the quiet sound of his voice and his brown arms and the way he sat in the canvas chair, waiting.

She said, "Why don't we get it and come back?"

Ryan smiled. "Why don't we?"

He called and reserved seats on an Eastern flight out of Miami. They had to hurry to make it. They packed and dressed inside a half hour. Denise remembered something as they were ready to go and they put the leftovers in the refrigerator for the maid: ketchup and mustard, pickles, oleo, bread, a ham shank and the two inches of Almadén red that were still in the bottle.

20

RYAN HAD TO WAIT WHILE RITA GOT THE COFFEE,
escaping, giving herself time to think, standing over
there by the tan coffee urn that matched the beige
tones and fabrics of the law office. She came back
past the palm tree plants on the file cabinets with
matching ceramic mugs and placed one on the desk
next to Ryan.

"Thanks," he said. "Look, you can't get in any
trouble. All you're doing, you're typing up a complaint and a summons. Nobody's going to ask who
typed it."

Rita sat down at the desk and made room for her
coffee mug. "You want to threaten him, is that it?"

"I want Mr. Perez to see he could get tied up in
court," Ryan said, "if Mrs. Leary decides she wants
to bring suit."

"Mrs. Leary, or you could call her the complainant," Rita said.

Ryan smiled. "That's what happens I get in a
lawyer's office. Okay—Denise could bring suit."

"Well, why doesn't she go ahead and do it?" Rita said. "If Perez is being such a prick about it."

"Because I don't think we have to. Going to court, it ties him up, it ties everybody up."

He could see Rita was trying to get out of it. Maybe she was mad, holding it in. She said, "I don't know. God, I've got a shit-load of work to get out today."

Ryan leaned closer to the desk. "It's two sheets of paper. What'll it take you, ten minutes? An ace typist."

Rita gave him a tired look. "Ace typist. I'm surprised you didn't bring a box of candy."

"Or a Baggie," Ryan said. "Okay, I'm asking you as a favor. I guarantee you won't get involved."

"You two must be pretty close by now," Rita said. "A week in Florida."

"Five days," Ryan said.

"Are you in love with her?"

"Yeah, I guess I am." He felt good saying it. Rita could do whatever she wanted.

She didn't say anything right away, looking at him with a thoughtful expression, maybe remembering the two of them together, feeling her impression of him, maybe appreciating him more than she had before. She said, "You're a nice guy, Jack. I just hope you don't fuck up."

*   *   *

Then, from earth tones and green plants to Jay Walt's purple crushed velvet and glass-topped chrome. Purple, with light-blue carpeting and the light-blue leisure suit and the clean light-blue Cadillac Seville outside the suburban office building. With Ryan's dirty light-blue Catalina parked next to it.

Where Ryan was sitting he could see the two cars through the window. He was thinking, Dark blue next time, or dark brown.

Jay Walt, in his desk-chair recliner, had his shoes off, his light-blue-socked feet crossed on his eight-foot sheet of glass desk.

"So what's the problem?" Jay Walt said. "It's done all the time. All you want to do is goose him, right? So mail him the complaint. Cost you thirteen cents."

"No, I want to see his reaction," Ryan said, "but I'm afraid I'd blow it. He sees I'm nervous, he's liable to think I'm pulling something."

"Which you are. Shit, come on, you serve paper every day with your nice boyish bullshit. What're you talking about?" Jay Walt thumbed his gold lighter several times to relight his cigar. "Hand it to him and play dumb."

"But he knows me," Ryan said. "That's the thing. It's my idea, he knows that, and I'm handing him the papers. You see what I mean? He'd try and finesse me, I'm standing right there."

Jay Walt began to nod and then grinned. "You haven't told me everything, have you, Jackie? You're working for the guy—what, now you're working for the broad? Hey, shit, I'd watch you too. What's this guy doing?"

"I don't work for him anymore," Ryan said. "You know how he is, he doesn't see he needs you, that's it."

"No fucking heart," Jay Walt said. "And you can't take him to court for fraud, because at one time you were part of it, right? Pissed off and you want revenge."

"She's the complainant," Ryan said, "I'm not. I can go to California for six months. Shit, I can walk away from the whole thing."

Jay Walt said, "Hey, Jackie? Bullshit. You got a good thing, broad with money coming, and you're not gonna let it out of your sight, man. What's the value of the stock?"

"Jesus," Ryan said, "that's what she wants to find out. Hand him a mandatory injunction and hope he'll want to sit down and talk instead of going to court."

"Keep the fucking lawyers out of it," Jay Walt said. "I don't blame you. But you got a problem. You want to jack the guy up without going near him. The only thing you can do in that case is mail it to him, as I said before."

"I was thinking, if you knew somebody I could rely on," Ryan said, "a bright young guy you think could do a quick study on Perez, give me his reactions, what he says—"

"Here? The assholes I got? You got to point them to the can they want to take a leak."

"—Mrs. Leary'd be willing to pay a hundred and a half. Maybe go two bills if she likes the report. Just between you and me."

Jay Walt turned his head against the backrest of his chair to look over at Ryan, waiting there patiently with his offer. Boy with a good reputation, honest, sincere, a little naïve maybe. Maybe not.

"In advance?"

"Say a hundred down."

"Who drew up the complaint, some law student?"

"I guarantee it's in order."

"Only the procedure's a little funny, huh?"

"You said yourself, it's done all the time."

The diamond on Jay Walt's little finger reflected a flash of purple as he extended his arm.

"Lemme have a look, Jackie. See if I like it."

They didn't ask Jay Walt to take his coat off, but as Mr. Perez walked over to the desk with the envelope he said, "Raymond, fix Mr. Walt a drink."

"Scotch and a splash'd be fine," Jay Walt said.

"Scotch and a splash," Mr. Perez said. "It still cold outside?"

"Not too bad," Jay Walt said. "Maybe forty-five, around there."

"That's cold," Mr. Perez said. He had his reading glasses on now and had taken the papers out of the envelope. Without looking up he said, "Raymond, hold that scotch and a splash."

Raymond Gidre, over by the bookcase bar, turned with the J&B in his hand.

Jay Walt, in his coat with the buckles and metal rings and epaulets, waited. He had only said to Mr. Perez, handing him the manila envelope, "This seems to be for you; some sort of legal matter." Trying to play dumb and keep his ass out of it as much as possible.

"'Complaint for Mandatory Injunction,'" Mr. Perez said, looking over at Jay Walt. "Some sort of legal matter, huh? 'To compel the disclosure of information . . . a summons to appear in Circuit Court, County of Oakland.' Yeah, I guess that's some sort of legal matter all right. Raymond, what would you say to taking this fat boy and throwing him out the window?"

"You open it," Raymond said, moving toward Jay Walt, "and I'll throw him. How far you want him to go?"

"I guess all the way down," Mr. Perez said.

"Might as well." He walked over to the room's smaller, regular-size window, snapped the shade up spinning on the roller, and raised the lower window flush with the top pane. "How's that?"

"That's good," Raymond said.

Jay Walt didn't believe it, looking from Mr. Perez to Raymond Gidre, who was close to him now, with his wet-down hair and sportshirt and mother tattoo. He could smell Raymond's hair tonic. He said, "Hey, guys, come on."

"I can run him right through there," Raymond said. "Got handles on his coat." Raymond grabbed the belt and one of the epaulets, almost jerked Jay Walt off his feet, and ran him across the room toward the window.

Jay Walt screamed. "Jesus Christ—come *on!* For Christ's sake, *wait!*"

Jay Walt's head banged hard against the window frame. "Shit," Raymond said. He backed him up, straining, clench-jawed, and pushed him half through the open window, Jay Walt squeezing against the sill with his knees to hold on, looking straight down seventeen floors to the Jefferson Avenue service drive, seeing the tops of cars moving, inching along, feeling the wind cutting his face.

"Son of a bitch is stuck."

"Hold him there," Mr. Perez said. "I believe he was saying his prayers."

"I don't know, he mentioned Jesus," Raymond said. "Ain't he a Jew boy?"

"I believe so. Ask him."

Raymond leaned close to Jay Walt's back. "Hey, are you a Jew boy?" Raymond looked up at Mr. Perez. "He nodded yes."

"Ask him was this his idea."

Raymond asked him. "He shook his head no," Raymond said.

"Ask him again."

"Nooo!" wailed Jay Walt, out in the wind.

"Ask him whose idea was it."

"Ryan!" Jay Walt screamed. "I don't know anything about it—honest to Christ!"

"Bring him in and shut the window," Mr. Perez said. He walked over to the bar and made himself a drink. When he came back, Jay Walt had edged away from the window and seemed to be holding on to his stomach, protecting himself.

"Slap him a good one," Mr. Perez said. "Get his attention."

Jay Walt didn't see it coming. Raymond gave him an open hand across the face that almost knocked him down. Jay Walt screamed as he got it.

"Some more."

He looked round and fatter in the coat, trying to cover up. "Please, please don't hurt me. I swear to God—"

He tried to turn, but Raymond caught him by the front of his coat and cracked him hard across the face. "Look at me, Jew boy," Raymond said. "Hey, look at me." Raymond grabbed him by the hair then, raising his face, Jay Walt moaning, trying to squeeze his eyes closed, and began slapping him with his yellow-callused palm, back-handing him on the return swing, raking the man's nose and cheekbones with his knuckles.

Mr. Perez sipped his drink and lowered it. "That's fine, Raymond." As Raymond stepped away, blowing on his hand, Mr. Perez said to Jay Walt, "Did you learn anything of value today?"

Jay Walt, his mouth open and swollen-looking, nodded and mumbled something.

"I can't hear you," Mr. Perez said.

"Yes, sir, I did, I didn't mean to—"

"Let me hear you say, I will never fuck with Mr. Perez again."

Jay Walt began to repeat the words.

"Speak up," Mr. Perez said. "I still can't hear you."

"I will never . . ."

"I will never fuck with Mr. Perez again, ever."

"I will never fuck with Mr. Perez again," Jay Walt said.

"Ever."

"Ever," Jay Walt said.

"I'm glad to hear that," Mr. Perez said. "Now wipe your nose and go home."

Ryan liked a dark business suit and white shirt with a suntan. It made the person look successful: sitting at a table in the Salamander Bar, quietly waiting to hear the outcome of a business deal. The subdued lighting was also good for suntans. He had a 7Up, then switched to a ginger ale and fooled with it, making it last, sucking at the ice in the bottom of the glass when Jay Walt came in.

"Wow," Ryan said, with reverence. "You look like you been stung by bees." He made a gesture of rising as Jay Walt wedged himself into the table and collapsed.

"We got to get out of here. No, I want a drink, Christ." He was gasping, barely moving his swollen mouth. "They open the window, Christ, try and push me out. This big son of a bitch starts hitting me as hard as he can."

"While you're out the window?"

"Seventeenth floor, I look down, Christ, I said, Hey, guys, come on, this isn't funny."

"What'd Perez say?"

"What'd he *say?* He tried to push me out the fucking window. Where's a waitress in this place?"

Ryan sat back in his chair. "So he didn't think much of the mandatory injunction, uh?"

* * *

Buying Jay Walt a couple of doubles and sitting with him gave Ryan time to plan his next immediate move. He gave Jay Walt another hundred dollars, saying he was awfully sorry it turned out the way it did—with Jay Walt getting some of his nerve back with the scotch and threatening to sue the son of a bitch—walked him over to the escalator, thanked him again, then crossed the lobby to the house phones.

When Mr. Perez came on, Ryan said, "Jay Walt just phoned me. Looks like you're gonna have *two* legal suits on your hands."

Mr. Perez said, "Don't you believe it."

"Not afraid to go to court, huh?"

"Why don't you come by and we'll talk about it," Mr. Perez said.

"If we can do it on the ground floor," Ryan said. "Maybe later on. There's something I got to do first."

"There is, huh? Son, you don't have anything pressing on you like I'm going to."

"You'd be surprised," Ryan said. "Why don't we have dinner together? I'll call you back." He hung up before Mr. Perez could say anything else.

That part was done, getting it set up.

Ryan went to a pay phone then to call Virgil Royal, with the odds heavy against Virgil answering or even finding him short of a few hours. Virgil said hello, with his lazy tone, and Ryan couldn't help but grin. Imagine being glad to hear Virgil Royal's voice. They talked for a minute and agreed on Sportree's in about an hour. Ryan said he'd find it.

"I don't see you doing much," Ryan said. "You want something, but I don't see you breaking your ass especially to get it."

"I'm being patient," Virgil said, "waiting till everybody make up their mind. You want a real drink this time?"

"No, this is fine." Ryan still had half a Coke. He watched Virgil nod to the waitress. She was over at the bar where several black guys were sitting with their hats on, glancing at themselves in the bar mirror as they talked and jived around. "What's this, the hat club?" Ryan said. "There's some pretty ones, but they can't touch yours."

Virgil was looking at him from beneath the slightly, nicely curved brim of his uptown Stetson. "I get my money, what's owed me, I'll give it to you," he said.

"I'll take it," Ryan said, "and everybody'll be happy. If we can get you to do a little work."

"What kind of work?"

"First, how much we talking about? What you say Bobby owes you?"

"Half."

"Half of what I heard he got is nothing."

"No, I'm telling you. Round it off, ten grand," Virgil said. "Now you tell me, how much we talking about? The whole deal."

"We don't know yet."

"But you got an idea. Explain it to me again, what the man does."

The hatbrim rose as the waitress put another orange drink in front of him. Virgil gave her a look that was warm but sleepy. She smiled taking his empty, like they had something going.

"All the guy does," Ryan said, "as I told you, he tries to make the beneficiary sign an agreement for his fee or give him power of attorney to make the stock transaction, you know, get certificates issued by the corporation, and according to what his percent is, stated in the agreement, he gets that much on the sale of the stock."

"How much is that?"

"Whatever he thinks he can get." Ryan paused. "Does it make any difference what the guy does? You want ten grand. Okay, I'm not going to argue with you, I respect your position in this."

"My position."

"I do. I'd like very much for you to go away and

never be heard from again. But you're here, and since you are, you might as well be doing us some good."

"Doing what?"

"Break in the guy's hotel room. Can you handle something like that?"

"Go on."

"Collect his papers. Every paper you see, you take. Whatever's in his briefcase, files, folders, a note on the back of an envelope, you take it. Something written on a matchbook cover, everything."

"All the man's papers."

"And it's got to be tonight. Around eight o'-clock, in there. Room 1705."

"You gonna have the man out for a while?"

"I hope so. I don't, I'll call you," Ryan said.

"That would be nice."

"Maybe bring a suitcase. Walk across the lobby you look like you're checking in."

Virgil gave him his lazy smile. "You gonna tell me how to do it?"

"Not if you know the way," Ryan said. "It's your show."

"And it's my ass if I get caught," Virgil said. "Must be very important stuff."

"Think of it like a paper drive. You go out collecting paper and bring it in and get ten grand," Ryan said. "I'll call you later."

*   *   *

It was five-thirty by the time Ryan got home. He sat down on the couch with his coat still on and called Denise.

"I just walked in," she said. "God, I'm dead."

"How'd it go?"

"I'm supposed to be sick and I come back with a tan. If you were the manager—you can imagine."

"If I was the manager," Ryan said, "I'd have you on the potato sacks. Listen, I'll be out later. The injunction thing didn't work—I'll tell you about it, it's kind of funny. I got hold of Virgil, that's set, and I hope I'm gonna meet Mr. Perez for dinner, get him away from the hotel. He hasn't called you?"

"I wasn't here all day."

"That's right. I've been trying to think, I still wish there was some place you could go for a while."

"I'm not going to hide," Denise said, "it's not worth it."

It irritated her when he brought it up, that she might need protection. Screw Mr. Perez, Denise said. She was through sitting alone with the shades drawn. It was a good attitude, but it made Ryan nervous.

He said, "All right, but don't open the door unless it's me. Or answer the phone unless I tell you before exactly when I'm gonna call. Okay?"

"Okay."

"Listen, when I come later, I could bring my toothbrush and a few things."

"Why don't you bring everything?" Denise said.

"Pretty soon. It won't be long."

"Hey, Ryan?" Denise said. "The money's a side issue now, isn't it? Like a bonus maybe, not something we have to have."

"Yeah, except it's right there."

"What I mean," Denise said, "they could threaten to break my legs or something, and if they do I'll sign anything they want. They can *have* the money, the fuckers. What're we out? So don't worry."

"I won't," Ryan said. "I'll see you later."

He called Mr. Perez, got him on the line, and gave him the sales pitch: the Paradiso on Woodward just north of Six Mile, softshell crabs, very good fish, steaks, or you can go Italian all the way . . . and greens. They actually cooked things like collards and escarole. . . . Fine. Seven o'clock.

Ryan turned on an FM station and listened to jazz while he cleaned up and changed from his business suit to a dark turtleneck and sportcoat. He got a handkerchief out of his top drawer and closed it. Then opened the drawer again and felt in under the jockeys. His hand came out with the .38 Smith and Wesson Chief's Special he'd bought three years before and had fired only a few times on a practice range. It was wrapped in green tissue paper.

He had never carried it during the three years, and even now the idea of the revolver, holding it, made him a little tense. Still, the hard weight of it felt good in his hand. If he was ever going to pack, now seemed like the time.

"How is it?" Ryan said.

He'd taken his time and didn't get there until almost eight. They were in the bar section of the Paradiso, in the back by a mirrored wall, already eating.

Mr. Perez looked up at him. "This is the spot, huh?"

"Always a crowd," Ryan said. "White tablecloths and good food."

Raymond Gidre was eating frog legs and digging into his double order of escarole cooked with bacon. He said, "About on a par with some nigger places we got back home."

Mr. Perez was still on his snails with a bottle of German white in front of him, wiping his French bread in the juice on the hot metal plate. It made Ryan hungry watching him. As Ryan sat down Mr. Perez said, "You look like you've been on a vacation."

"I took the lady to Florida for a few days," Ryan said. "Get her straightened out."

"Also looks like we're going to bullshit awhile," Mr. Perez said. "I thought we might get down to facts."

"Okay," Ryan said, "how about this? You tell us what the stock is, Mrs. Leary cashes it in and gives you ten grand for your trouble."

"That's what I was afraid of," Mr. Perez said, pushing the metal plate away from him.

"Or," Ryan said, "we take you to court on the injunction. The first way saves time and legal fees. The second way, you don't get anything."

"That first way also saves you from being prosecuted as part of the act, get your nose rubbed in it." Mr. Perez looked at his wristwatch. "Raymond, you going to make the hockey game, you better get moving."

Raymond looked at his own watch. "Yeah, I guess I better. You can get a cab all right?"

"I don't see why not." Mr. Perez said to Ryan, "Raymond's never seen a hockey game before."

"I been looking forward to it," Raymond said. He was finishing off his escarole, mopping up the juice with bread. When he got up, wiping his mouth with his napkin, he was still chewing. "I'll see you later on."

Ryan and Mr. Perez watched him hurry along

the bar to the front of the restaurant and out toward the entrance. Why? Ryan was thinking.
Leaves his boss here and goes to a hockey game.

Mr. Perez said to Ryan, "Now then. I think
you're in over your head. I think you're being naïve
or somebody's giving you the wrong advice. I let
you take me to court, you'll find out quick there's
no grounds for an intent to defraud or anything
that violates a statute. I'm making a business pro-
posal to Miz Leary. She can accept it or reject it,
there's no coercion. There's not a hint, a smell, of
criminal intent. If you're going to tell me a lawyer
drew up that complaint, then I say you're bluffing.
In fact, what you're doing, you're fucking up. I offered you thirty grand, but you see more. The thing
is you're not big enough to see more, because there
isn't any way you can get it."

"You're worrying about what you think I want
out of this," Ryan said, "and you start assuming
things. Maybe I don't give a shit if I get anything or
not. Maybe she doesn't either, it's not your concern.
All you've got to decide is if you want ten grand or
nothing."

"I see I better talk to the lady again," Mr. Perez
said. "Point out she's getting some half-assed advice from a process server who doesn't know what
he's doing."

"You've already talked to her, and she wasn't too

impressed," Ryan said. "I told her what you wanted, and for some reason you getting the whole thing sounded to her like a piss-poor deal."

"You and I discussed possibilities, that's all," Mr. Perez said. He poured himself a little more wine. "Being realistic, what would she think of going halves?"

"At one time that might've sounded fine. Well, acceptable maybe. But now, see, she's made you a counter-offer. Ten grand," Ryan said. "So now it's up to you."

"You're right there, it's up to me," Mr. Perez said. "It's always been up to me. I could be dining at Commander's Palace this evening instead of this place. I'm here because this is my business. Now you come along, try and fuck up things—it's like you're telling me I don't know what I'm doing."

"I've got a feeling," Ryan said, "I could go back to Probate Court, look up the guy who left the stock in the first place, Anderson, dig around, locate his heirs. I find out what the stock is, all the talking's over, isn't it?"

"Or, I could have Raymond drop by and see you," Mr. Perez said. "How does that sound?"

"Throw me out the window? I'm on the first floor."

Mr. Perez shrugged. "Or we could wrap it up tonight. Meet with the lady, she signs an agreement that we split it down the middle. Then it's just a matter of some paperwork. Everybody's happy, we shake hands and go home."

Some paperwork. Something occurred to Ryan he hadn't thought of before. He said, "First, before anything's done, the stock's got to be transferred to her name, through probate."

"It does, huh? What stock? Transferred by whom?"

The waitress said, "Red snapper. I was able to get your tail piece."

"I went ahead and ordered," Mr. Perez said. "I hope you don't mind."

"And your cottage fries and vegetable." Making room for them on the table, the waitress said to Ryan, "Are you gonna order, hon?"

Mr. Perez looked at her for the first time.

"Not right now," Ryan said. He wanted her to finish and move off.

Mr. Perez gave him a put-on surprised look. "You're not going to eat? I thought this was the best restaurant in town."

"I'll let you know," Ryan said to the waitress. He felt awkward, unsure of himself, and didn't know why. Mr. Perez, with his dinner in front of him, squeezing lemon on his snapper, was in control again. The man was practiced, good at it. He made a little ceremony of tasting the fish and again acting surprised.

"Not bad, not bad at all." He did the same thing

with the escarole. "Yeah, you might be right for once."

"If we go to court," Ryan began, "get it into probate . . ." He hoped that was enough; he wasn't sure how to make an explicit threat out of it.

"My friend," Mr. Perez said, "there is no stock until the lady signs the agreement. There is no way you or the court can find out what it is. If I'm subpoenaed, I'll say it again in court, 'What stock? What stock is it you want transferred to her name? Your honor, I don't know what they're talking about.' You understand?"

"Yeah, but I guess we're not communicating," Ryan said. He pushed his chair back and got up. "I hope you don't mind eating alone."

"Not at all," Mr. Perez said. "In fact, I enjoy it. We're through, anyway, aren't we?"

Shit, Ryan was standing there with his hand on the back of the chair and couldn't think of anything to say. He wanted to give the guy a good parting shot and walk away with the words hanging in the air.

"Well, call if you want the ten grand. Otherwise, let's forget the whole thing." That seemed about right. He was walking away from the table.

"Fine," Mr. Perez said, "I'll call if I need you for anything."

Ryan kept going, along the bar to the front and past the reservation desk to the foyer. The son of a bitch, he'd call if he needed him. What'd he mean, if he *needed* him? He got his raincoat from the checkroom lady and a couple of mints from the dish on the tobacco counter.

It was cold outside, misty. Almost eight-thirty. It was too early to call Virgil. He started along the sidewalk to the restaurant's parking lot, getting a buck out of his pocket.

If I need you for anything.

Like nothing Ryan said had impressed him or changed his way of thinking. Business as usual. Sitting there eating his dinner. Sends Raymond off to a hockey game. Ryan stopped.

He turned and ran back into the foyer of the restaurant. There were magazines on the tobacco counter, *Host of the Town*, what to do in Detroit, if anything, but no newspaper. Sorry, the checkroom lady said. In the phone booth Ryan got Olympia's number from information and dialed it.

"Hi, what time's the game start, eight-thirty?"

The Wings were on the road, the voice told him. At Montreal tonight.

He dialed Denise's number and listened to it ring. He said, Come on, answer it. Forget what I said and answer it. The phone continued to ring.

21

"IT'S A HOTEL LOBBY," VIRGIL SAID. "You never seen one before?"

Tunafish brought his gaze back and looked straight ahead, toward the bank of elevators. "I never seen this one before. It's the first time I been here."

It was Virgil's first time in the Pontchartrain, too, but he didn't bother to mention it. He said to Tunafish, "Yeah, we here." Like what was the big deal? "Anybody ask, we going up to see a man. See if he want his walk shoveled."

They got off the elevator on 17 and walked down the hall looking at room numbers, Tunafish saying them out loud, beginning with 1725.

"Oh-five," Virgil said and stopped by the door. He knocked, giving the door panel three light taps, and waited. "Hey, I don't believe nobody's home," he said, and reached in his coat pocket for his ring of keys and was going through them when Tunafish touched his arm.

"Somebody coming."

Virgil looked past him, his hatbrim brushing the door frame. A chambermaid had appeared from somewhere and was coming down the hall pushing a linen cart. Virgil slipped the ring of keys back into his pocket. His hand moved inside his jacket and remained there.

Approaching them, the maid said, "Good evening," with the trace of an accent.

"How you doing?" Virgil said, looking over his shoulder as she moved past them with the cart, a heavyset woman in a white uniform, white anklets, and black crepe-soled shoes. Virgil kept watching her. When she stopped at the next door and took a sheet of paper out of her pocket, he said, "Hey, mama?" She looked up. "Yeah, come here, will you? I wonder you could open this door for us. My friend forget the key."

"Uh-oh, shit," Tunafish said. He didn't like the look on the fat ugly woman's face, puzzled, frowning a little. She came over to them, though, her hand in her pocket, probably holding on to the passkey.

"You stay with Mr. Perez?" she said.

"Yeah, I'm his brother come to visit him," Virgil said. "Open the door, Mama." He brought out from under his jacket Bobby Lear's gleaming nickel-plated .38. The maid didn't see it right away. She said, "You his *brother?*" Then she saw it.

"Oh, my God," and her hand went up to her mouth.

"Open the door, please," Virgil said. "Nobody want to hurt you." Getting the key out and putting it in the door, she looked like she was going to cry. Virgil patted her shoulder gently. "Come on, Mama, it's cool," assuring her again as they entered the suite and Virgil steered her into the front closet, asking why would anybody want to hurt a pretty woman like her.

As Virgil closed the door to the closet, Tunafish walked over close to it and said, "You make a sound, we come in there, we both of us gonna rape the ass off you. You hear?"

"Get a suitcase," Virgil said, going to the desk. "Look in the bedroom."

They used Mr. Perez's black Samsonite two-suiter. Virgil cleared off the desk, taking loose papers, folders, and notebooks, scratchpads, and everything in the desk, including hotel stationery and the room-service menu, and dropped everything in the suitcase open on the floor. Tunafish made them a couple of scotch and Coca-Cola drinks. Virgil had to jimmy open Mr. Perez's locked attaché case. Right on top was a Beretta three-eighty, nice little mean-looking piece. Virgil slipped it into his jacket. He dumped the papers and file folders, lists of names and addresses, in the suitcase and went looking for more, finding a telephone-address book and a note pad with some writing on it in the bedroom and copies of *The Wall Street Journal* and *Business Week* in the bathroom. Virgil said, Shit, grinning, and took the roll of toilet paper. He took the Gideon Bible, some more magazines, and the folded laundry bags in the closet, and topped off the load in the suitcase with a painting on the wall he liked of a cat out in a sailboat with the mast broken off and this terrible motherfucker storm coming at him. Virgil sat down and had his scotch and Coke drink, wondering if the cat made it, then wondering where the cat had got the sailboat, if it was his or if he'd stolen it someplace and was trying to get away, shit, when the storm got him.

Coming out of the elevator, the first thing they saw was a bellman coming right at them. Tunafish hung back, letting Virgil get ahead of him with the suitcase.

Reaching for it, the bellman said, "Can I get you a cab?"

"No, we got a car." Virgil let him have the suitcase, the bellman almost dropping it as he took the grip.

"It's a heavy one."

"Full of money." Virgil grinned.

The bellman laughed.

About the time Virgil got home to his apartment

on Seward, on the near west side, and began going through the papers, wondering what he had, Ryan was trying to stay alive.

Raymond Gidre had said, "His place, huh?" And Mr. Perez had said, "No, *her* place." Raymond had said, "How do you know he won't go home?" Mr. Perez had said, "Take my word for it." In the restaurant before Ryan had joined them.

Now Raymond was sitting in the Hertz car in front of the Leary woman's apartment building in Rochester. There were lights in windows, but he wasn't sure if any were hers or if she was home. Mr. Perez had said not to go to her apartment. It would be good to sit up there and wait for him, watch the look on the Leary woman's face. It was cold in the Hertz car, sitting there with the motor and the lights turned off. "Wait there," Mr. Perez had said. "He comes, you don't have to say a word to him."

Raymond was looking forward to it. He had a 9 mm. Mauser Parabellum, official eight-shot German Luger, under his coat and a twelve-gauge Weatherby pump gun leaning against the seat with the walnut stock on the floor.

But, damn, it was cold.

The vestibule of the apartment building, through the glass door, looked warm. Except it was lit up.

He doubted he'd be able to take the Weatherby in there.

After a few minutes the idea of a warm place won out over the shotgun. Then don't take it. What would he need it for if he's standing there as Ryan walked in? He got out of the Hertz car, leaving the Weatherby inside with the door unlocked, and crossed the parking area to the front entrance of the apartment wing. Maybe there was a light switch.

There wasn't, though. It was probably inside the door that had to be buzzed to let you in. Raymond turned around. He couldn't see much outside through his reflection on the glass door, just the shapes of cars, some highlights in the darkness. He'd be seen from out there, though, for sure. He looked up at the light fixture. Hell, it was only about a foot out of reach. He got out his German Luger, pointed it up there at arm's length, rose to his toes as he shoved the six-inch barrel through the opening in the fixture and poked it against the light bulb. Hardly made a sound as the vestibule went dark. There. Raymond leaned against the wall to wait. It was a little warmer in here, but not much.

Ryan was anxious to get to Denise's. Careful, but in a hurry, waiting for traffic lights to change, going through an amber-turning-red in the middle of

Rochester and finally coming to the street that climbed the rise to the apartment buildings, looking for a light in Denise's window as he turned into the parking area in the middle of the complex. Ryan got out and angled through the rows of parked cars toward the entrance. It was here, coming to open pavement, he sensed something wrong, something different. If there had been only one apartment building here he might not have noticed the light out in the vestibule. But he looked around at the other entrances, five of them in the U-shaped complex, and there was a light in every entrance but this one.

Ryan had stopped before he saw the glass door swing into the darkness of the vestibule and the figure appear—somebody coming out, pointing at him, pointing something—and he was moving, running back to the protection of the car rows, as Raymond began firing the German Luger at him.

Son of a bitch, something had spooked him. Raymond came out to the pavement and paused, listening, before he crossed to the first row of cars. He'd fired three rounds, louder than hell in the closed-in area between the buildings. Now the only thing Raymond could hear, standing between two cars, was his own slow breathing, in and out of his nose. Some lights were going on in the building opposite him. Probably in all the buildings. He wondered if Ryan was going to run over to one of those lit-up entrances and start pushing buzzers. Raymond hoped he would. Get him in there banging at the inside door, screaming for help, and shoot him through the glass.

Raymond moved out into the open toward the next row of cars and that flushed him, hearing his quick running steps first, and there he was, going for daylight, running past the cars to the little street that led down the hill to the main road. Raymond held his German Luger straight out in front of him with both hands and squeezed off three rounds, shit, seeing Ryan still on his feet and hearing the glass pop in a car windshield.

He needed the Weatherby pump gun. He also needed to get the Hertz car the hell out of here, before the flashing lights appeared, or he might never get back to it. He'd be giving Ryan an extra half-minute start, but that was all right, he'd be in the open for a time, anyway, if he was running for town, spooked good now, in a panic, running to find a policeman or somebody to help him.

Raymond got on him in less than a half minute, more like twenty seconds, flying out of there in the Hertz car with the lights off, down the little street and squealing the tires in a hard left onto the main road and across the railroad tracks, heading for the streetlights and neon signs a block away, and there he was on the left-hand side, going past Morley's Drugs. Raymond swung the Hertz car into a filling station that was closed for the night, switched the motor off, and got out with the Weatherby pump gun.

He kept to the right side of the street, hurrying to catch even with Ryan, seeing him now and again past the cars parked on the street. Ryan was moving at a fast walk, looking back over his shoulder, a dark figure over there, in and out of the glow of streetlights and illuminated signs. Raymond didn't see any people on the street except for some way down, a block away, and a few cars going by. He had the pump gun out in plain sight, not caring if anybody saw him with it. What were they going to do, take it away from him? Near the middle of the block, approaching the center of town, Raymond was ready to make his move.

He waited for a car to come along going south, the direction he was headed, stepped out in the street, and ran along with the car maybe fifteen or twenty yards, using it for cover, then let the car go on and started across the street, timing it just right and seeing the dumb look of surprise on Ryan's face—Raymond standing out there with a big goddamn Weatherby raised at him. Ryan was moving as Raymond fired. Then Raymond was moving, pumping the shotgun, throwing himself across the hood of a parked car. He fired again and blew the plate-glass window out of a place called Bright Ideas as Ryan kept going.

Within a block and a half, running in the street about a dozen strides behind Ryan on the sidewalk, pumping and throwing down on him with the twelve-gauge, Raymond shot out the windows of Bright Ideas, Mitzelfelds department store, the box office of the Hills movie theater, a couple of car windshields and a pair of headlights before Ryan got around the corner and was out of sight. The son of a bitch was quick, moving and ducking into doorways and behind cars. Maybe he'd grazed him, cut him up some. He'd run him down and find out. People were coming out on the street, standing in front of places now. Raymond stood still on the sidewalk, his back to the streetlight, as a white police car with a gold emblem wailed by north flashing blue lights, probably answering a call from the apartments. With the sound fading, Raymond ducked around the corner after Ryan, digging twelve-gauge shells out of his coat pocket.

The wail of the police car lifted Ryan and he stopped to listen—Christ, saved—he could see it swerving after Raymond, running him down, the pair of young, alert Rochester police officers out of the car with drawn revolvers—

Yeah?

Bull*shit*, the police car was still going, the nice sound trailing after it, stretching thin and not doing him one bit of good, what those guys were paid to do, for Christ's sake—and Ryan was moving again, running past the back-street shops, the once-Victorian houses that now had artsy paint jobs and craftsy signs. All closed, silent, dark. No place to go in and hide and tell somebody to quick, call the police. The guy was crazy, running down the fucking main street firing a shotgun, Christ, people *watching* him.

You're doing it all wrong, Ryan told himself, much too late. From the beginning, running. He was still running and didn't have time to stop and think. Coming to a corner, the cross street lined with old trees, he wished to God he knew what he should do, keep going, cut left or right, what? He wanted to hide somewhere, but he didn't want to get trapped. His side ached and his stomach hurt. He ran toward the house on the corner with the sign in front, *Objects & Images*. Quick decision, he'd break in if he had to, use the phone and wait there in the dark. But not in time. The twelve-gauge sound hit the air flat and heavy and the shot ripped against the side of the house directly behind Ryan, jerking his head around to see the crazy bastard on him again, one house away, coming in mean, hard prison-farm condition, mind made up nothing was going to stop him. It scared the shit out of Ryan, fear slugging him to pump his legs faster. Christ, how'd he get here, doing it all fucking wrong, an ex-con with a slide-action shotgun coming down on him. His stomach hurt, something hard pressing on his intestines. He put his hand on his stomach, still running, and felt the grip of the .38 Smith that he had absolutely forgot all about.

Cutting across the front lawn of the corner house, he wanted to get behind something, but was afraid to stop, so he kept running, down the cross street lined with trees now. He wished he knew what he was doing, instinctively knew the way to take the guy. Get behind something. Get behind a tree and hit him going by. Except what if he missed and there was crazy Raymond swinging around with the shotgun? The shotgun made an awful noise and tore out whole plate-glass windows and ripped shingles off houses and could take the top of your head right off, like the man at the Wayne County Morgue who'd killed himself with a shotgun. He remembered the smell of the morgue and remembered, in that moment, what the smell was like. Bad breath. A sick person's breath. A whole tiled room full of it. He didn't want to get there, end up on a metal-tray table naked, lying in the cold-room with fifty naked people, his clothes in a paper bag between his legs.

Ryan stopped in the middle of the tree-lined street, pulled out the .38 Smith and turned around, extended it with both hands, like the cops on TV did, and when he saw Raymond, coming across the lawn, coming out of the line of trees to the pavement, Raymond charging directly up the street at him, three houses away, Ryan fired. He started to turn, to run, and saw Raymond stop. Ryan fired again, he fired four times again as fast as he could pull the trigger, the revolver alive, jumping in his hand. The sound died away. Raymond stood there. He wouldn't fall down. Ryan squeezed the trigger again, hard, and heard the hammer click on an empty chamber.

Less than three houses away, less than a hundred feet, Raymond said, "That all you got?"

22

THE DOOR TO SUITE 1705 STOOD OPEN. The chamber-maid was there, a man from Security, and the hotel's first assistant manager, who stood in the middle of the room staring at the wall above the sofa. Mr. Perez came out of the bedroom, finally taking off his topcoat and throwing it over a chair. He went to the bookcase bar and began making himself a drink.

"They took one of the paintings," the assistant manager said. He seemed mildly surprised as he realized it.

Mr. Perez came away from the bar with his drink. "They did, huh? That's the first indication of genuine concern I've heard from you. As I recall, it was a print of a Winslow Homer. A photographic *re*print."

"Mr. Perez, I just noticed it. That's all. I didn't mean to imply—"

Mr. Perez wasn't finished. "Two men, two nigger men, come in here and steal valuable documents and you're worried about a picture you can get in a ten-cents store."

"I wasn't *worried* about it."

"You let anybody you want come in your hotel?"

"Well," the assistant manager said, "the problem, we can't actually screen everyone who comes in. You can understand that."

"I understand I've been robbed," Mr. Perez said. "That's what I understand. What I'd like to know is what you're gonna do about it."

"Well, we'll call the police, of course. If you can give them a list of what was stolen—"

"A *list?* My friend, they stole"—Mr. Perez almost said, "my whole goddamn business," but stopped in time—"papers, documents, beyond commercial value in themselves."

The assistant manager didn't understand. "Not notes then, or stock certificates?"

"I mean records and proposals that can't be duplicated and are worth, conservatively . . . several million. That's why, sir, I hope you don't mind my asking what you're gonna do about it. Or do I have to sue your ass for some kind of negligence?"

"Mr. Perez," the assistant manager said, "you know the hotel can't be responsible for anything left in the room. That's why we have safe deposit boxes."

"That's a sign," Mr. Perez said. "You can bring it to court with you and show it to the judge."

It was not the assistant manager's hotel. When Mr. Perez moved out, someone else would move in. He said, "As I mentioned, we'll call the police, and it's possible your . . . documents will be recovered. If you'll give me a list of what was taken—I know they'll also want to question you."

Mr. Perez knew it, too. He wanted to threaten and kick ass, impress and intimidate the assistant manager; but he didn't want to talk to the police just yet, or perhaps ever, for that matter. He knew who'd taken the papers, or *had* them taken; that wasn't hard to figure, though it did surprise him. But now, what would the two niggers do if they read in the paper tomorrow about *Jack C. Ryan, Process Server, Found Shot to Death*? Better wait and see.

"I'll let you know," Mr. Perez said to the assistant manager. "Good night."

"You'll give me the list of items?"

"That's right. Then you can call the police. But not before I tell you."

"If you prefer to do it that way," the assistant manager said.

"I prefer everybody out," Mr. Perez said.

Jesus, he'd no sooner closed the door and walked over to his chair when somebody started knocking and he had to walk all the way back to open the door.

"Now what?"

Raymond Gidre came in.

*   *   *

Driving back to Detroit in the Hertz car, once he'd slipped past the blue flashers that were all over the place and screaming up the Interstate toward Rochester, Raymond kept telling himself, You hit him. You must've.

So by the time he was sitting with Mr. Perez and had heard about the niggers breaking in and was holding a cold drink on his lap, Raymond was convinced Ryan was lying dead somewhere in a wet ditch. He told Mr. Perez it was so because he thought it would make him feel better. Mr. Perez was more itchy than he'd ever seen him. His skin was blotchy from drinking and the red veins in his nose were sticking out. Even sitting in the chair he was hunched forward, wouldn't let himself relax.

"What do you mean you *think* you got him? You either got him or you didn't."

"I know I hit him," Raymond said, "on account of the blood."

"What blood?"

"See, I must've hit him good when he started running again, but as I told you, it was dark. He cut through some yards and come to a street where there's this donut place open—counter where you get your coffee and different kinds of donuts you order to go or else take over to a table there."

"Raymond," Mr. Perez said, "where was the blood?"

"In this place I'm telling you about. The boy works there's standing by the pay phone, dialing it, till he sees what I got. Then he like to shit. I said to him, 'Where's he? Man come in here.' He points to a door leads out back. Then I see the blood on the counter where he must've put his hands, smeared on it. Out back was a field and then a ravine full of scrub and shit. That's where I figure he's laying."

Mr. Perez waited a moment. "You didn't go find out?"

"I couldn't. A squad car come in the alley as I was standing there, starts shining a spot all around. They was others, you could see the blue flashers over the other side of the field and up by the apartments, you could hear them all over. Was time I had to get out of there."

"So they find him and he's alive," Mr. Perez began.

"I don't see how he could be."

"He gives them your name and address. You get rid of the gun?"

"Jesus, you know what that Weatherby cost me?"

"You know what it could? Twenty years."

"I'll dump it somewhere."

"There's a river out there, the Detroit River," Mr. Perez said. "That's where you put it. On your way over the bridge to Windsor, Canada, where you're gonna be staying awhile."

"I'm pretty sure I got him."

"Raymond, check into a motel, then call me, give me the number and I'll be in touch with you." Mr. Perez seemed calm now, because he knew what he was doing. He was patient with Raymond, because it was the way to handle him.

"Want me to leave right now?"

"In a minute. Bring the phone over here."

Mr. Perez dialed Ryan's number. When the answering service came on, he hung up. "Not home."

"I told you where he's at," Raymond said. "In the field."

"Or at the police station," Mr. Perez said. "Or the lady's apartment."

"Was cops all over there."

"You remember Miz Leary's number?"

"I never had it."

Mr. Perez looked over at the bare, cleaned-out desk. "You certain you didn't write it down someplace?"

"I never even saw it."

Mr. Perez sat back in the chair. It wasn't going to do any good to blame Raymond or curse or break things. If Ryan was alive—or even shot-up some—and got hold of the papers, he'd learn the name of the stock and the show would be over. Not only that, Ryan would likely press charges—assault with a deadly weapon or attempted murder—and here'd come the police looking for two ex-cons who'd done it before in Louisiana. If Ryan was alive, it was time to go. And start compiling another list of names to get himself back in business again, which could take him three or four months, at least. On the other hand, if Ryan was lying dead in the weeds, if Raymond wasn't bullshitting him . . .

"Raymond, fix me one, will you please?"

. . . he'd be free to work on Miz Leary some more and, goddamn it, get her signed up this time. But if Ryan was out of it . . .

"Make it a good one, Raymond."

. . . the flunky niggers wouldn't know what to do with the papers and most likely throw them away. He'd still have to spend months, time and money, making up a new list.

For the most part, Mr. Perez's reasoning was sound. Where he missed was assuming what the flunky niggers would do. He didn't know Virgil Royal.

When Ryan came in, Denise clung to him. He put his arms around her and they held on to each other.

"You're gonna get all dirty."

"Where *were* you?—I heard the shots, I knew it had to be you as soon as I heard the noise."

"Raymond was waiting."

"Did they get him?"

"I don't know. He chased me—the guy's crazy, running down Main firing a shotgun, people watching him. I couldn't believe it—blowing out store windows."

"You're soaking wet."

"I came through that field back of here, it was all mud and crap."

"You're covered with *blood*." She had backed away to look at him. "My God, are you shot?"

"No, it's from broken glass. Just my hand, it's not bad. I must've got some on my face."

"You look like you were in a war."

"I feel like it."

He got his clothes off and took a shower. Denise came in while he was drying himself, and he stopped and kissed her and held her again, wrapping the towel around both of them. It felt good under there, and he knew it was going to get a lot better once they talked a little and got that out of the way.

He sat in bed with the covers up around his waist watching her undress. She was neat, folding her slacks over the back of a chair as she told him about the police being here, squad cars outside more than an hour while they questioned the tenants.

"What'd they ask you?"

"If I'd seen anything, recognized anyone. Or if I

knew of anyone in the building that might be involved. I didn't know where you were, I wasn't sure. I kept thinking, I'll hear from you soon. If I don't, I'll do something."

"What were you going to do?"

"Call the police and tell them."

He didn't want to get into that now.

"You look good, still tan."

"You don't know how glad I was to see you." In her white bikini panties now in the lamplight, taking off her work shirt, very natural about it, but still keyed up and in her mind, concerned about him, no bra, good, those neat breasts, white, and the slim tan body, hooking her thumbs in the panties now. He loved the word *girl*. She was a girl. She was more than that, way more, someone who talked to him with quiet awareness in her eyes, the person in there looking out as they looked at each other and talked and didn't have to finish sentences—which was beyond his comprehension, to feel natural, more himself, because of a closeness to someone else—but what made it even better, he was always conscious of her girlness. He wanted to touch her and hold her, and when he did he couldn't touch and hold her enough.

"What're you waiting for?"

"I'll be right back." She went out of the room, still in her panties. Ryan lay back, settling his head on the pillow.

He began to think of Raymond again, what Raymond would do if he hadn't been picked up—Raymond out there loose, reporting to his keeper, and Mr. Perez throwing him a fried shrimp and patting him on the head. Jesus, call the police and get those two put in a cage, quick.

No, he had to hear from Virgil first. If Virgil got the papers, the list—okay, then call the police. If he didn't—shit, then what? Get Raymond arrested, involve Mr. Perez if that was possible. Go on. And Mr. Perez fingers you as an accomplice. Or he doesn't get arrested but says fuck this, it isn't worth it, and takes off. And nobody ever gets to touch the hundred and fifty thousand. Sitting there.

He had to quit thinking. Or else call Virgil right now.

"I stuffed newspaper in your shoes so they wouldn't curl up," Denise said, coming into the room as he rolled out of bed. "Where you going?"

"I got to make a phone call."

"You always talk on the phone naked?"

"Not always." He thought of Virgil, his hat shading his face, Virgil doing something, letting the phone ring. Virgil not home yet. There was a *click*. The voice said, "How you doing?"

"The other way around," Ryan said. "How'd you do?"

"Say ten thousand, huh, for all this paper?"

Ryan let his breath out, relieved, all the worrying for nothing. "You got it."

"Yeah, I got it. I'm looking at it."

"Any problems?"

"No problems," Virgil said, "some questions in my mind. Like what is it in here worth the money? Worth how much?"

Ryan felt himself tense. He kept his voice calm, though. "You said ten thousand, your figure, right? I said I wasn't going to argue with you. Remember?"

"I remember how easy you said it. Worth ten thousand to you."

"I agreed with you. Why argue?"

"But maybe worth more, huh?"

"I thought we made a deal. You holding me up now, seeing if you can get more?"

"I'm asking you, worth how much?" Virgil said. "Or worth how much to somebody else?"

There it was. Ryan came up with a pretty good imitation of a laugh. He said, "Hey, you want to see if you can get some bids? You don't even know what you're selling."

"But you know," Virgil said, "and so does the man used to have it. Think about can you go any higher than ten and maybe I'll call you back."

"You want to discuss it," Ryan said, "okay, but I've got to see what you've got first. Virgil?" He was saying it as Virgil hung up.

Ryan got a cigarette from the counter and lit it going into the bedroom. The lamp was turned off, Denise was in bed.

"Virgil's holding us up."

"He got the papers?"

"He doesn't know what he's got, but he thinks it's worth more than ten."

"Why don't you come to bed?"

He stubbed the cigarette out in an ashtray on the nightstand and got in next to her.

"Warm me," Denise said.

"I should've known better, handing him something like that."

"Let's not talk about it anymore tonight, okay?" Denise said, moving close to him.

"You know who he's gonna call now."

"Let's not talk about anything unless, you know, you want to say something . . . good."

"You feel good."

"So do you," Denise said in the darkness. "I know the feel of you now. I could be blindfolded and pick you out in a crowd, you know that? In a locker room at the Y. I'd feel my way along, just feeling arms and maybe chests. I love to touch your chest . . . and your flat stomach, and your . . . thigh." She waited. "Where are you?"

"You haven't said that in a while."

"I'm not saying it for me this time, I'm saying it for you. Where are you?"

"I'm here."

"No, you aren't," Denise said, "not yet. But I'm going to get you here." She did, too, touching him and saying, close to him in the darkness, "What do we need?"

"Here we go," Virgil said.

"Here *you* go," Tunafish said. "You doing it."

Virgil picked up the phone and dialed a number, glancing at the phone book open next to him. The suitcase and most of the papers were on the floor of Virgil's living room. The Gideon Bible was on the coffee table. The picture of the cat on the boat with the busted mast and the storm coming was on the wall over Virgil's hi-fi system. He had given the .32 Baretta to Tunafish, making him take it.

Tunafish watched Virgil. He wanted a smoke, but Virgil didn't have any. He didn't like it at all, getting into something else now, thinking each time, Okay, when it's over he won't need me no more. Then Virgil would call him again. Add them up, the things he was in.

Shooting Lonnie.

Following the man. Getting nothing for it.

Stealing the other man's papers.

Add stealing the panel truck for shooting Lonnie.

Stealing the papers. What else?

Having the man's gun in his pocket.

Now some other shit going down.

Virgil said, "Yeah, 1705, please."

Add what the police didn't know about him, Tunafish was thinking, to what they did know. Right now, extortion, Bonzie's idea, making the phone calls to the mamas: bring money to save their little girls. Tunafish saw himself in shit up to his chin with the chance of it covering his head any day now. The police kept worrying him about the extortion, telling him what Jackson would be like for the next three to five. Asking him which mamas was it he had called and which Bonzie had called, asking him what did he want to hang around with Bonzie for, asking him how Virgil was doing, slipping Virgil in, asking if he'd seen Virgil lately. Asking did he want to tell them anything was bothering his mind.

"Line's busy," Virgil said, his hand over the phone. He straightened in his chair then, getting ready. "No, she can ring now." Virgil waited, then seemed to smile. "Who am I speaking to, please?"

"Who do you want?"

Tunafish, sitting in his leather coat, deep in a chair, could hear the man's voice.

"You the man lost something this evening?"

There was a pause. "Yes, I lost something."

"Well, I'm selling scrap paper," Virgil said. "Paper that's gonna get scrapped if nobody wants to buy it. You dig?"

* * *

Mr. Perez placed a call to the Elmwood Motel in Windsor, Room 115.

"Me again, Raymond. You in bed?"

"Almost. I been looking out the window, I don't see a thing to do. You know, coming here"— Raymond laughed—"I seen a sign, you know what it said?"

"What'd it say, Raymond?"

"It said 'Chinese and *Canadian* Food.'"

"You'll have something to do tomorrow," Mr. Perez said. "One of our nigger friends in the paper business called up."

"You don't tell me."

"Wants to sell my own property back to me. I asked him how much. He said he already had a bid of ten thousand. I said all right, I'd give him fifteen. He said if I could pay fifteen I could pay twenty."

"What he had in mind, huh?"

"To him, all the money in the world. I said all right, twenty."

"He believe you?"

"He wants to, so he does."

"You ask him if he'd take a check?"

"They don't think about how a person goes about getting twenty thousand dollars together. They think anybody staying here must be rich and rich people have money in their pockets."

"He's coming tomorrow?"

"No, says he'd soon as not walk in the hotel carrying my suitcase. I said you walked out with it, it didn't bother you none. He wants to meet us two o'clock a place called the Watts Club Mozambique."

"The what?"

Mr. Perez repeated the name. "On a street called Fenkell. Look it up in your directory."

"No problem."

"You go look at the place in the morning, then we'll meet and talk about it."

"That sounds good," Raymond said. "I'll see you tomorrow."

Mr. Perez hung up.

Less than a minute later the phone rang. When Mr. Perez answered, Raymond said, "I forgot to ask you, what do you think they mean, *Canadian* food?"

There had been time to think during the night and time to think after waking up with Denise and finally getting out of bed to shower and get dressed. They didn't talk about Virgil or Mr. Perez or any of it until they were sitting at the counter with juice and coffee and Ryan told her he was going to call the police.

"Good," Denise said. "I'll get the number."

Ryan was stirring his coffee. "I don't mean the

cops here. I've been thinking, maybe the best thing would be to call Dick Speed first. Tell him what's happened, you know, get him in on it instead of going right to the local cops and trying to explain why a guy was shooting at me. You see what I mean? It's pretty involved."

"Whatever way you want to do it," Denise said, "as long as we get it over with."

"He knows about most of it. I'll ask him what he thinks we should do, if we've got a chance of involving Mr. Perez—" Ryan stopped. "Shit, I can't tell him the whole thing. How do I explain I sent a guy to burglarize a hotel room?"

"Don't tell him that part," Denise said, "just tell him about Raymond. All we want is for them to leave us alone. It doesn't have to have anything to do with Virgil . . . does it?"

"I don't know. Once I open it up . . ."

"Call him." Denise reached for the phone on the counter and moved it closer to Ryan. "You know you'll have to sooner or later."

Ryan lit a cigarette first, getting ready, before dialing the number. He asked for Dick Speed and could hear sounds, voices in the Squad Six offices as he waited. Then Speed was on the line. They said hello and how's it going, fine, and Ryan got to it, saying, "I want to talk to you about something. A guy tried to kill me."

"I believe it," Dick Speed said. "Which one?"

"You remember the two guys from Louisiana you looked up for me, Perez and a Raymond Gidre?"

"Hold on a second."

Ryan could hear voices again, Dick Speed asking someone for a file, saying it was right there on the desk. Denise was watching him expectantly. He looked at her and shrugged. "He told me to hold on."

"Okay," Dick Speed said. "Perez and Gidre tried to kill you."

"No, it was just Raymond . . . Gidre."

"With what?"

"A shotgun." Ryan told him about it briefly, the high points, the breaking glass. He didn't mention shooting at Raymond; he'd save that.

"You reported it to the police?"

"That's what I'm doing. Aren't you the police?"

"The Rochester police," Dick Speed said. "Outside Detroit I don't give a shit who tries to kill you."

"Look, I'm calling you because it's kind of an involved situation," Ryan said, "if you know what I mean. I'm not sure what all I should tell them."

"You mean if you should tell them about the papers were stolen from room 1705, the Pontchartrain Hotel, at approximately eight-fifteen last night?"

"Jesus," Ryan said. There was a silence.

"You still there?"

"I'm here."

"How'd you like to go someplace with me this afternoon?" Dick Speed said. "Maybe eyeball the guy tried to shoot you. How's that sound?"

"I don't believe it," Ryan said. "How could you know all that, I mean about the papers?"

"How come you know they were stolen?" Dick Speed said. "You want to answer that?"

"I told you it was complicated."

"Isn't it, though," Dick Speed said. "You want to go with me or not?"

Ryan felt tired, like he hadn't gotten enough sleep.

"I'll go."

He listened, nodding, then hung up the phone. Denise was waiting.

"Well?"

"Well, I talked to the police," Ryan said.

23

"YOU MENTIONED, TALK ABOUT SMALL WORLDS," Dick Speed said. "We get Tunafish on this attempted extortion that's very flimsy, in fact not worth a shit, but long as we're talking to him, he's right there, why not play let's make a deal? Drop the beef, save him some of the best years of his life, we say, if he'll talk to us about his brother-in-law and try and recall if Virgil *was* actually with Tunafish a certain night or was he visiting somebody at a hotel. Tunafish says, What hotel? It got a little confusing about hotels before Tunafish says, The man talk to you? We say yeah, he did, not knowing who the fuck he means at all. See, we're trying to put Virgil in the hotel where Bobby Lear was shot dead and Tunafish's talking about, it turns out, the Pontch. Says he went up there with Virgil, yeah, thinking he was gonna see a man, and so on. We say right, you haven't done nothing. He wants you to go with him to make the drop, fine. Says carry the man's gun, do it, what he tells you. Your soul is now spotless, free of sin." Dick Speed looked out his side window. "They went in there at one-twenty-five. All we need now's your other two friends."

The bar was across the street from where they sat in Dick Speed's unmarked Ford. A brick building with a glass-brick window and a painted sign that said *Watts Club Mozambique*. A smaller sign said *Jazz Nightly*. The place didn't look to be open or doing business, though several people had gone in and come out during the twenty-five minutes they had been waiting. It was cold in the car, dull gray outside, the street of storefronts dirty and old-looking, a street that had been handed down, Ryan remembering it as a Jewish neighborhood, and was now nearly all black.

"Very active at night around here," Dick Speed said. "Down at the corner of Fenkell and Livernois was where we almost had another riot last summer, you remember? The bar-owner comes out, shoots a spook in his parking lot."

"I remember reading about it," Ryan said.

"Very touchy for a while. A guy was pulled out of his car, going home from work, the guy didn't even know what the fuck was going on. Some foreign guy, an ethnic you say now, gets the shit beat out of him and dies in the hospital."

After a few moments Ryan said, "Saint Gregory's,

it's around here somewhere. I used to play basketball there in the seventh and eighth grade. It was about maybe half black then."

"You ever go there to Confession?"

"No, why?" Ryan looked at him and saw the dumb-innocent expression. "Oh. Yeah, I forgot. You want to hear it?"

"I already did, from the Tuna," Dick Speed said. "He didn't mention you in particular. I mean your name isn't written down anywhere, but—Jesus, that's about the dumbest thing I ever heard of a supposedly intelligent person doing. How much you pay 'em?"

"Nothing yet. Virgil was supposed to get something if we made it."

"I asked you how much."

"Ten grand."

"Jesus Christ, you know what you're talking about?"

"What's the amount? It's breaking and entering, isn't it? I mean to Virgil, what's that? Looking at it relatively. He's taking something from a guy, he's not taking money, information that legally belongs to somebody else."

"You think that's the way your lawyer's gonna plead it?"

"I don't know"—it was dumb and it wore Ryan out trying to make it sound rational—"I made a bad call, I admit it. Now what?"

"Now what, it's up to Virgil and the Tuna," Dick Speed said. "They get their ass in the cogs, and got to sweat and pray they don't take you with 'em. We'll see what we can do. So far you've been pretty lucky."

"That I've got you on my side?" Ryan couldn't help saying it. He sat there while Dick Speed gave him a grim look.

"You gonna be a smartass now?"

"No, I'll be good," Ryan said.

"Boy, I don't know about you." Dick Speed was shaking his head.

Ryan let it go and sat quietly. He didn't know why he did things like that, antagonized people. Maybe to see their reaction. He wasn't serious; he was kidding. Right now would be the time to tell Speed he had a gun on him, watch him go through the roof. He'd almost left it home when he stopped to change his shoes, but he reloaded it instead— thinking of Raymond, knowing he was going to see Raymond again, and Virgil—and stuck it back in his raincoat pocket. He didn't mention it to Speed, though, or show it to him. He figured the guy had enough to think about.

They didn't talk much after that. At two, Dick Speed said, "Okay, where are they?"

About ten after, Ryan said, "There's one of them. Raymond Gidre." He was coming toward them on the sidewalk. Three cars away, in front of them, he crossed the street to the bar.

"Where's the other one?" Speed said.

By a quarter after, they were pretty sure Mr. Perez wouldn't be taking part today.

Virgil took some time deciding where Tunafish should sit with the suitcase. Tunafish said, You making the deal, you sit with it. Virgil said no, he would be observing the transaction. The man, whoever came, would see the suitcase. He could look in it if he wanted. When the man gave him the money, Tunafish was to bring it to Virgil and then watch the man, with his hand in his pocket holding his new little Baretta. If it didn't go down right, if the man didn't hand Tunafish the money or if he tried to grab the suitcase and run, Virgil would step in and kill the deal. Step in from where, though?

Watts Club had a U-shaped bar extending to a small bandstand that faced the restrooms. It was a strange layout: tables on this side of the bandstand along the bar, and tables on the other side, in the back of the place. The best seat in the house would be in front of the door to the men's room. Virgil thought at first that's where he should be, inside the men's. Place Tunafish so that whoever came would have to sit or stand with his back to the door and Virgil could cover him easy, keeping the door open an inch. But he couldn't see himself waiting in the men's room very long with that disinfectant pissy perfume smell.

So he decided he'd sit around on the other side of the U-shaped bar with his back to the wall, where there were paintings of naked African ladies and a buck straddling a bongo drum, beating the shit out of it. Virgil placed Tunafish at the end table closest to the toilet—so the man would have to walk all the way in—put the suitcase on a chair, got Tunafish a rum and Coke, and walked around the U-shaped bar to the stool he liked. From here he could look directly across the two bar sections to see Tunafish sitting at the table. Virgil ordered a tall vodka and orange juice from the lady bartender. The manager or somebody was straightening up behind the bar, counting change, and two other employees were around somewhere, one of them in the checkroom that served as a front office.

There were no other patrons in the bar besides Virgil and Tunafish when Raymond Gidre walked in at ten minutes past two.

The first thing Raymond did was count the house. Four, no, five that he could see.

He stopped at the bar and said, "Let me have a Jim Beam and 7Up if you will, please."

The lady took a long time to make an easy drink

and charged him a buck seventy-five for it. Jesus Christ, in a nigger place. He saw Mr. Perez's suitcase on the chair and the boy sitting next to it, round fuzzball head sticking out of a leather coat with big shoulders. Boy with a drink in front of him and his hands in his pockets.

Another boy with a hat and sunglasses sitting across the other side of the bar like he was a nigger cowboy, riding the barstool with his big orange drink. That one, Raymond said to himself. The skinny boy had the suitcase, but the cowboy was the one to watch.

Raymond took his drink and walked over to Tunafish. He said, "How you doing? Your hands cold?"

Tunafish, looking up at him, said, "My hands? What?"

Raymond placed his drink on the table. He reached into his coat, brought out his German Luger and shot Tunafish in the face, twice.

Virgil was several beats off, thinking it was still the preliminary stage when it was almost over. He did have his hand on Bobby Lear's nickel-plated automatic and he got it up over the edge of the bar. He was looking at Raymond and couldn't believe what was happening. He had been patient and planned it—

Raymond was half-turned to him, extending the Luger. He fired twice again and blew Virgil off the stool, his head hitting against the high breasts of a painted African lady on the wall.

The manager and the lady bartender, in the pen of the U-shaped bar, standing by the cash register, didn't move. If it wasn't a robbery, they assumed it was dope business. The employee in the coatroom stood by the counter of the half door. No one in the place screamed; no one said a thing.

Picking up the suitcase, Raymond was thinking, Shit, them peckerheads'd never make it the night in New Iberia. He knew the four people were watching him as he walked down the length of the bar, turned to the right past the tables, and reached the inner glass door that opened into the vestibule. About twenty paces in twenty seconds.

It took Virgil that long to push himself from the wall to the bar and slide along the rounded edge on the blood coming out of his chest. He thought the man would turn around to make sure. He hoped the man would, seeing him past the nickel-plated barrel extending from his arm. The arm, across the bar, and his free hand, hanging on to the rounded edge, held him up. Somebody would see him, but he wanted the man to see him, ready this time. He hadn't been ready before. He wished he could do it again, start over, be waiting here, the man comes in—he'd have to have hit the man coming in to beat him. Better than hitting the man going out and that was all the chance he had left in the whole fucking

world left to do, shit, when he'd just learned the
natural way to do things and had only fucked up
this one time, being a little late, a little too patient—
the man was almost out. Virgil concentrated and
began squeezing the trigger of the nickel-plate,
hearing it loud close to him and seeing the man
seem to jump like somebody had kicked him in the
ass, the man pushing through the door, not stopping or turning, gone, with the glass door swinging
back in.

The manager and the lady bartender and the employee back of the coat-check counter still didn't
move or say anything.

There were patrol cars on the side streets at both
ends of the block and a Seventh Squad detail in unmarked cars parked within sight of the bar entrance. Officially this was their stakeout, to recover
stolen property and apprehend the suspects. With
the sound of gunfire it was the Seventh Squad that
radioed its units and got the show going.

It took a few moments for Ryan to realize what
was happening, hearing the shots and the voice on
the radio repeating numbers and saying, "Move
in . . . move in!" He didn't recognize the sound of
the first four shots as gunfire or relate the sound to
the sudden static-y words coming over the radio.
Dick Speed was already out of the car. Ryan got out

his side and slammed the door and heard Dick Speed say, "Stay in there!" But at that moment there were more gunshots from inside the bar, four or five, Ryan counted. He saw the Colt Magnum in Dick Speed's hand. The door to the bar opened. Raymond was out on the sidewalk with the suitcase. Ryan saw the two Seventh Squad plainclothesmen in the street about twenty yards away, and beyond them a squad car with its flashers spinning blocking the intersection and the cops getting out, hurrying this way.

Dick Speed, the closest one to Raymond, said, "Stand where you are—drop it!"

Raymond was coming out from between two cars parked in front of the place, the suitcase in one hand and the Luger in the other—coming the way Ryan remembered him coming the night before, but staggering, bumping against the trunk lid of a car. Ryan had his .38 out, pointing it at Raymond.

Dick Speed, not ten feet from Raymond now, was holding his Mag extended in both hands. Ryan heard him say, "Drop it, motherfucker, you're dead!"

Raymond stopped. He took a step, tried to, then buckled, as though dragged down by the weight of the suitcase, and fell on top of it. Ryan could see blood on the back of his suit coat. Dick Speed circled him, moved in, and pressed the Mag against the back of Raymond's head.

"Let go of the gun."

The two Seventh Squad detectives moved in. One of them put his foot on the wrist of Raymond's outstretched arm and pulled the Luger out of his hand. The other one ran inside the bar. Within the next half minute there were uniformed policemen all around them. One of them, Ryan realized, was staring at him and seemed about to say something or make a grab for him. But it was Dick Speed, getting up from Raymond, who spoke.

"What's that?"

"What?" Ryan said.

"In your hand."

"Oh." He stuck the .38 back in his raincoat pocket.

"You recognize this man?"

"It's Raymond."

Dick Speed continued to give him the look, relaying a no-bullshit warning to stay out of it, until he turned abruptly, spoke to one of the uniformed cops, then went into the bar.

Ryan heard the Seventh Squad detective, kneeling over Raymond, say, "He's dead. Or else he's holding his breath." Ryan stared at Raymond, at the suitcase partly under him.

"What happened to him?"

The Seventh Squad detective looked up at him. "He's been shot. What do you think happened to him?" He pushed Raymond off the suitcase, rolling him onto his back on the wet pavement. Raymond's eyes were closed. His hand still gripped the suitcase until the detective pried his fingers loose.

The suitcase was free, lying on its side in the street. Ryan could take two steps and touch it with his foot. He got a cigarette out and lit it. There were sirens coming, getting louder. He saw black people on the sidewalk edging in to get a look past the parked cars. The suitcase lay there. None of the cops touched it. They'd come over and look down at Raymond and say something or shake their heads. Pick it up, Ryan kept thinking.

But maybe there wasn't anything in it and that's what started the shooting.

No, Raymond wouldn't have come out with it. Mr. Perez's papers were in there. A sheet with Denise's name on it and the name of the stock.

Nobody paid any attention to the suitcase. Ryan drew on his cigarette. For a moment he wondered about Virgil and Tunafish, if they were all right. He wanted to go inside and find out, but he didn't want to leave the suitcase. He felt responsible for it. What if somebody walked off with it? He stooped down and set it upright as he rose, then stepped away from it, chickening out with the cops standing around him. There was more noise and confusion than before. Good. But he wished the cops would turn around or walk away for a minute. A van-type ambulance, an Emergency Medical Service unit, was rolling toward them now, its dome lights revolving, siren dying. The van edged past to bring the rear end to Raymond's body. Ryan picked up the suitcase again, as if to get it out of the way. A cop glanced at him, but didn't say anything, the cop not sure who he was. Ryan set the suitcase down at his side. The cigarette had burned almost to the filter. He had to do it now or forget it. Open the suitcase and give it a quick look. Not out here, Christ no. He couldn't walk down the street with it, get on a bus. There was only one place. He picked up the suitcase, not looking at the cops or the medical attendants now and walked around the EMS unit to Dick Speed's car.

Ryan got in the back seat with the suitcase, jammed himself in there with it, half-turned with his back to the EMS unit outside, feeling hidden and for the moment safe. It passed through his mind the suitcase might be locked and the key in Raymond's pocket—being loaded into the ambulance—but it wasn't locked, it clicked open and there were Mr. Perez's files and letters and legal documents, and a flattened roll of toilet paper, all in a jumbled pile the way they'd been thrown in. Going through the papers at random, without a plan, he found several sheets bearing Mr. Perez's letterhead, *F. X. Perez and Associates, Investment Consultants*, his name on agreements and letters to corporations, and blank sheets of hotel stationery. Ryan set aside, on his lap, the letterhead sheets he took out, and dug into the loose papers, hoping to see Denise's name or Robert Leary's underlined or circled in red. There were files labeled with names of corporations and others marked Indianapolis, Fort Wayne, Chicago, Detroit . . . a list of maybe a dozen names in the Detroit file . . . *there*, Robert Leary, Jr., and the address on Arden Park. There were handwritten notes and initials next to the names that Ryan couldn't make out. There were notebook sheets with names and addresses: Jay Walt's, Ryan's, Denise's address and phone number in Rochester. He didn't know what to look for. He needed time to start at the top and go through each sheet of paper if he had to—before they gave it back to Mr. Perez. Would they?

Sure, once he proved it was his. Why not?

Ryan wasn't sure about that or what Mr. Perez would do now; but he began folding Mr. Perez's letterhead and the agreement forms with his name on them, and the Hotel Pontchartrain stationery, and sticking them in the inside pocket of his sportcoat. They were bulky in there but flat underneath the raincoat. The siren made him jump, going off right outside as the EMS unit pulled away. He didn't look around, though. He didn't turn until somebody opened the door behind him.

"Is that your property?"

Dick Speed was standing there with one of the Seventh Squad detectives.

"I was just looking through it."

"I can see that. I asked you was it yours."

"No, not really."

"Not really. What's that mean?"

"You know whose it is, for Christ's sake." That was a mistake, he shouldn't have said it.

"You can identify it as who it belongs to?"

"I've never seen it before."

"So what you're doing," Dick Speed said, being an official smartass now with his hair and leather jacket and big gun, "you're going through some-body's property that doesn't belong to you."

"I guess so," Ryan said. Act nice. Then when they were alone, driving downtown, he'd talk his friend into letting him go through the papers. Just while they were in the car.

"Detective Olsen here'll take it in his custody," Dick Speed said, and Ryan's hopes died.

He got in the front seat and they took off. He didn't say anything for several blocks, until they were turning off Livernois onto the Lodge Freeway.

"How come all of a sudden, all the help you've given me on this, you want to act like a prick?"

"How come you haven't asked about your friend Virgil?" Dick Speed said. "You got him into this, don't you want to know how he is?"

He'd forgot about Virgil. "You saw him—is he okay?"

"He's dead."

"Virgil? Come on—"

"You want to know about Tunafish? He's dead too. Raymond Gidre, from New Iberia, Louisiana. Three guys dead by gunshot over a suitcase, you want to know how come I'm acting like a prick."

They didn't talk after that. Ryan thought about Virgil, about the times he'd been with him and the time he'd met Tunafish. He couldn't picture them dead and was glad he hadn't gone in to see them. Most of the way downtown, though, Ryan thought about the suitcase, wondering what would happen to it.

24

WHAT HAPPENED THAT TIME IN NEW ORLEANS, THEY'D had a Jew lawyer they were dealing with and Mr. Perez had lost his patience and wound up an accessory to murder. He had been new in the business and had not yet learned to avoid risks by shifting the brunt of them to someone else.

The situation wasn't unlike the present one: a woman who'd inherited stock and didn't know it and her adviser, the Jew lawyer, telling her to hold out and get it all. He had promised the Jew lawyer a commission and had paid him in advance by check on two occasions. That was the first mistake. He'd met the Jew lawyer several times in the Jung Hotel and had been seen with him, in the company of Raymond. Another mistake. The Jew lawyer—in his unpressed seersucker suit, talking and chewing with his mouth open, waving his fork around with red-bean gravy stuck to it—had said, "No, it seems to me it's a question of my client paying *you* a commission, what we deem is equitable based on the value of the stock." Raymond had given him what was equitable in the Jew lawyer's car parked on Lee Circle, five rounds in the chest as the Jew lawyer was shaking his head no for the last time. The final mistake, pissant thinking, having Raymond staying in the same hotel room with him to save money in those early days—and being there when the police busted in and three of them knelt on Raymond, holding his arm twisted behind him, while the fourth cop poked around and found Raymond's Army Colt .45 in the toilet tank.

Mr. Perez made lists of eventualities now. One column, if everything worked perfectly. The other column, if everything didn't.

If everything worked perfectly, Raymond would take the suitcase from the two niggers and that was that. How he did it was up to Raymond. Mr. Perez let Raymond do the heavy work any way he wanted because it was Raymond's business. He knew how to scare the shit out of people and get things done.

If everything didn't work perfectly, there was a chance Raymond could get (a) killed; (b) injured, hospitalized, or in need of medical attention; (c) arrested; (d) arrested and injured. The risks were pretty much all Raymond's.

There was also a chance, if everything didn't work perfectly, if Raymond messed up and was arrested, the police might try to involve Mr. Perez. Or it might be the niggers' lucky day and somehow they'd stomp or shoot Raymond. But by anticipating these risks, Mr. Perez was able to minimize them. He was reasonably confident Raymond would walk in with the suitcase. If the niggers came instead, he'd offer them a drink, sit down, and work out a deal. If the police came, he'd offer them a drink and ask if they'd recovered his stolen property yet. "Raymond? You don't tell me. He did *that?* Well, officer, it was a lucky thing he had a gun, wasn't it? Dealing with people like that. No, I simply asked Mr. Gidre if he would speak to them for me. Very frankly, I don't mind telling you, I was afraid to myself." Mr. Perez made up lines and rehearsed them.

He had been convicted and served time once, because he had been impatient and not properly prepared. It wasn't going to happen twice.

The other thing he did during a high-risk period— just in case he was being watched—was maintain an appearance of business as usual.

This time, what Mr. Perez did, he rented an Avis car, drove out to the A&P supermarket in Rochester, and asked Denise Leary if she'd like to have lunch with him. Denise hesitated, then said okay. "But I'm surprised. I thought you'd be busy today."

Mr. Perez smiled. "Too busy to see my most important client?"

They met at one-thirty and drove to the Burger Chef on the south end of Main. The script Mr. Perez had worked out: he'd play with her today, get her to feel he wasn't such a bad guy after all. Then, while she was relaxed, see if he could plant some doubts in her mind about Ryan and work him loose.

But Denise didn't give him a chance. They both ordered Ranchers, and as soon as they were seated, while Mr. Perez was still undoing his paper napkin, she said, "Something you should understand. I don't care that much about the stock or what it's worth. If I don't get it, I'm not out anything, am I? I mean, I haven't lost anything. But I'll go along with Ryan, whatever he wants to do."

"Even if he wants to maneuver you out of the whole thing?" Mr. Perez said.

"Why do you say that?"

"Because I know him. While he was working for me he went along with anything I suggested."

"That was before."

"Before what? I'm talking about a week ago. See, he acts intelligent enough, he's polite, gives you a nice smile. But it turns out he's a street hustler inside, man trying to live by his wits on a fifth grade education."

Denise shook her head, eating fries and then dabbing her mouth with a napkin. "Look, and I know what you're trying to do, too. You're wasting your time. You don't know anything about Ryan and me. But even if it was true, if he's trying to maneuver me as you say, I still wouldn't be out anything, because I don't have my heart set on the money. I don't need it."

"Everybody needs money," Mr. Perez said. "Perhaps not a hundred and fifty thousand, but some of it would be nice, wouldn't it?"

"The whole thing is," Denise said, "you look at money differently than I do. You'd push somebody out a window to get it. And if you said you were going to push me out, I'd give it to you. Because I honest and truly, whether you believe me or not, don't care about the money."

"Then why don't you sign the agreement with me?" Mr. Perez said.

"Because it's up to Ryan," Denise said, "and for some reason he thinks you're a tinhorn asshole. But let's keep in touch, okay?"

It shouldn't be this difficult, Mr. Perez thought then and at times later on. Why is it? How did it get out of hand?

The process server. Ryan.

It was the first time in Mr. Perez's career he had misjudged anyone to the degree that it might cost him money. (Even on the New Orleans deal, the woman with the Jew lawyer, he had kept in touch with her while he was in Angola and got her to sign an agreement.) When the feeling gnawed at his insides, he took Gelusil tablets and blamed it on northern cooking. He would not admit his misjudgment as long as Mrs. Leary ate her fries with ketchup in the corner of her mouth and didn't care about the money. He had to fool with her some more, stroke her, treat her kindly. If that failed, all right, then open the window. He was playing with children, was the trouble. They were unpredictable and threw him off his game.

He said, "If you insist on Mr. Ryan advising you, that's fine. But why don't the three of us sit down, forget anything was said before that might've made somebody mad, and get this thing worked out. What do you say?"

"If it's all right with Ryan."

"Can you call him?"

"He's supposed to call me later."

"Where is he, out serving paper?"

"No, he's doing something with the police." Denise cut into her hamburger patty. "Mine's a little well done. How's yours?"

"The local police, here?"

"The Detroit police," Denise said, taking a bite of the hamburger patty but watching Mr. Perez. "I mentioned, I thought you'd be busy today."

Mr. Perez saw it coming. Her delivery wasn't bad at all, good timing, playing it dumb, but with the glint of awareness in her eyes if he wanted to notice it. Nice touch with the hamburger being well done.

Well done—it was a piece of shit, but served as a nice piece of business.

He said, "Where was it I'm supposed to be busy today?" And she says:

"Buying a suitcase."

He had to smile at that. She was good. "Tell me something," Mr. Perez said. "Why should I pay to get my own property back?"

"I don't think you're gonna get it back," Denise said.

"Why not? It's mine."

"Because Ryan'll be there and you won't."

"How can he claim it if it isn't his?"

"I'm not saying he will," Denise said. "What he'll do is identify the man who tried to kill him. Your friend Raymond."

"Now we're talking about something I don't know anything about," Mr. Perez said. "What's it got to do with me, or the suitcase?"

"You better finish your Rancher," Denise said. "They pick you up, you might not get anything to eat for a while."

Mr. Perez smiled at her again, watching her dab a couple of fries in the ketchup on her plate.

"Honey, you're pretty good, you know that? But I'll make you a bet I have my suitcase back before the day's over."

"How much?"

"A dollar," Mr. Perez said.

Ryan didn't know if he was supposed to stay or leave. Nobody told him anything. He hung around, looking in the squad room offices that were crowded with old desks. Seeing guys in their shirtsleeves with sidearms drinking coffee. Looking at mug shots of black guys on the wall. Watching a fairly attractive black girl operate a Xerox machine. Dick Speed would pass him without a word, very busy, coming in and out of his office, going into Olsen's office a couple of times where the suitcase was open on a table. Ryan watched them through the glass picking up papers, looking at them. After about a half hour of being quiet and polite, letting them play their grade school game with him, Ryan left.

The place reminded him of a grade school he'd gone to in Detroit—the principal's office, waiting, looking up at the picture of George Washington, the high windows that reached to the ceiling, the solemn gray sky outside. He wasn't a little boy anymore and didn't have to say please and thank you and kiss ass if he didn't want to. He left.

He didn't go far, though. He went to a coffee house across from the Athens Bar on Monroe, a block from police headquarters, ordered a cup of Turkish, and shot bumper pool. Shit, he was still waiting around.

He phoned Denise and told her what had happened and what was going on. She told him about having lunch with Mr. Perez and he felt good again. He didn't have to be down. If he was down it was because he chose to be down, and that was dumb.

Denise said, "If they don't want to talk to you, what're you hanging around for? We've got better things to do."

"Right," Ryan said. "But what exactly did you have in mind?"

Denise said, "Go home and pack your bag, and when you pick me up I'll tell you."

That's what he did. In fact, he got out most of his summer clothes, his jeans, lightweight stuff, and packed them in the twenty-nine-dollar Sears footlocker, reactivating it, no longer a coffee table, something to put his feet on. It was a good feeling.

But then he sat down and got up and walked around the silent apartment and looked out the window. It was after seven, nearly dark outside.

He phoned Dick Speed.

And Speed, with a tone of mild surprise, said, "Where'd you go? I look around, you're not here."

"I didn't know I was supposed to wait."

"Did I say it was okay for you to go?" Still playing the game, punishing the bad boy.

"You want me to come down and wait some more?"

"You're too late," Dick Speed said. "You waited, you'd have seen your friend Mr. Perez."

"You picked him up?"

"No, he walked in by himself. Had a very interesting discussion—not with me so much, with Olsen. Left a few minutes ago."

"Can I ask you," Ryan said, trying hard to sound calm, "did you give him the suitcase?"

"Let's talk about it in the morning," Dick Speed said. "I'm about to piss on the fire and head for the ranch."

"Dick, come on, for Christ's sake, just tell me, will you?"

"There're a few things I want to sit down and talk to you about, as I'm sure you know, you rascal. Long as you're not gonna leave town, there's no rush."

A good sign, the light side of the cop beginning to shine through again.

Be calm and show him a little humility. "Dick, if I can ask you to wait just fifteen minutes, okay? Please."

"Well," the son of a bitch said, "all right, I'll be here. But don't putz around."

"I'm leaving now."

"And, Jackie?" Dick Speed said. "Bring the papers you took out of the suitcase."

It was quiet in the squad rooms this time. The offices that Ryan could see, with their worn, cluttered desks butted against each other, were empty. He didn't like offices at night with fluorescent lights on. Offices were depressing enough with people in them. He didn't like waiting in offices either, sitting in a straight chair by the desk; he felt at a disadvantage. "Sit down," Dick Speed had said, and walked out. Ryan sat with the papers he'd taken from the suitcase, Mr. Perez's letters and the hotel stationery, in a manila envelope on his lap. He didn't know where Dick Speed had gone—until he got up, dropped the manila envelope on the desk, and walked out, not to leave, to move around. There was more room in the squad rooms' outer office where he had waited this afternoon, but there wasn't anything to look at he hadn't seen before: the mug shots on the wall, a calendar, the Xerox machine, the coffee maker.

He heard Mr. Perez's voice.

Ryan turned. He saw Dick Speed through the glass partition of Detective Olsen's office, where the suitcase had been this afternoon. Dick Speed was alone, looking down at something on the desk.

"Hey, Ryan, come here!"

He called to him before he saw Ryan through the glass, then waved for him to come in.

A tape recorder was on the desk.

Ryan saw it—Dick Speed fooling with it, rewinding, then stopping the tape—but he didn't see the black Samsonite two-suiter anywhere. He looked around the office again to be sure.

"You want to hear an act," Dick Speed said, "listen to this."

"You gave it to him, huh?"

"What?"

"His papers. When he was here."

"That was part of the act, walking in, showing he's got nothing to hide."

"If you didn't pick him up, how'd he find out?"

"He says he went to the bar to meet his friend Gidre and they told him what happened. He even went to the morgue and identified Gidre before he came here."

"To see if Raymond had the suitcase," Ryan said.

"So he walks in and wants to know if we recovered his property. Well, we've got a few questions to ask him first, three people getting killed over a suitcase he says is his." Dick Speed punched a button on the tape recorder.

PEREZ: . . . that the theft was reported. Naturally I told the hotel management.

"That's Perez," Dick Speed said. "The other one's Olsen, questioning him. You'll hear me a few times."

OLSEN: The management. Who'd you tell, exactly?

PEREZ: I don't know, some assistant. Young fella with slick hair and pointed shoulders in his coat.

OLSEN: Pointed shoulders. You asked him to report the robbery to the police?

PEREZ: I assumed he would, something's stolen from a room. Wouldn't you?

SPEED: Did you know Mr. Gidre was carrying a gun?

PEREZ: I told him, I said, "Raymond, I'd just like you to talk to them." I don't mind telling you I was afraid to, not knowing anything about them, who they were. I said just talk to them nice, see if we can come to some kind of agreement.

SPEED: You didn't answer my question. Did you know Mr. Gidre was carrying a gun?

PEREZ: No, I didn't.

SPEED: Did you know he owned a gun?

PEREZ: I believe he might've told me that, yes. But I didn't know he was carrying it with him today. See, I spoke to him about it last night.

OLSEN: You said you spoke to one of them on the phone. Do you know which one?

PEREZ: I don't know. They all sound alike to me.

OLSEN: Did he ask you for money?

PEREZ: He said he wanted to meet with me and have a talk. I suppose feel me out, see how much he could get.

OLSEN: Were you willing to pay him?

PEREZ: Within reason.

OLSEN: If it was just to talk, why do you suppose they had the suitcase with them?

PEREZ: That's what concerns me right now, if it is my suitcase and if my documents and papers are in it. See, I don't know if they might've been trying to pull something.

SPEED: Mr. Gidre apparently took the suitcase from them. He'd know, wouldn't he, if he was taking the right one?

PEREZ: Well, it was a Samsonite, black. Fairly good size. That the one you have?

OLSEN: Were your initials on it?

PEREZ: No, I don't believe on that one.

OLSEN: Can you describe the contents?

PEREZ: Well, as I said, there were letters, legal documents, pretty much all of a business nature.

OLSEN: Uh, did any of the letters, or any of the papers, have your name on them?

PEREZ: Of course they did. My name, my business stationery. There might've been some hotel stationery in there, too. The Pontchartrain.

Dick Speed looked at Ryan. Ryan kept staring at the tape recorder.

OLSEN: What does your business letterhead say?

PEREZ: What does it say? It says my name, "F. X. Perez and Associates. Investment Consultants."

OLSEN: You're sure you had letterhead stationery in the suitcase.

PEREZ: I didn't keep it in the suitcase, *they* put it in. If my letters and stationery aren't in there, then the niggers took 'em out or lost 'em, I don't know. All I do know is they cleaned out every piece of paper I had in the hotel room.

OLSEN: That seems unusual, doesn't it? Taking only papers. Was anything of value taken?

Dick Speed looked at Ryan, grinning, anticipating Mr. Perez's answer.

PEREZ: Of *value*? Like a wristwatch or something? Christ Almighty, they took my *business*!

As Olsen began to speak, Dick Speed said, "More of the same." He punched the rewind button and the tapes raced in reverse. "We asked him to describe his business. He told us. We asked if he had ever contacted a Mrs. Robert Leary. He said yes. Had he ever met Robert Leary? No. Or Virgil Royal? He said he'd never heard of Virgil Royal. Then what did he think happened at Watts Club Mozambique this shitty afternoon at ten after two? He said, 'It sounds to me like a misunderstanding.' Do you like that? A misunderstanding."

"If they both had guns," Ryan said, "I can see it. They shoot people."

"All three had guns. None of them registered."

"So what did you do with him? Perez."

"Took his statement and let him go."

Ryan asked the question. "With his suitcase, uh?"

And waited while Dick Speed watched the take-up reel spin with the tape on it and pressed the OFF button.

"We gave him every opportunity to identify it as his property, but he couldn't. At least, not to our satisfaction."

"You mean you didn't give it to him?"

"We told him if he'd reported it stolen and given us a description . . ." Dick Speed paused, taking the reel off the recorder and slipping it into a box. Ryan watched him.

Answer the fucking question.

". . . but to just walk in and claim something, that put a different light on it. He got irritable and important then and said he demanded we hand over his property. I told him we'd be happy to, if we had it, if and when he identified it properly."

"What'd he say then?"

"He said if we didn't hand it over, he'd get us served with an injunction and take us to court."

"He probably will, too. He knows what he's doing."

"Well, we know what he's *been* doing. I reminded him his friend or employee killed two people during an attempted robbery. *Robbery!* He started to go into it being his property and all that again. And I said, 'You already served time for accessory to murder, didn't you? In the state of Louisiana?' I can thank you for having that one."

"Did it stop him?"

"Well, for the time being. But since he wasn't at the scene with Gidre, and if there's no way to prove he actually hired or induced Gidre to kill them, I don't see how we'd be able to pin an accessory on him." Dick Speed turned from the desk and started out of the office. "Come on. I'll tell you something, though. I can read that asshole and I don't care for him. And if I can't nail him, then at least I can let the air out of his tires, if you follow me. Slow him up."

Going into Dick Speed's office, Ryan saw the manila envelope on the near side of the desk, where he'd dropped it. He reached over and picked it up as he sat down.

Dick Speed was swiveling around in his chair. He said, "What's that?" Then seemed to realize what it was and shook his head. "Never mind, don't tell me. What's in the suitcase is what we found in it. I don't want to have to explain anything else or have to arrest anybody for petty theft and have to appear at Frank Murphy on my day off and hang around Common Pleas all morning."

"I appreciate it," Ryan said.

"I hope to Christ so," Dick Speed said, "you dumb shit. I hope you know where your ass'd be if I wasn't sitting here."

"I know," Ryan said, nodding. "I appreciate it, I really do." He took a cigarette out and lit it. Sitting back then, he blew the smoke out slowly.

Dick Speed was watching him. "But what?"

"Nothing," Ryan said. "I was just wondering if the suitcase was still around."

"Why?"

"Well, if it is—is it?"

"Go on."

"If it is, you think it would hurt anything if I looked through it? You can watch me if you want. I mean, I'm not going to take anything, I just want to look up something."

"That's all?"

"Well, maybe use your Xerox machine."

"Jesus," Dick Speed said.

"I'll even pay for it," Ryan said. "Give you a dime a sheet."

25

THEY MET IN THE CAFETERIA of the old Casino on Belle Isle in the Detroit River, a big yellow-brick pavilion from 1910 that had been recently cleaned of grime and graffiti, a warm place on a cold spring morning for people living on pensions and social security. Ryan liked to come here.

The three of them, Ryan, Denise, and Mr. Perez, sat with their coffee by the French windows, looking out at the river and the freighters and the green shoreline of Canada across the stream, taking their time getting to it. There was no hurry. It would be done now.

"I was over in Windsor this morning," Mr. Perez said, "my first visit to Canada. I had to pick up Raymond's things. Boy traveled light, he didn't have too much with him."

"Why?" Denise said.

Mr. Perez turned from the window. "Why what?"

"Why are you bothering with his things?"

"It's no bother. I'll take them to his family sometime, his mama and daddy. There might be something personal they'd want to keep."

"Maybe his shotgun," Ryan said.

Mr. Perez stirred his coffee. "You don't find people like Raymond every day."

"Thank God," Denise said.

"Most always cheerful, had a good disposition," Mr. Perez continued. "Boy liked to eat, too, I'll tell you."

"It sounds like you're gonna miss him," Ryan said.

"You bet your life I am. Till I find somebody else as good and easy to get along with."

"Then you're still in business," Denise said.

Mr. Perez gave her a surprised look. "Isn't that why we're sitting here? You called me, honey, I didn't call you. I must have something you want."

Ryan said, "You get all your stuff back?"

"You were there, weren't you?" Mr. Perez said. "You saw the police take it?"

"I wondered if you claimed it yet. Or had the nerve."

"The nerve?" Mr. Perez smiled. "That's what it's all about. How you stand up and pull it off, keeping a straight face. Getting my property back may take me a little time and a trip to the courthouse, but I'll get it back, don't worry about that."

"You owe me a dollar," Denise said.

"Yes, I do, don't I?" He smiled again, digging out a wad of bills and handing her one. "I've got a feeling we can quit bullshitting each other and put it on the table, the three of us here. How's that sound to you?"

Denise smiled back at him. "As you say, that's what it's all about."

"You're a good one. I hope you see through this fella before too long."

"Be nice," Denise said. "Remember, it's no-more-bullshit time."

"So as we look at it, we see that you need me and I need you," Mr. Perez said. "And since neither one of us is gonna bend and we're sick and tired of wasting time, why don't we meet right here"— touching the center of the table with his finger— "and split it down the middle? Fifty-fifty."

"You do have a lot of time in this," Ryan said.

Mr. Perez nodded. "More than I've ever spent before on a case."

"A case, huh?"

"Whatever you want to call it."

"Okay, for your time, as a finder's fee," Ryan said, "Mrs. Leary'll give you ten thousand. How does that sound?"

Mr. Perez shook his head slowly and seemed tired. He said, "Come on," and looked at Denise. "Fifty-fifty. You get roughly, no, not so roughly, seventy-five thousand dollars for signing a paper.

How long would it take you to make that working at the A&P?"

"Tell him," Denise said.

Ryan had let Mr. Perez talk because he wanted the man to have his hopes up reasonably high when he let him have it.

"Denver Pacific," Ryan said.

Mr. Perez looked at him. "What?"

"Denver Pacific. That's the stock. Fifteen hundred shares."

"How'd you find out? The niggers?"

"What difference does it make?"

"I suppose," Mr. Perez said. "Well, as I told you, if I strike out, I don't stamp my feet and carry on. I say thank you very much and go on to the next one."

"Mrs. Leary means it about the ten thousand finder's fee," Ryan said. "After all, if you hadn't come along . . ."

Mr. Perez nodded, thoughtful, somewhere far away. "That's very generous of Miz Leary."

"It's nothing," Denise said.

Ryan said, "I suppose it took you a little time to work up that list of prospects. You got a duplicate at home?"

"Unfortunately," Mr. Perez said, "I carry my office with me. Everything. But I'll get my papers back, don't worry about that."

"It could be months before you get a court date,"

Ryan said. "And then you've got to hope for a favorable decision." He waited a moment. "What would your list of prospects be worth to you right now?"

He was taking the Xeroxed sheets, folded once, out of his inside coat pocket. Mr. Perez, sitting very still, was watching Ryan's hands, seeing the list of corporations and names of lost stockholders unfolded and turned toward him so that he could see the list clearly and identify it and know exactly what it was.

"Would you say twenty thousand?" Ryan asked.

Mr. Perez did not hesitate, though he said it quietly. "More like ten thousand."

"Tell you the truth, that's what I had in mind," Ryan said. He dropped the sheets on the table, in front of Mr. Perez. "Mrs. Leary owes you ten; you buy these, you owe me ten—that makes us even, doesn't it?"

Ryan and Denise got up from the table. Going past Mr. Perez, Ryan's hand touched the man's shoulder. He said, "Mr. Perez, it was nice doing business with you."

Outside, going through the archway and down the sweep of steps, Denise said, "I don't know why, but seeing him sitting there, I felt sorry for him."

"I don't know why, either," Ryan said. "You see him this afternoon, he'll be eating somebody up."

They reached the car that was angle-parked at the curb, facing the casino.

"Mr. Ryan . . ."

It came from behind them, from Mr. Perez standing in the arch of the front entrance. They turned to see him and watched him raise his hand holding the sheets of paper.

"Wonder if you'd like to find some people for me."

Ryan held the door handle, his thumb on the button. It was a funny feeling, knowing he could walk back to the man standing there with his list of names, knowing the man would pay him whatever he asked and never mention Denise or Raymond or Virgil. Ryan opened the door and got in the car.

Driving away, Denise said, "For a moment I thought you were going to take him up on it."

Ryan looked over at her and smiled and shook his head, but he didn't say anything.

ELMORE LEONARD
THE UNDISPUTED MASTER
OF THE CRIME NOVEL

RAYLAN
A Raylan Givens Novel

Available in Paperback and eBook

DJIBOUTI

Available in Paperback and eBook

ROAD DOGS

Available in Paperback and eBook

COMFORT TO THE ENEMY AND OTHER CARL WEBSTER STORIES

Available in Paperback and eBook

MR. PARADISE

Available in Paperback and eBook

THE HUNTED

Available in Paperback and eBook

FIRE IN THE HOLE
Stories, Including One Featuring Raylan Givens

Available in Paperback and eBook

GOLD COAST

Available in Paperback and eBook

MR. MAJESTYK

Available in Paperback and eBook

CUBA LIBRE

Available in Paperback and eBook

MAXIMUM BOB

Available in Paperback and eBook

RIDING THE RAP
A Raylan Givens Novel

Available in Paperback and eBook

PRONTO
A Raylan Givens Novel

Available in Paperback and eBook

RUM PUNCH

Available in Paperback and eBook

GET SHORTY

Available in Paperback and eBook

TISHOMINGO BLUES

Available in Paperback and eBook

KILLSHOT

Available in Paperback and eBook

FREAKY DEAKY

Available in Paperback and eBook

BANDITS	Available in Paperback and eBook
GLITZ	Available in Paperback and eBook
STICK	Available in Paperback and eBook
CAT CHASER	Available in Paperback and eBook
SPLIT IMAGES	Available in Paperback and eBook
CITY PRIMEVAL	Available in Paperback and eBook
THE MOONSHINE WAR	Available in Paperback and eBook
HOMBRE	Available in Paperback and eBook
THE SWITCH	Available in Paperback and eBook
OUT OF SIGHT	Available in Paperback and eBook
SWAG	Available in Paperback and eBook
LaBRAVA	Available in Paperback and eBook
VALDEZ IS COMING	Available in Paperback and eBook

NOW AVAILABLE

52 PICKUP	Available in Paperback and eBook
BE COOL	Available in Paperback and eBook
GUNSIGHTS	Available in Paperback and eBook
THE HOT KID	Available in Paperback and eBook
LAST STAND AT SABER RIVER	Available in Paperback and eBook
PAGAN BABIES	Available in Paperback and eBook
TOUCH	Available in Paperback and eBook
UNKNOWN MAN #89	Available in Paperback and eBook
UP IN HONEY'S ROOM	Available in Paperback and eBook

Available wherever books are sold.